P9-CDG-160

MR. PRATT

Published May, 1906
Second Printing, July, 1906
Third Printing, October, 1906
Fourth Printing, November, 1906
Fifth Printing, February, 1907
Sixth Printing, August, 1907
Seventh Printing, November, 1907
Eighth Printing, February, 1908
Ninth Printing, September, 1908
Tenth Printing, January, 1909
Eleventh Printing, February, 1911

MR. PRATT

A NOVEL

By JOSEPH C. LINCOLN

Author of

"Cap'n Eri," "Partners of the Tide," Etc.

With Frontispiece

By HORACE TAYLOR

A. L. BURT COMPANY

PUBLISHERS ∴ NEW YORK

HORACE TAYLOR

To

MY FRIEND

GILMAN HALL

NOTE

The germ from which the yarn of "Mr. Pratt" developed was contained in a short story by the author, which appeared in "Everybody's Magazine." In that story, "The Simplicity of It," the "Heavenly Twins" were middle aged men, and their characters—as well as their names—were not those of Hartley and Van Brunt. But they did try to live the "Natural Life," and Mr. Solomon Pratt then, as in the present instance, assisted in the attempt and told the tale.

J. C. L.

Hackensack, N. J., March 28, 1906.

CONTENTS

MR. PRATT

CHAPTER I

THE MASTERS

I HEARD about the pair first from Emeline Eldredge, " Emmie T." we always call her. She was first mate to the cook at the Old Home House that summer. She come down to the landing one morning afore breakfast and hove alongside of where I was setting in the stern of my sloop, the *Dora Bassett,* untangling fish lines. She had a tin pail in her fist, indicating that her sailing orders was to go after milk. But she saw me and run down in ballast to swap yarns.

" My sakes! Mr. Pratt," says she; "have you heard about Nate Scudder? "

" Yes," I says. " Ever since I come to Wellmouth."

" I mean about what him and his wife has just done," says she. " It's the queerest thing! You'll never guess it in the world."

"Ain't been giving his money to the poor, has he?" says I, for, generally speaking, it takes a strong man and a cold chisel to separate Nate Scudder from a cent.

"Oh! ain't you the funniest *thing!*" she squeals. "No indeed! He's let his house to some city folks, and——"

"Ain't that the cook calling you?" I asks I'm a homeopath when it comes to Emmie T.; I like to take her in small doses—she agrees with me better that way.

It was the cook, and Emeline kited off after the milk, only stopping long enough to yell back: "Folks say they're dreadful rich and stylish. I'll tell you next time I see you."

Well, I cal'lated she wouldn't—not if I saw her first—and didn't pay no more attention to the yarn, except to think that June was pretty early for city folks to be renting houses. There was only three or four boarders at the Old Home so far, and I was to take a couple of 'em over to Trumet in the sloop that very day.

But, while we was on the way over, one of the couple—sort of a high-toned edition of Emmie T. she was—she turns to her messmate, another pullet from the same coop, and says she, "Oh say!" she says. "Have you heard about the two young fellers from New York who've rented that Scudder house on the—on the—what do they call it? Oh, yes! the Neck road. I heard Nettie Brown say they were too dear for anything. Let's drive past there to-morrow; shall we?"

So there it was again, and I begun to wonder what sort of critters Nate had hooked. I judged that they must be a kind of goldfish or he wouldn't have baited for 'em. Nate ain't the man to be satisfied with a mess of sculpins.

I landed the boarders at Trumet and they went up to the village to do some shopping. Then I headed across the harbor to shake hands with the Trumet light keeper, who is a friend of mine. His wife told me he'd gone over to town, too, so I come about and run back to the landing again. And I'm blessed if there wa'n't Nate Scudder himself, setting on a mackerel keg at the end of the wharf and looking worried.

I hadn't hoisted the jib on the way down, and now I let the mainsail drop and went forward.

"Hello, Nate!" I hailed, as the *Dora Bassett* slid up to the wharf.

He kind of jumped, and looked at me as if he'd just woke up.

"Hello, Sol!" he says, sort of mournful. Then he turned his eyes toward the bay again and appeared to be starting in on another nap.

"Hear you got some boarders over to your home," I says, heaving him a line as a hint for him to come out of his trance and make me fast.

"Yes," says he, paying no attention to the line.

"Come early in the season, ain't they?" says I, grabbing hold of one of the wharf spiles and bringing my boat alongside easy as I could.

"Ya-as," says he, again. Then he fetched a long breath and opened his mouth as if he was going to go on. But he didn't; all that come out of the mouth afore it shut up was another "Yes."

I made the *Dora Bassett* fast myself and climbed on to the wharf.

"Are they cal'lating to stay long?" I asks. He'd got me interested. Seemed to have the "yes" disease bad.

"Hey?" says he. "Oh—er—yes."

I was a little mite provoked. Not that I was hankering to have Nate Scudder heave his arms around my neck and tell me he loved me, but I didn't know any reason why my pumps should suck dry *every* time I tried 'em.

"Humph!" I grunted, starting to walk off.

"Well, be careful of yourself; look out it don't develop into nothing worse."

"What do you mean?" he sings out, seeming to be waked up for good, at last.

"Oh," says I; "I judged by the way you kept your mouth shut that you had sore throat and was afraid of getting cold. Good day."

Would you believe it, he got up off that mackerel keg and chased after me.

"Hold on, Sol!" he says, kind of pleading. "Don't be in such a hurry. I wanted to talk to you."

I had to laugh; couldn't help it. "Yes," says I, "I kind of suspicioned that you did, from your chatty remarks. If you'd said 'yes' nine or ten times more I'd have been sure of it."

"Well, I did," he says. "I wanted to ask you—I thought I'd see what you thought—you see——"

Here he kind of faded away again, and stood still and wiped his forehead.

"Look here, Nate Scudder," I says, "for a man that wants to talk you make the poorest fist at it of anybody ever I see. Why don't you try singing or making signs? I wouldn't wonder if you got ahead faster."

He grinned, a feeble sort of lop-sided grin, and tried another tack.

"You was speaking of them boarders of mine," he says.

"Yes; *I* was," I says.

"They come day afore yesterday—early," says he.

"Um-hum. So I heard," I says.

He fidgeted a minute or so more. Then he took me by the arm and led me back to the keg.

"Sol," he says, "set down. I want to ask you something. By gum! I *got* to ask somebody. I'm—I'm worried."

"Yes?" I said, giving him a little of his own medicine.

"Yes. Them boarders—they worry me. Me and Huldy set up till nigh eleven o'clock last night talking about 'em. She thinks maybe they stole the money, and I don't know but they're crazy, run away from an asylum or something. You've seen more city folks than I have, being around the hotel so. See what you think.

"'Twas this way," he went on; "I got a letter from the feller in New York that I sell cranberries to. He said a couple of friends of his wanted to come to a place in the country where 'twas quiet.

Did I know of such a place round here? Well, course I wrote back that 'twas nice and quiet right at our house. There wa'n't no lie in that, was there, Sol?"

"No," I says. "I should say 'twouldn't be shaving the truth too close if you'd said there was more quietness than anything else down on the Neck road."

"Well," he goes on, not noticing the sarcasm, "I wrote and never got a word back. Me and Huldy had given up hearing. And then, yesterday morning, they come—both of 'em. Nice lookin' young fellers as ever you see, they are; dressed just like the chaps in the clothes advertisements in the back of the magazines. The biggest one—they're both half as tall as that mast, seems so—he took up his hat and says, kind of lazy and grand, like a steamboat capt'n:

"'Mr. Scudder?' he says.

"'That's my name,' says I. I was kind of suspicious; there's been so many sewing-machine agents and such round town this spring. And yet I'd ought to have known *he* wa'n't no sewing-machine agent.

"'Ah!' he says. 'You've been expecting us then. Has the luggage come?'

"What in time did I know about his 'luggage,' as he called it?

"'No,' says I. ''Tain't.'

"'Oh, well, never mind,' he says, just as if a ton or two of baggage didn't count anyway. 'Can you give us two sleeping rooms, two baths, a setting room, and a room for my man?'

"'Two *baths?*' says I. 'Can't you take a bath by yourself? You seem to be having lots of funny jokes with me. Would you mind saying what your name is and what you want?'

"He looked me over sort of odd. 'Beg pardon,' he said. 'I thought you were expecting us. Here's my card.'

"I looked at it, and there was the name 'Edward Van Brunt,' printed on it. Then I begun to get my bearings, as you might say.

"'Oh!' I says. 'I see.'

"'So glad, I'm sure,' he says. 'Now can you give us the sleeping rooms, the baths, and the room for my man?'

"'Humph!' says I, lookin' back at the house behind me; 'if me and Huldy bunked in the henhouse and the chore boy in the cellar, maybe we could accommodate you, that is, all but the baths.

You'd have to take turns with the washtub for them,' I says.

"He laughed. He was so everlasting cool about things that it sort of riled me up.

"'Perhaps you'd like to hire the whole shebang?' says I, sarcastic, pointing to the house.

"He looked at it. It looked sort of cheerful, with the syringa over the door and the morning-glories hiding where the whitewash was off.

"'Good idea!' he says. 'I would.'

"Well, that was too many for me! I went into the house and fetched out Huldy Ann—she's my wife. There ain't many women in this town can beat her when it comes to managing and business, if I do say it.

"'How long would you want the house for?' says Huldy, when I told her what was going on.

"'A month,' says Van Brunt, turning to the other city feller. 'Hey, Martin?' T'other chap nodded.

"'All right,' says Van Brunt. 'How much?'

"Thinks I, 'I'll scare you, my fine feller.' And so I says, 'A month? Well, I don't know. Maybe, to accommodate, I might let you have it for two hundred.' I sort of edged off then, thinking sure he'd be mad; but he wa'n't—not him.

" 'Two hundred it is,' he says, and fished out a little blank book and one of them pocket pens.

" 'Name's Scudder?' he asks.

" 'Yes,' says I. 'Nathan Scudder. One T in Nathan.'

" And I don't know as you'll believe it, Sol," says Nate, finishing up, " but that feller made out a check for two hundred and passed it over to me like 'twas a postage stamp. What do you think of that?"

I didn't know what to think of it. On general principles I'd say that a man who wanted to board with Nate and Huldy Ann Scudder was crazy anyhow; but of course these fellers didn't know.

" It beats me, Nate," I says. " What do *you* think?"

" Blessed if I know!" says Scudder, with another of them long breaths. " All I'm sure of is that they're up home, with the parlor blinds open and the carpet fading, and me and Huldy's living in the barn. She's doing the cookin' for 'em till this 'man' of theirs comes. Land knows what kind of a man he is, too. And that check was on a New York bank, and I've just been up to Trumet here with it and the cashier says 'twill be a week afore I know whether it's good or not. And I can't make out whether them two are thieves, or lunatics, or what. And Huldy can't neither. I never was so worried in *my* life."

I kind of chuckled down inside. The idea of anybody's skinning Nate Scudder was the nighest to the biter's being bit of anything I ever come across. And just then I see my two passengers coming.

"Well, cheer up, Nate," I says. "Maybe you'll get the reward, whether it's lunatics or thieves. Only you want to look out and not be took up for an accomplice."

He fairly shriveled up when I said that, and I laughed to myself all the way out of Trumet harbor. One thing I was sure of: them two New Yorkers must be queer birds and I wanted to see 'em.

And the very next afternoon I did see 'em. They come down the Old Home pier together, walking as if they didn't care a whole continental whether they ever got anywheres or not. One of 'em, the smallest one—he wa'n't more'n six foot one and a ha'f—looked sort of sick, to me. He had a white face, and that kind of tired, don't-care look in his eye; and the bigger one sort of 'tended to things for him.

"Good morning," says the big one—the Van Brunt one, I judged—cheerful enough. T'other chap said, "Good morning," too.

"Morning," says I.

"Can you take us out sailing?"

"Why—er—I guess so," I says. "I don't know why I can't, if you feel like going. Course——"

I hadn't finished what I was going to say afore they was in the boat. Now, generally speaking, there's some bargaining to be done afore you take folks out for a three-dollar sail. You naturally expect it, you know—not so much from boarders as from towners, but still, some. But not for these two—no, sir! It was this powerful suddenness of theirs that hit me betwixt wind and water, same as it had Nate. Made me feel sort of like I'd missed the train. Stirred up my suspicions again, too.

'Twas a nice day; one of them clear blue and green days that you get early in June. The water wa'n't rugged, but just choppy enough to be pretty, and the breeze was about no'theast, givin' us a fair run down the bay.

"This is grand!" says the big fellow, as the *Dora Bassett* begun to feel her oats and lay down to her work.

"Cæsar! Van," said the other one; "why do you bring me down to earth like that? Grand! Bleecker next!" He hollered out this last part in a kind of screechy sing-song. Then they both laughed.

I looked at 'em. There wa'n't nothing to laugh at, so far as I could see, and the "Bleecker" business didn't appear to have no sense in it, either. They made two or three other speeches that sounded just as foolish. Thinks I, "I wonder if Scudder's right?" They didn't look like lunatics, but you can't always tell. Old man Ebenezer Doane went to church of a Sunday morning just as sensible acting as a Second Adventer *could* be; but when he got home he fired the bean-pot at his wife, chased his children out door with a clam hoe, and they found him settin' a-straddle of the hen-house singing "Beulah Land" to the chickens. These fellers might be harmless loons that had been farmed out, as you might say, by the asylum folks. There was that "man" that Nate said was coming. He might be their keeper.

"I understand you've got a friend coming," says I, by way of ground bait.

"Friend?" says the big one. "*Friend?* I don't understand."

"Scudder said you had another man coming to his house," says I.

He smiled. "Oh, I see." Then he smiled again, a queer lazy kind of a smile, like as if he was amused at himself or his thoughts.

"I don't know that I should call him a friend, Mr.—er——"

"Pratt," says I. "Solomon Pratt."

"Thanks. No, I wouldn't go so far as to call him a friend; and yet he's not an enemy—not openly." He smiled again, and the other chap—whose name I found out was Hartley—Martin Hartley—smiled too.

"He's the man Van here belongs to," explained the Hartley one. They both smiled again.

I kind of jumped, I guess, when he said that. It began to look as if the asylum idea was the right one, and this feller that was coming *was* the keeper.

"Hum," says I, and nodded my head just as if the whole business was as plain as A B C. "Do *you* belong to anybody?" I says to Hartley.

"I did," says he, "but he's doing time."

"Doing time?" says I.

"Yes," says he, explaining, kind of impatient like. "Up the river, you know."

I chewed over this for a minute, and all I could think of was that the feller must be in a clock factory or a watchmaker's or something.

"Watches?" I asks.

Hartley seemed to be too tired of life to want to answer, but his chum did it for him.

"No," says he. "I believe it was pearl studs on the showdown."

Well, this was crazy talk enough for anybody. I didn't want to stir 'em up none—I've always heard that you had to be gentle with lunatics—so I went on, encouraging 'em like.

"Studs, hey?" says I.

"Yes," says he. "He was a British beast, and Martin was all balled up in the Street at the time—away from his apartments a good deal—and the B. B. annexed everything in sight."

"Go 'long!" says I, for the sake of saying something.

"Beg pardon," says he.

"Nothing," says I; and we stopped talking.

They seemed to enjoy the sail first rate, and acted as rational as could be, generally speaking. They didn't know a topping lift from a center-board, so far as boat went, but that wa'n't strange; I'd seen plenty of boarders like that. But never afore had I seen two that acted or talked like them.

We got back to the wharf along about dusk, and I walked with 'em a piece on their way to Nate's. I was keeping a sort of old bach hall just outside the village and so it wa'n't much out of my way. They had me guessing and I wanted more time to work on the riddle.

We cut across Sears's meadow, and the frogs was beginning to squeal and the crickets to chirp. To me them early summer noises are as cheerful and restful as a teakettle singing or a cat purring. But, all at once, Hartley, the sick one, stopped and held up his hand.

"Heavens, Van!" he says. "It sounds like the ticker," and he said it *so* prayerful and sad.

Van Brunt shook his head. "Don't it?" says he. "I can see the tape running off that tree. 'Green Apples Preferred, 106 bid and 8 asked.' Is there *no* escape?" he says.

I left 'em on the hill by the Baptist burying ground. I watched 'em walking down the road, big and straight and handsome, and I pitied 'em from the bottom of my heart.

"Sol Pratt," says I to myself, "here's a lesson for you. You're old and homely and your bank account is nothing, minus a good deal, divided by naught; but don't you never complain again. S'pose you was good-looking and rich, but out of your head, like them two poor young chaps. Dear! dear!"

And I thought about 'em and pitied 'em all that evening, while I was frying my herrings for supper. I hope I'll get credit somewheres for all that pity.

CHAPTER II

THE MAN

I SEE 'em pretty often during the next week. They used to loaf down to the landing of a morning, smoking cigars, and with their hands in their pockets. Crazy or not, there was a something about 'em that kind of got me; I own up I begun to like 'em, in spite of their top-hamper being out of gear. As a general run I don't hanker for the average city boarder. He runs too much to yachting clothes and patronizing. Neither the clothes nor the airs set well; kind of look like they was second-hand and made over for him by the folks at home. When one of that kind is out sailing with me, and begins to lord it and show off afore the girls, the *Dora Bassett* is pretty apt to ship some spray over the bow. A couple of gallons of salt water, sliced off a wave top and poured down the neck of one of them fellers is the best reducer I know of; shrinks his importance like 'twas a flannel shirt.

But Nate Scudder's private patients wa'n't that

kind. Not that they wa'n't dressed. Land sakes! I don't s'pose they wore the same vests two days running. But they looked like they was used to their clothes, not as if they'd just been introduced and didn't feel to home in 'em. And they didn't patronize none to speak of; called me "Skipper" and "Sol" just as sociable as could be. And as for the girls, they never looked twice at any of the hotel ones. Them two skittish females that I took over to Trumet used to get in their way and beg pardon and giggle, hoisting flirtation signals, so to speak, but Van Brunt and Hartley wouldn't even come up into the wind; just keep on their course like they was carrying the mail. 'Twas these two females that first named 'em "The Heavenly Twins"; 'twas shortened later to "The Heavenlies."

Every time I took the Heavenlies on a cruise the more certain I was that they were loons—harmless and good-natured, of course, but loons just the same. Most generally they carried a book along with 'em and read it out loud to each other. They'd read a spell and then stop and break out with, "By Jove! that's so. He's right, isn't he?" You'd think that book was a human almost, the way they went on about it. I've heard a minister do the same way over the Scriptures; but this wa'n't the Bible, the name of it was "The Natural Life." I borrowed it once to look at, but 'twas all foolishness to me; telling about money being a cuss, and such rot. I've been cussed considerable sence I first went to sea, but not by money—no, *sir!*

But Van Brunt would read three or four fathom of rubbish out of "The Natural," and then heave to and say:

"Odd we didn't think of that afore, Martin. It *doesn't* count for much, does it? Well, we're through with it now, thank God! Look at that sunset. Have a smoke, skipper?"

And then he'd pass over a cigar that had cost as much as ten cusses a box, if I'm any judge of tobacco.

One night, just as we were coming into port, Van says to me:

"Sol," he says. "We may want you and the boat to-morrow. My man'll let you know in the morning. Meanwhile just dodge the nautical bunch at the hotel, will you?"

I was a good deal shook up. I'd almost forgot that keeper.

"Man?" says I. "Oh, yes, yes! I see. Is he here now?"

"No; coming to-night, I believe. By-by. Just consider yourself engaged till you hear from us."

They walked off and left me thinking. Thinks I, "It's a fair bet that that keeper don't let you two go boating by yourselves again."

So the next day about half-past nine, when I'd just about decided to let some of the boarders have the *Dora Bassett*, I looked up from my fish lines and here was a feller coming down the wharf.

He was a kind of an exhibit for Wellmouth, as you might say. Leastways he was bran-new for me. Six foot two over all, I should judge, and about two foot in the beam. Cast a shadow like a rake handle. Dressed up fine and precise, and prim as a Sunday-school superintendent. He *looked* sort of gospelly, too, with his smooth upper lip and turned-down mouth, and little two-for-a-cent side whiskers at half mast on his cheeks. But his eyes was fishy. Thinks I, "No sir-ee! I don't want to subscribe to no *Temperance Advocate*, nor buy 'The Life of Moses and the Ten Commandments,' nor I don't want to have my tintype took neither."

He stood still by the stringpiece of the wharf and looked me over, kind of grand but well-meaning, same as the Prince of Wales might look at a hoptoad.

" 'Ello," says he.

" Hello, yourself," says I, keeping on with my work.

" Mr. Edward 'as ordered the boat for 'alf past eleven," he says.

" I want to know," says I. " How'll he have it —fried? "

" Beg pardon? " says he.

" You're welcome," says I. I can stand being patronized, sometimes, if I'm paid for it, but I didn't see this critter developing no cash symptoms.

" My good man," he says; " you don't understand me. I said that Mr. Edward 'ad ordered the boat for 'alf past eleven."

" I know you did. And I asked if he'd have it fried."

He seemed to be turning this over in his mind. And with every turn he got more muddled. I'd concluded by this time that he wa'n't a book agent. *What* he was though I couldn't make out nor I didn't much care. He riled me, this feller did.

" Look 'ere," says he, after a minute. " Is your name Pratt?"

" Yup," I says. " On Thursdays it is."

"Thursdays?" says he. "Thursdays? What—what is it on Fridays?"

"*Mister* Pratt," says I, pretty average brisk.

He seemed to be more muddled than ever. He looked back towards the hotel and then at me again. I had a notion he was going to sing out for help.

"My man," he says, again. "My man——"

"Humph!" I interrupted. "Well, if I'm your man whose man are you?"

And, by time! he seemed to understand *that!* "I'm Mr. Edward Van Brunt's man," says he, "and Mr. Edward 'as ordered the boat for 'alf——"

And then *I* begun to understand—or thought I did. 'Twas the keeper. Well, in some ways he looked his job.

"O—oh!" says I. "All right. Yes, yes. I heard you was coming, Mr.—Mr.——"

"'Opper," says he; "James 'Opper."

"Proud to know you, Mr. Opper," says I, which was a lie, I'm afraid.

"Not Hopper," he says. "'Opper."

"Sure! Opper's what I said," says I.

He got red in the face. "'Opper," he says. "Haitch—o-p-p-e-r."

"Oh, Hopper!" I says.

"Of course. 'Opper," he says.

I felt as if I'd been sailing a race and had made a lap and got back to the starting buoy.

"All right," says I. "What's an H or two between friends? How's your patients, Mr. Opper Hopper?"

"Look 'ere, my fine feller," he says. "You're too fresh. For a 'a-penny I'd come down and put a 'ead on you."

And right then I give up the idea that he was a retired parson. Parsons don't talk like that.

"You would?" says I. "Well, you go on putting ''eads' on the poor lunatics you have to take care of and don't try any of your asylum games with me. 'Twould be safer for you and wouldn't interfere with my work. What do you want?"

"I'm Mr. Edward Van Brunt's vally—" he says—"'is man-servant; and 'e 'as ordered you to——"

"His man-servant!" I sung out, setting up straight.

"Of course. Didn't I says so? His vally; and——"

Well, I'd made a mistake, I judged. If he was a servant he couldn't be the keeper. I ca'lated 'twas best to be a little more sociable. Besides, I was curious.

"Humph!" says I. "I guess I'd ought to beg your pardon, Mr. Opper——"

"*'Opper!*" he fairly hollered it.

"All right. Never mind. Come on aboard and let's talk it over."

So aboard he come, making a land-lubber's job of it, and come to anchor on the bench in the cockpit, setting up as stiff and straight as if he'd swallowed a marlin-spike. Then we commenced to talk, me dropping a question every once in awhile, and him dropping h's like he was feeding 'em to the hens.

"What kind of a servant did you say you was?" says I, breaking the ice.

"A vally, Mr. Edward's vally."

"Vally, hey?" says I. "Vally! Hum! I want to know!"

I guess he see I was out of soundings, so he condescends to do some spelling for me.

"V-a-l-e-t," says he. "Vally."

"Oh!" says I. "A *vallet*. Yes, yes; I see."

I knew what a vallet was—I'd read about 'em in the papers—but this feller's calling it a "vally" put me off the course. He was nothing but a foreigner, though, so I made allowances. I give him a cigar that I bought at the grocery store on the way down, and we lit up. Then he commenced to tell about himself and how he used to work for a lord once over in England. According to his tell England was next door to Paradise and the United States a little worse than the other place. "Gawd forsaken" was the best word he had for Yankeeland.

"I suppose you'll quit when the keeper comes," says I.

"Keeper?" says he. "W'at keeper?"

"Why, the feller from the asylum. How long has your boss and his messmate been crazy?" I asks.

"Crazy?" he says. "Crazy? W'at do you mean?"

"Look here," says I. "You tell me straight. Ain't Van Brunt and Hartley out of their heads?"

"Out of their 'eads? 'Eavens, no!" He was so upset that he couldn't hardly speak for a minute. Then he commenced to tell about the Heavenlies, and 'twa'n't long afore I begun to see that 'twas Nate Scudder and me that needed a keeper; we was the biggest loons in the crowd.

Seems that the Twins was rich New Yorkers—

the richest and high-tonedest kind. Both of 'em had money by the bucket and more being left to 'em while you wait. They lived on some Avenue with a number to it and they done business in the " Street," meaning that they dickered in bonds and such things, I gathered. Also I gathered they didn't have to work overtime.

" But, if they ain't crazy what made 'em come down here to live? " says I, " at Nate Scudder's? "

Well, that was a kind of poser, even for Mr. James Opper Hopper Know-it-All. He commenced to tell about society and pink teas—I guess 'twas pink; might have been sky-blue though—and races and opera parties and stocks, and " strenuous life " and the land knows what. It seemed to simmer down finally to that book " The Natural Life." Seems there was a kind of craze around New York and the cities, stirred up by that book, to get clear of luxury and comfort and good times and so on, and get to living like poor folks. Living the " Natural Life," the valet called it.

" So? " says I, thinking of how I had to scratch to keep body and soul together. " I've been right in style all my days and didn't know it. Hum! going cranberrying and fishing and clamming and taking gangs of summer folks out on seasick parties is the proper thing, hey? And your boss and his chum want to live simple?"

Yes, he said they wanted to live real simple.

"Well," says I, "if Huldy Ann Scudder cooks for 'em that's the way they'll live."

He went on with another rigmarole about how the Heavenlies had lived in New York. Cutting out everything about himself and that British lord—which was two-thirds of the yarn—there was some stuff about a girl named Page that interested me. Seems *she* was the real thing in society, too. Had money and good looks and fine clothes—all the strenuous nuisances. And she was engaged to Hartley once, but they had a row or something and broke it off. And now she was engaged to Van Brunt.

"But, see here," I says, puzzled. "If she's engaged to Van why ain't he to home courting her instead of dissipating on baked beans and thin feather beds over to Scudder's? Why ain't he to home in New York getting ready to be married?"

Well, the marriage, so James said, was to be arranged later. Near as I could find out Van and this Agnes Page had mighty little to do with the marrying. 'Twas their folks that was fixing that up. Agnes herself had gone to Europe with her ma. When she was to home she was great on charity. She done settlement work, whatever that is, and her one idea in life was to feed ice cream to children that hankered for fishballs and brown bread. This wa'n't exactly the way Lord James give it out, but 'twas about the sense of it.

"Yes, yes," says I. "But how does Hartley like chumming around with the feller that's going to marry his old girl?"

It appeared that that was all right. Hartley and Van was chums; loved each other like brothers—or better. Little thing like a girl or two didn't count. Hartley was kind of used up and blue and down on his luck and suffering from the Natural Life disease; he wanted to cut for simplicity and Nature. So Van, havin' a touch of the Natural himself, come along to keep him company.

"But this Page girl?" says I. "How does she feel on the Natural Life question?"

"Oh, she believes in it too," says his Lordship. "Only she's more interested in 'er charity and 'elping the poor and heducating 'em," says he.

I fetched a long breath. "Well, Mr. Opper—Hopper I mean—" I says, "you can say what you want to, but I'll still hang on to my first notion. *I* think the whole crew is stark, raving crazy."

I'd noticed that he hadn't been pulling at my cigar much—a good five-cent Bluebell cigar 'twas too. Now he put it down, kind of like 'twas loaded.

"My good feller," he says. "Would you mind if I tried one of me own weeds? 'Ave one yourself," says he.

I took the cigar he handed me. It was one of Van Brunt's particular brand.

"Humph!" thinks I, "your bosses may be simpletons for the love of it, Brother James, but not you. No, sir-ee! *You're* in it for the value of the manifest."

In another half hour or so the Heavenly Twins showed up alongside. And then 'twould have done you good to see that valet's back get limber. He bowed and scraped and "Sirred" till you couldn't rest. They spoke to him like he was a dog and he skipped around with his tail between his legs like he *was* one—a yellow one, at that.

When we'd passed the point out comes that everlasting book and the Twins got at it.

"Van," says Martin Hartley, setting up and taking notice; "the Natural Life for mine. I envy the lucky devils who've had it all their lives."

'Twa'n't none of my affairs, but I shoved my oar in here—couldn't help it.

"You fellers ain't getting the real article—not yet," says I. "There's a hotel over back of the village where the boarders get the *ginuine* simple life—no frills included," I says.

They was interested right off.

"Where's that, skipper?" says Van Brunt. "What's its name?"

"Well," says I, "folks round here call it the poorhouse."

Then they both laughed. Good nice fellers, as I said afore, even if they *was* crazy.

CHAPTER III

TOO MANY COOKS

IT was a day or so after that that I see Nate Scudder again. I'd been out in the sloop with a parcel of boarders—they were beginning to get thicker at the Old Home now, same as the mosquitoes—and on my way home I met Nate driving down the Neck Road. He was in the carryall and I hailed him as he come abreast of me.

"Hello, Nate!" I says. "Taking the air, are you?"

He pulled up his horse—it didn't take a hard pull—and, while the critter leaned up against the shafts and took a nap, Nate talked to me. It appeared that there'd been more or less trouble down his way. Huldy Ann and Lord James hadn't agreed any too well.

"You see," says Nate, taking a calico handkerchief out of his hat and swabbing his bald head with it, "it's that valet feller—he's too stuck-up to live."

I wa'n't going to fight with him on that point, so he went ahead with his yarn.

" He come parading out to the barn," says Nate, " and give out that he'd been appointed cook in Huldy Ann's place. Well, she'd been sort of laying herself out, as you might say, to please them two up at the house—giving 'em spider bread and dried apple pie for breakfast, and the like of that—and it riled her to be chucked overboard that way. So she got sort of sarcastic. That Opper man, he——"

" His name's Hopper," I says.

" He don't call it so, then."

" That's all right. Him and I had a spelling match here t'other day and Hopper it is," I says.

" Well, then, this Hopper feller he lorded it round, asking where the double biler was and complaining that he couldn't cook steak without a charcoal fire, and so on. Huldy took him down, I tell you!

" ' Charcoal your granny!' says she. ' I've fried more steak than you've got hairs on your head, and a plain wood fire always done me,' she says.

" He cooked that steak, and say! I'll bet the

Iron-Jawed Man I see once at a dime show up to Boston couldn't have got away with it. Tough! Why, the pesky idiot never pounded it a bit! How do you expect to get tender steak if you don't pound it? Haw! haw!"

When he got through laughing he went to say that him and Huldy had decided to go over to her sister's at Ostable for a visit.

"We've been intending to go for a good while," he says. "And now we can do it without its costing much. Pay for the house goes on whether we're there or not, and the railroad fare'll be more than made up by the saving in our own grub. I'm a peaceable feller, anyhow," says he, "and there'd be no peace while Huldy and that Britisher was together."

"Case of too many cooks spoiling the soup, hey?" says I.

"Soup!" he says. "Well, you wait a little spell. If they ain't chasing around after a new cook inside of a week I'm a Jonah, that's all."

He was right. Couple of days later I heard from Emmie T. that the Twins had hired Hannah Jane Purvis to do the cooking for 'em. Hannah Jane's late lamented had been cook on a

Banks boat when he was young, so I suppose she cal'lated she'd inherited the knack. But I had my doubts.

I was getting real chummy with the Heavenlies by this time, so one afternoon I walked up to the Scudder place to see 'em. They were sprawled out on the piazza chairs with their feet on the railing and they hailed me as friendly as if I was rich as they was, instead of being poorer than Job's turkey. I noticed Lord James tiptoeing around in the parlor, so I naturally mentioned him.

"Your valet man, here," I says; "he wa'n't quite to the skipper's taste as cook, hey?"

They both laughed, Van Brunt with his big good-natured "Ha, ha!" and Hartley with that quiet chuckle of his.

"James," said Van, "is a glittering success in the wardrobe, but he dislikes to hide his talents under a kitchen bushel."

"James," said Hartley, "appears to apply the same methods to trousers and steak."

"Presses both of 'em, don't he?" I says, thinking of Scudder's yarn.

"Flat as a board," says Van. "Besides which, this is supposed to be a pleasure cruise for Martin and me, and James serves with the cheerful dignity of an undertaker. He's too complex; we yearn for simplicity and rest."

I grinned. "Well, you've got the simplicity with Hannah, ain't you?" I asked. "I ain't saying nothing about the rest."

Both of 'em groaned. I knew Hannah Jane Purvis, and she had the name of talking the hinges off a barn door.

"Lord!" says Van. "Let's change the subject. By the way, Martin; it's odd that Agnes hasn't written."

Hartley was setting out towards the front of the porch where the sun could get at him. Now he shifted back into the shadow of the vines.

"Is it time for a letter to reach here?" he asked.

"Why, yes. I should think so. She was to reach New York on the first and sail on that day. She would probably write on the steamer. It was a fast boat and, allowing that the letter came back immediately—well, I don't know that it *is* time yet."

He began to whistle. I gathered that 'twas the Page girl he was talking about. The valet had told about her going on a trip to Europe. But it struck me that, for an engaged man, Van Brunt was the easiest in his mind of anybody ever I see.

I've never been engaged myself, but judging by them I've known who was, he'd ought to be shooting telegrams to Europe faster than you could shake 'em out of a pepper box.

Neither of 'em spoke for a minute. Then Hartley asked, quiet as usual, "Have you written her, Van?"

"Oh, yes; dropped a line the other day, telling her we were safe and duly housed and so on. Whooped up the joys of the 'Natural' and begged her to 'go thou and do likewise.' Which she would like to do, probably, but which also—if I know her highly respected mamma—she won't."

"Where did you address your letter?" Hartley asks, after a little.

"Liverpool, care of her usual hotel. She'll get it all right—always provided she hasn't already organized a settlement colony of small Hooligans in the Liverpool slums. But there! Let's forget morals and matrimony. Heigho! Wonder what's doing in the Street? Not that I care a red."

They seemed to have forgot me altogether. But I was interested in their talk all the same, and I've tried to put it down just as I heard it. 'Twas queer talk, but they was queer folks, and I was learning how the big-bugs done their courting. From what

I'd heard so far I liked the Wellmouth way full as well.

The front gate clicked. Van Brunt looked up. "Great Scott!" says he, "it's the phonograph."

'Twas Hannah Jane Purvis coming home from the next house with a dishpan full of peas. Hannah was a kind of scant patterned critter without much canvas on her poles and her sleeves most generally rolled up. She had brindled hair clewed back so tight off her forehead that her eyes wouldn't shut good, and the impression you got from the first look at her was that she was all square corners—not a round one in the lot

"Well!" says she, coming up into the wind in front of the piazza and looking at me hard. "I do believe it's Solomon Pratt. Why, what a stranger you *be!* I ain't seen you for I don't know when."

I didn't know when either and I didn't try to remember. "Sufficient unto the day is the trouble belonging to it," the Scriptures say, if I recollect it right, and 'twas enough for me that she'd seen me this time. She comes over, dishpan and all, and planks herself down on the steps right in front of Van Brunt's chair. There ain't nothing shy or unfriendly about Hannah Jane; she's the most folksy female I ever come across, and always was.

"My sakes!" says she, turning round to Van, "I see Mr. Pratt come in here and I *couldn't* make out who 'twas. Thinks I, 'They've got company and I must get there quick.' So back I put, and I don't know as I've got a full measure of peas 'cause it seemed to me that some of 'em spilled off the top when Cap'n Poundberry was emptyin' 'em in. I hope not, 'cause peas is high now. Not that it makes any difference to well-off folks like you, Mr. Van Brunt, but——"

"Hadn't you better go back and pick 'em up?" asks Van, solemn as an owl.

"Oh, land of love! no. There wa'n't enough for *that*. Besides I want to see Mr. Pratt. Well, Mr. Pratt," says she. "I suppose you're surprised enough to find me working out. Dear! dear! I don't know what Jehiel—he that was my first husband—would have said; nor my second one neither. But there! we can't none of us never tell what's in store for us in *this* world, can we?"

I made some sort of answer; don't matter what. She went ahead lamenting over what a come-down 'twas for her to work out. You'd think she'd been used to marble halls to hear her. She settles the dishpan between her knees and starts in shelling peas, talking a blue streak all the time. She was a whole sewing circle in herself, that woman.

"Jehiel was such a quiet man," she says, after a spell. "He scarcely ever talked." (Didn't have a chance, thinks I to myself.) "When he died—did I ever tell you how Cap'n Samuels—my first husband as was—come to die, Mr. Hartley?" says she.

Hartley had took up the Natural Life book and was trying to read it. Now he looked up and says, mournful but resigned, "No, Mrs. Purvis, I believe we have never had the pleasure."

"The pleasure was wholly the Cap'n's," says Van Brunt under his breath. If Hannah Jane heard him she didn't let it worry her.

"Well," she says, "'twas this way: Captain Jehiel—him that was my first husband—was the most regular man in his habits that ever was, I guess. Every Saturday night all the time we was married—and we was married eleven year, not counting the two after he was took sick—he always had baked beans for supper. I used to say to him, 'Jehiel,' I used to say, 'ain't you tired of baked beans? I should think you'd turn into beans, you're so fond of 'em.' But he never did and——"

She stopped for a second to get her breath. Van cut in quick.

"That wasn't the cause of his death, then?" he asks, very grave.

"Who—what?"

"Turning into beans? Of course not. I believe you said he didn't turn."

"I said he never got *tired* of 'em. Course he didn't turn *into* 'em. Whoever heard of such a thing? Well, as I was saying; every Saturday night we had 'em, and one night—'twas the last one, poor thing—" She stopped to unfurl her handkerchief and mop her eyes.

"Pray go on, Mrs. Purvis," says Van, very polite. "You were saying 'twas the last bean——"

"I said 'twas his last well *night*. There was *beans* enough, land knows! Well, I had 'em on the table and he set down. 'Hannah,' says he, 'I don't feel like beans to-night.' I looked at him. It wa'n't because they wa'n't good beans. I'm always as particular as can be about cooking beans. Always put such to soak over night on a Friday, and then Saturday morning I take 'em and put 'em in the bean-pot along with some molasses and a nice chunk of pork. You can't be too particular about your pork. 'Don't,' I used to say to the man that drove the butcher cart; 'don't,' says I, 'give me nothing but fat pork. Might's well have plain lard and be done with it. Give me,' says I, 'a streaked chunk; streak of lean and a streak of fat.' Then I put 'em in the oven and bake 'em all day and by night they're ready. So when Jehiel says to me, 'Hannah, I don't feel like beans,' I set and looked at him."

"Did he look like 'em?" asks Van.

Hannah Jane switched round on the step and stared at him. But he was as sober as a church and just running over with sympathy, seemed so, so she sniffed and went on.

"He looked *sick,*" she says, "and I could see that he *was* sick too. So I got him to bed and *what* a night I put in! Oh, the hot jugs to his feet! Oh, the running for the doctor! We had Dr. Blake here then, Mr. Pratt. You remember him, don't you? Great big tall man with gray whiskers. No, wait a minute. 'Twas Dr. White that had the whiskers; Dr. Blake was smooth-faced. No, seems to me he had a mustache. I remember he did because he was engaged to Emma Baker's sister's girl and she used to say that when she once got him for good he'd have to raise more beard than that. She said a doctor without a beard was like a soft biled egg without—without—without something or 'nother in it. Strange I can't think! An egg without something in it——"

"Chicken, possibly," suggests Van.

"No, indeed. Salt! that's what 'twas. A soft biled egg without salt in it. Now you'd ought to be as careful about biling eggs as you had about anything else. Way some folks bile eggs is a sin and shame. I've et eggs so hard that you could build a stone wall out of 'em, seems so; and then again I've et 'em when I've actually had to *drink* 'em. Now when *I* bile eggs I always—let me see; I wa'n't speaking of eggs when I fust started. Where was I?"

"You were telling us about beans, I believe, Mrs. Purvis," purrs Van again, sweet and buttery as can be. "I seem to have a dim recollection of beans, Mrs. P."

"Oh, yes, yes! I was going on to tell of Jehiel's sufferin's, Mr. Van Brunt. If I could *only* begin to give you an idea of that poor critter's agony. Why, he—who's that at the back door?"

'Twas the neighbor's boy, as it turned out, come to borrow a cupful of sugar, but he took Hannah

Jane away from us, which was a mercy. She dropped the dishpan and went inside.

Van Brunt looked after her. "Will some one please inform me," says he, "whether I've been at a clinic, or a funeral, or just a cooking-school session?"

"Humph!" says Hartley. "Unfortunate interruption. Now we shan't learn what became of the long-suffering Jehiel."

"Oh, he died," says Van. "*I* wanted to find out what became of those beans."

"I understand now why they put 'At Rest' on Jehiel's gravestone," I says.

Hartley turned to me. "Skipper," he says, "you mustn't think that Van and I are altogether cold-blooded because we refuse to weep over the departed Samuels. The lady has cheered us with happy little memories of this kind ever since she agreed to demean herself and make 'riz biscuit' at four-fifty per. She began with her cousin, who died of small-pox, and she's worked down through the family till she's got to her husband."

"Yes," says Van, "and he's only her first. We shall hear later how Number Two fell into a stone-crusher or was boiled in oil. Lord!"

"Hank Purvis had five brothers," says I; "and

they've all died within the last ten year. You've got more funerals coming to you."

It was quiet for a few minutes. Out back we could hear Hannah Jane laying into the neighbor's boy because he tracked mud on the kitchen floor.

"It was no use," says Van, decided. "I refuse to renew my subscription to *The Daily Morgue.* All those in favor of parting with the Widow Purvis at once, immediate, P. D. Q., will say 'Aye.' Contrary minded, 'No.' It's a vote. Hannah is erased. What shall we do, Martin—go back to James and dignity, or feed ourselves?"

Hartley seemed to be thinking. "Skipper," says he to me, "you can cook. I—even I, the interesting invalid—can eat your chowder and like it and come back for more. Will you come and help us out? What do you say?"

Van Brunt sat up straight. "Martin," says he, "you're as comforting as the shadow of a great rock in a—in a—something or other. You're a genius. Pratt, you've got to come here and live with us. We need thee every hour, as Mrs. P. sings at five A.M., which is her ungodly time for getting out of bed. It's settled; you're coming."

"Well, now; hold on," says I. "Some ways

I'd like to, and, if you want plain cooking, why, I guess likely I can give it to you. But business is business and there's my boat and my living for the summer. You're here only a month, as I understand it, and——"

That didn't make no difference. I could fetch the *Dora Bassett* along too, Van said. Hartley explained that they intended to stay through the summer, anyhow, perhaps later. He went on to tell that he and his chum was what he called "redeemed conventionalities," or some such name, and that they intended to stay redeemed. They'd hitched horses and agreed to find the Natural in all its glory. And the Natural they was *going* to find if it took a thousand year.

" And while we're giving you the story of our lives, skipper," says Hartley, with one of his half smiles, " I want to say right here that our present surroundings aren't all that fancy painted 'em. They're too much in the lime light." This was just one of his crazy ways of saying things; I was getting used to 'em a little by now. " We're too prominent," he says. "The populace are too friendly and interested."

" Also," says Van, " the select bunch of feminines from the hotel have taken to making our front walk a sort of promenade. Martin and I are naturally shy; we pine for solitude."

There was more of this, but I managed to find out that what they wanted was a quieter place than Scudder's. A place off by itself, where they could be as natural as a picked chicken. I agreed to try and help 'em find such a place. And I said, too, that I'd think about the cooking idea. Money didn't seem to be no object—I could have my wages by the hod or barrelful—just as I see fit.

"Well," says I, getting up to go. "I'll see. Let me sleep on it for a spell, same's you fellers have done on Nate's pin-feather beds. But I ain't so sure about your staying all summer. How about that young lady friend of yours, Mr. Van Brunt? She may take a notion to send for you to introduce her to the King of Chiny or the Grand Panjandrum with the little round bottom on top. Then you'd have to pack up and cut your cable."

Van, he looked hard at me for a minute. I thought first he was mad at me for putting my oar in where it wa'n't supposed to be. Then he laughed. "Sol," says he, "that young lady and I are kindred spirits. For a year I'm natural and happy, and she can nurse her Hooligans and go on charity sprees. Then—well, then we fall back on our respected parents and wedded—er—bliss. Hey, Martin?"

Hartley, in the shadow of the vines, lit another cigar and nodded. But he didn't say nothing.

For the next three or four days I chased around trying to find a house and lot where them Heavenly lunatics could be natural. I located a couple of bully summer places, all trees and windmills and posy beds and hot and cold water and land knows what. But they wouldn't do; they "smelled of coupons," Van said. What they really wanted, or thought they wanted, was a state's prison in a desert, I judged.

For a week or ten days we kept the hunt up, but didn't have no luck. Whenever I'd think I'd uncovered a promising outfit the Heavenlies would turn to and dump in a cargo of objections and bury it again. After five or six funerals of this kind I got sort of tired and quit. It got to be July and their month at Nate's was 'most over. I was up there the evening of the Third and I happened to ask 'em if they wanted me and the sloop for the next day. There was to be a Fourth of July celebration over to Eastwich, and some of the boarders wanted to go and see the balloon and the races and the greased pig chase, and such like. If the Twins didn't care I'd take the job, I said. But they took a notion to go themselves. Van said 'twould be an excuse for me to give 'em another chowder, if nothing more. So, on the morning of the Fourth we started, me and Van Brunt and Hartley and Lord James, in the *Dora Bassett.* Talk about cruises! If I'd known—and yet out of it come— But there! let me tell you about it.

CHAPTER IV

THE PIG RACE

I DON'T cal'late that I ever had a better run down the bay than I done that morning. 'Twas a fair wind, and a smooth sea, not the slick, greasy kind, but with little blue waves chasing each other and going " Spat! spat! " under the *Dora Bassett's* quarter as she danced over 'em. And that's just what she did—dance. There wa'n't any hog-wallowing for her; she just picked up her skirts, so to speak, and tripped along—towing the little landing skiff astern of her—like a sixteen-year-old girl going to a surprise party.

An early July morning on the bay down our way is good enough for yours truly, Solomon Pratt. Take it with the wind and water like I've said; with the salt smell from the marshes drifting out from the shore, mixed up with the smell of the pitch-pines on the bluffs, and me in the stern of a good boat with the tiller in my hand and a pipe in my face—well, all right! That's *my* natural life; and I don't need no book to tell me so, neither.

The Heavenlies enjoyed it, and they'd ought to. 'Twas clear then, though it got hazy over to the east'ard later on. But then, as I say, 'twas clear, and you could see the schooners strung out on the skyline, some full up, with their sails shining white in the sun, and others down over the edge, with only their tops'ls showing. Far off, but dead ahead, just as if somebody had dipped their finger in the bluing bottle and smouched it along the bottom of the sky, was the Wapatomac shore, and away aft, right over the stern, was the Trumet lighthouse, like a white chalk mark on a yellow fence, the fence being the high sand bank behind it.

The Twins laid back and soaked in the scenery. They unbuttoned their jackets and took long breaths. They actually forgot to smoke, which was a sort of miracle, as you might say, and even Hartley, who had been bluer than a spoiled mackerel all the morning, braced up and got real chipper. By and by they resurrected that book of theirs and had what you might call a Natural Life drunk. I never see printing that went to a person's head the way that book seemed to go to theirs. I judged 'twas kind of light and gassy reading and naturally riz and filled the empty places same as you'd fill a balloon.

Everybody was happy but Lord James, and I could see that he wa'n't easy in his mind. He set about amidships of the cockpit and hung onto the thwart with both hands, like he was afraid 'twould bust loose and leave him adrift. If the *Dora Bassett* had struck a derelict or something and gone down sudden I'll bet they'd have dredged up that Hopper valet and the thwart together. And then they'd have had to pry 'em apart. His Lordship wa'n't used to water, unless 'twas to mix with something else.

By and by Hartley shoves both hands into his pockets, tilts his hat back and begins to sing. More effects of the Natural Life spree, I suppose, but 'twas bully good singing. Might have been saying most anything, calling me a short lobster for what I know, 'cause 'twas some foreigner's lingo, but the noise was all right even if I did have to take chances on the words. I cal'late to know music when I hear it.

"Good!" says Van, when his chum stopped. "Martin, you're better already. I haven't heard you sing for two years or more. The last time was at the Delanceys' 'At Home.' Do you remember the Dowager and 'My daughter'? Heavens! and 'My daughter's' piano playing! Agnes told the Dowager that she had never heard anything like it. You and she were together, you know. Give us another verse."

But Martin wouldn't. Shut up like a clam and reached into his pocket for a cigar.

"That was A No. 1, Mr. Hartley," says I. "I wish you could hear Solon Bassett play the fiddle; you'd appreciate it."

Van he roared and even Hartley managed to smile. As for Lord James he looked at me like I'd trod on the Queen's corns.

Blessed if I could see what there was funny about it. Solon *can* play like an Injun. Why, I've seen him bust two strings at a Thanksgiving ball and then play "Mrs. McLeod's Reel"—*you* know, "Buckshee, nanny-goat, brown bread and beans"—on t'other two, till there wa'n't a still foot in the hall.

We made Eastwich Port about noon and had dinner. I cooked up a kettle of chowder—fetched the clams along with me from home—and 'twould have done you good to see the Heavenlies lay into it. Lord James he skipped around like a hopper-grass in a hot skillet, fetching glasses and laying out nine or ten different kind of forks and spoons side of each plate, and opening wine bottles, and

I don't know what all. When he hove in sight of the wharf that morning he was toting a basket pretty nigh as big as he was. I asked him what it was.

"Why, the 'amper," says he.

"The which?" says I.

"The lunch 'amper, *of* course," he says. "The 'amper for the heatables."

Well, I wondered then what in the nation was in it, for 'twas heavier than lead. I remember that the heft of it made me ask him if he'd fetched along some of the late Hannah Jane's left-over riz biscuit. But now I see why 'twas heavy. There was enough dishes and truck for ten men and the cook in that basket. We had my chowder and four kinds of crackers with it, and chicken and asparagus, and nine sorts of pickles, and canned plum pudding with sass, and coffee and good loud healthy cheese, and red wine and champagne. When I'd hoisted in enough of everything so my hatches wouldn't shut tight, and was pulling on one of the Twins' cigars, I says to Van——

"Mr. Van Brunt," says I, "is this part of what you call the Natural Life?"

"You bet, skipper!" says he. *He* hadn't finished the chowder end of the layout yet.

Well, I heaved a sigh. 'Twas kind of *un*natural to me, having come on me all to once; but I cal'lated I could get used to it in time without shedding no tears. Didn't want to get used to it too quick, neither; I wanted the novelty to linger along, as you might say.

When the dinner was over—the Heavenlies was well enough acquainted with the family to nickname it "lunch"—I started in to help his lordship wash dishes. The Twins sprawled themselves under a couple of pine trees and blew smoke rings.

"Hurry up there, messmate," says I to the valet; "I want to get through time enough to run up to the fair grounds and see that greased pig race."

Hartley had been keeping so still I cal'lated he was dropping off to sleep, but it seems he wa'n't. He set up, stretched, and got to his feet.

"I'll go with you, skipper," says he. "Might as well do that as anything. I've never seen a greased pig race. They don't have 'em on the Street."

"Chase nothing but lambs there," drawls Van Brunt, lazy, and with his eyes half shut. Then he turned over and looked at his chum.

"Great Cæsar! Martin," he says, "you don't

mean to tell me that you're going up into that crowd of hayseeds to hang over a fence and watch some one *run,* do you? Why any one on God's earth should *want* to run," he says, "when they can keep still, is beyond me; and why you, of all men, should want to watch 'em do it—that's worse yet. Come here and be natural and decent."

But Hartley wouldn't do it. His blue streak seemed to have struck in again and he was kicking the sand, nervous-like, with his foot.

"Come on, Van," he says. "I want the walk."

"Not much," says Van. "Walking's almost as bad as running. I'll be here when you get back." And he stretched out on the pine needles again.

It may be that Hartley did want that walk, same as he said, but he didn't seem to get much fun out of it. Went pounding along, his cigar tipped up to the visor of his cap, and his eyes staring at the ground all the time. And he never spoke two words till we got to the fair grounds.

There was a dickens of a crowd, five or six hundred folks, I should think, and more coming all the time. Everybody that could come had borrowed the horses and carryalls of them that couldn't and had brought their wives and mothers-in-law and their children's children unto the third and fourth generation. There was considerable many summer folks—not so many as there is at the cattle show in August—but a good many, just the same. I counted five automobiles, and I see the Barry folks from Trumet riding round in their four-horse coach and putting on airs enough to make 'em lop-sided.

Hartley gave one look around at the gang and his nose turned up to twelve o'clock.

"Gad!" says he, "this, or something like it, is what I've been trying to get away from. Come on, Sol. Let's go back to the boat."

But I hadn't seen so many shows as he had and I wanted to stay.

"You wait a spell, Mr. Hartley," says I. "Let's cruise round a little first."

So we went shoving along through the crowd, getting our toes tramped on and dodging peddlers and such like every other minute. There was the "test your strength" machine and the merry-go-round and the "ossified man" in a tent: "Walk right up, gents, and cast your eyes on the greatest marvel of the age all alive and solid stone only two nickels a dime ten cents," and all the rest of it. Pretty soon we come to where the feller was selling the E Pluribus Unum candy—red, white and blue, and a slab as big as a brick for a dime.

Hartley stopped and stares at it.

"For heaven's sake!" says he. "What do they do with that?"

"*Do* with it?" says I. "Eat it, of course."

"No?" he says. "Not really?"

"Humph!" I says. "You just wait a shake."

There was a little red-headed youngster scooting in and out among the folks' knees and I caught him by the shoulder. "Hi, Andrew Jackson!" says I. "Want some candy?"

He looked up at me as pert and sassy as a blackbird on a scarecrow's shoulder.

"Bet your natural!" says he. I jumped.

"Lord!" says I; "I cal'late he knows you."

Hartley smiled. "How do they sell that—that Portland cement?" says he. "Give me some," he says, handing a half dollar to the feller behind the oil-cloth counter. The man chiseled off enough for a fair-sized tombstone and handed it out. Hartley passed it to the boy. He bit off a hunk that made him look like he had the mumps all on one side, and commenced to crunch it.

"There!" says I. "That's proof enough, ain't it?"

But he wa'n't satisfied. " Wait a minute," says he. " I want to see what it *does* to him."

Well, it didn't do nothing, apparently, except to make the little shaver's jaws sound like a rock crusher, so we went on. By and by we come to the fence alongside of the place where they had the races. The sack race was on, half a dozen fellers hopping around tied up in meal bags, and we see that. Then Hartley was for going home again, but I managed to hold him. The greased pig was the next number on the dance order, and I wanted to see it.

Major Philander Phinney, he's chairman of the Eastwich selectmen and pretty nigh half as big as he thinks he is; he stood on tip-toe on the judge's stand and bellered that the greased pig contest was open to boys under fifteen, and that the one that caught the pig and hung on to it would get five dollars. In less than three shakes of a herring's hind leg there was boys enough on that field to start a reform school. They ranged all the way from little chaps who ought to have been home cutting their milk teeth to " boys " that had yellow fuzz on their chins and a plug of chewing tobacco in their pants' pocket. They fetched in the pig shut up in a box with laths over the top. He was little and black and all shining with grease. Then they stretched a rope across one end of the race field and lined up the pig chasers behind it.

"Hello!" says Hartley, "there's our Portland cement youngster. He'll never run with that marble quarry inside of him."

Sure enough, there was the boy that had tackled the candy. I could see his red head blazing like a lightning bug alongside of a six-foot infant with overalls and a promising crop of side whiskers. Next thing I knew the starter—Issachar Tiddit, 'twas—he opens the lid to the pig box and hollers "Go!"

The line dropped. That little lone pig see twenty odd pair of hands shooting towards him, and he fetched a yell like a tugboat whistle and put down the field, with the whole crew behind him. The crowd got on tiptoe and stretched their necks to see. Everybody hollered and hurrahed and "haw, hawed."

Now I've been calling the place where they had the races and so on a field. Well, twa'n't really a field, but just part of the course where they had trotting matches on cattle show days. There was a fence on each side of it and across the ends of the section they was using there was ropes stretched. Back of the fences was the crowd on foot, and back of the ropes was more of 'em, but behind these ropes likewise was lots of horses and wagons and carry-alls and such. Every wagon was piled full of people and amongst 'em I could see the Barry coach, with the four gray steppers prancing up and down in front of it and old Commodore Barry and his son on the front seat with the women folks behind.

Well, when that pig started he made a straight course for the lower end of the field, but the sight of the horses and all scared him, I guess, and he jibed and back he come again. Half a dozen of the pig chasers—them that was nearest to him when he come about—ran into each other and piled up in a heap, squirming like an eel-pot. They got up in a jiffy and started over again, meeting the gang that was coming back on the second lap.

By the time that pig had made three laps round that course he was a candidate for the hogs' lunatic asylum. Twice he'd been grabbed, once by the ears and once by a leg, but his liveliness and the grease had got him clear. About half of the boys had given up the job, and was making for harbor behind the fence; covered with sand and grease, they was, and red and ashamed. The crowd was pretty nigh as crazy as the pig, only with joy. Even Hartley was laughing out loud—first time I'd ever heard him.

That little chap with the red hair had been right up with the mourners till the third round; then he was stood on his head in the scuffle and left behind down by the ropes in front of where the Barrys was. The rest of the chasers were scattered around the other end of the field, with the pig doing the grand right and left in and out amongst their legs. One of the boys—that big lanky one whose cheeks needed mowing—made a flying jump and dove head first right on top of the critter's shiny black back. In a shake he was the underpinning, so to speak, of a sort of monument of boys, all fighting like dogs over a woodchuck.

Next thing I knew the pig shot out from underneath the pile same as if he'd been fired out of a cannon. He was squealing when he begun to fly and squealing when he lit, but his running tackle hadn't been hurt any. Down the field he went and the only one of the chasers in front of him was that little red head. He makes a grab, misses, and the pig keeps straight on, right into the crowd of men and horses and carriages.

"Look out!" yells everybody. "Let him go!" But that little shaver wa'n't built that way. Under the ropes he dives, right where the jam of wheels and hoofs was thickest. The Barry coach horses rared up and jumped and backed. You could hear wheels grinding and men yelling and women screaming.

I was one of the first over that fence, but, quick as I was, that Hartley invalid was quicker. As a general thing he moved like 'twas hardly worth while to drag one foot after the other; but now he flew. I could see his big shoulders shoving folks over like they was ninepins. Under the ropes he went and in where the tangle was the worst. And then it closed up into a screeching, kicking whirlpool like. Down he went and I lost sight of him.

Everybody on the grounds was crazy, but I cal'late I was the worst Bedlamite of the lot. Somehow I felt responsible. 'Twas me that told about the Fourth of July doings first and got him over there. 'Twas me that coaxed him into staying for the consarned pig business. And I kind of felt that I was his guardian, as you might say, now that Van Brunt wa'n't along. Yes, and by ginger, I *liked* him! Course I thought of the poor little boy, too, but I'm free to say 'twas Hartley that I thought of most.

For the doings of the next two or three minutes you'll have to ask somebody else. All's I remember real well is catching hold of Issachar Tidditt's Sunday cutaway and ripping it from main truck to keelson. You see, Issachar was trying to back out of the tangle and I was diving in. Next thing I'm sure of is hanging onto the bridle of one of the Barry horses and playing snap the whip with my feet, up and down and over and under.

She cleared up some finally and there was a ring of folks jamming and pushing and climbing between wheels and under wagon bodies, and in the middle of the ring was Hartley, kneeling on the ground and looking pretty middling white and sick, with a dripping cut over his eye, and with that little shaver's red head in his lap. And old Doc Bailey was there, but how or when he come *I* don't know. Yes, me and the pig was there, too, but the critter was out of commission, being dead, and I was too busy to think *where* I was.

"How is he, doctor?" asked Hartley anxious.

The Doc didn't answer for a minute or so; he was bending over the boy, sponging and swabbing like all possessed. Poor little chap; he looked white and pitiful enough, stretched out there amongst that crowd of strangers and not a soul of his own folks around to look out for him. And he was such a gritty little mite. I looked at him; chalk white he was, and still, with his eyes shut and his breath coming kind of short and jerky. And—well, *my* breath got jerky, too.

"How is he?" says Hartley again.

Just as he said it the boy stirs and begins to breathe more regular. The doctor seemed to feel better.

"He'll come round all right now," says the Doc. "'Twas the kick that knocked him out. The pig got the worst of it and that saved him. There are no bones broken. But he'd have been trampled to death afterwards if it hadn't been for you, sir. Better let me fix up that cut."

But the Twin shook his head kind of impatient. "'Tend to the boy," he says. So the doctor went on with his sponging and swabbing and pretty soon the youngster opens his eyes.

"Did I get him?" says he.

"What's that?" asked the Doc, stooping over.

"Did I get the pig? Is the fiver comin' to me?"

Well, you'd ought to have heard the crowd

laugh. Somebody sings out, "Three cheers for the kid," and they give 'em with a whoop.

"What's the matter with youse?" says the youngster, setting up and looking around, dizzy like. "Aw, cut it out!" he says, when they begun to holler some more. "Did I get the pig?"

"You bet you did," says the doctor, laughing. "You're a spunky little rooster. Whose boy are you, anyway? Belong in Eastwich?"

"Naw," says the little feller, like he was plumb disgusted. "N'York."

Hartley smiled. "A brother outcast," says he, looking up at me.

Major Phinney had been shoving through the crowd and now he was in the front rank, where, so they tell me, he used to be in war time—after the fighting was over.

"He's one of them Fresh Air boys," says the Major, puffing, but pompous. "There's a summer school of 'em been started just outside the town here. Couple of New York women brought the tribe down last week. This one's one."

Little red head turned to Hartley. "Say," says he, "don't you tell her."

"Tell who?" says Martin.

"The teacher. Miss Agony."

"Miss *which?*"

And just then here comes Issachar, his cutaway hanging graceful and ornamental from the collar, and piloting a mighty pretty and stylish young woman to the front. She breaks loose from him and runs for'ard and flops down on her knees.

"Why, Dennis! Why, *Dennis!*" she says. "How could you run away and behave like this? Are you hurt? Is he——"

She looks up at Hartley as she begins to ask the last question. And he was staring at her as white as a sheet of paper.

"Why, *Agnes!*" he says. And she went white, too, and then red. "Oh!" says she. And then "Oh!" again. "Oh, *Martin!*"

CHAPTER V

THE CRUISE OF THE "DORA BASSETT"

AFTER that there was a kind of tableau, same as them they have at church sociables. Here was Hartley staring at the young woman, and the young woman staring at him, and the boy staring at both of 'em, and me staring at the three, and the crowd around doing grand double-back-action staring at the whole of us. Then the party broke up, as you might say.

Hartley, red as a beet now, got up and bowed. The young woman got up too and held out her hand in a doubting sort of way. But afore he could take it, she seemed to remember something, or changed her mind, for she dropped the hand and turned to the boy, who was on his feet by this time looking down at the relics of his clothes. And between grease and sand and dirt and rags they made a ruin that was worth looking at—made you think of a rubbish pile with a red danger lantern on top.

"You naughty boy!" says she. "How could you do so? If you knew how frightened Miss Talford and I have been. Are you hurt, dear?"

"Naw," says the dear, brisk and disgusted. "Sure I ain't."

The young woman fidgeted around him, petting and "pooring" him and pinning him together, so to speak. Hartley fidgeted too, not seeming to have his bearings at all. He acted to me like he wished he was ten thousand miles away; and yet I cal'late he didn't really wish it neither. The doctor and Major Phinney were fussing around and the crowd kept getting bigger and closing in.

"If you'll excuse me, Miss," says I, interfering as usual where 'twas none of my affairs, "I think perhaps 'twould be a good idea if we went somewheres where 'twan't so popular. Maybe we might go into one of the rooms at the hall or somewheres."

"Why, of course!" says Hartley, grabbing at the notion like 'twas a rope I'd thrown out to him. "We'll go to the hall. Ag—Miss Page, let me present my friend, Mr. Solomon Pratt."

So 'twas the Page girl, after all. I'd guessed as much, though how she come to be in Eastwich when she'd ought to have been in Europe was more'n I could make out. She looked up at me and reached out her little hand with a kid glove on it. Likewise she smiled—not with her mouth alone, same as an undertaker meeting the relatives of the departed, but with her eyes too. 'Twas the right kind of a smile. I'm vaccinated and not subject to women folks as a rule, but I'd have done considerable to get a deckload of them smiles.

"I'm very glad to know you, Mr. Pratt," says she, just as though she meant it. And we shook hands—really shook 'em.

Afore I could get over that shake and smile enough to be sensible, Major Philander shoved her arm into his and headed for the hall. Drat his figurehead! You never could beat that old image when there was a pretty woman around. Hartley looked kind of set back like. Then he takes the boy by the hand and falls into the Major's wake. Me and the doctor trailed along behind.

The Doc kept talking about what a brave thing the Twin's diving under the horses was, but I didn't hear more than half of it. I was watching the Page girl's hat and thinking how much prettier 'twas than the ones them boarder girls at the hotel wore. And yet there wa'n't a quarter so many feathers and ribbons and doodads on it.

The little chap was chirping up to Hartley all the way. What worried him was when he was going to get his five dollars. Martin told him he'd get it all right. He'd advance it himself and collect it afterwards.

"What's your name, son?" says he to the youngster.

"Denny," says the boy.

"Denny? Dennis, you mean? Dennis what?"

"Aw, I don't know. Plain Denny, I guess."

"Where do you live in New York?"

"Over around Cherry Street most of the time. Me and the old man used to hang out in the back room of Mike Donahue's place on Mott Street till he got sent up. Then I got to sellin' papers and doin' shines and things. Sometimes I'd take a shy at the Newsboys' Home nights. That's where Miss Agony—Miss Page, I mean—found me. I'm one of the Fresh Air kids over to her place."

"Many more like you over there?"

"Sure! nine or ten of us; girls and all. We been here a week now. I skinned out of the winder this mornin' and hoofed it over here. Wanted to see the show. Gee! what a gang of jays!

You're the guy what put up the candy for me, ain't you?"

"Shouldn't wonder. Do you like your teacher?"

"Bet your life. She's a peach. So's the other one; Miss Talford her name is."

"Humph! What do they call you over on the East Side when you're at home?"

"Redny," says the little shaver.

Hartley looked down at him and smiled one of his quiet grins.

"Bully for you, Redny!" says he. "You're a brick."

We got through the crowd and into the hall finally. Shutting the door was a job. The folks outside seemed to think they'd been cheated. I'd like to have got rid of Philander, but you couldn't do that without a block and tackle; he stuck to Miss Page like a kedge anchor to mud bottom. The doctor was putting a strip of sticking plaster on Hartley's forehead. The cut wa'n't nothing but a scratch, I'm glad to say.

After a spell I see my chance and I cornered the Major and commenced to talk politics. He was hankering for the county representative nomination and I knew his soft spot. Hartley and the

Page girl got together then, but they didn't seem to know what to say.

I heard her explaining that she hadn't gone to Europe at all. Her ma had been took sick; nothing to speak of, I judged, spell of "nerves" or the like of that. So Agnes and her chum, this Margaret Talford, had seen the chance they'd been waiting for and had got their poor children tribe together and come down and took the Lathrop place at South Eastwich. Seems Miss Talford had hired it afore, intending to go the Fresh Air v'yage alone, long's she couldn't get Agnes to go it with her.

"But how is it that you're here?" says she. "I thought you were at the mountains."

Hartley explained that, at the last moment, he had decided to try the seashore. He was at Wellmouth for the present, he said.

"But you should have known I was here," she says. "I wrote to—to Ed, of course—before I left the city. Oh, I see! I sent the letter to your Adirondack address. But it should have been forwarded."

Hartley stammered a little, but he said quiet that he was afraid perhaps Van Brunt hadn't thought to send word to have his mail forwarded.

" I see," she says. " That's like Ed."

Martin seemed to think 'twas too, but all he said was, " He's written you very faithfully. His letters, of course, have gone to Liverpool."

Well, that was about all. We had to be going. I said good-by and we started for the door. Miss Page came over and held out her hand.

" Mr. Hartley," says she, " I want to thank you for saving Dennis; Major Phinney told me about it. It was brave. And I'm glad that you're not hurt."

She was pretty nervous, but a good deal less flustered than he was when he took her hand.

" It was nothing, of course," he says, hurried like. " That youngster was worth picking up. Good morning, Miss Page."

He stopped a second to say something about Van Brunt no doubt coming over to see her in a day or so. And then we left the hall and headed for the street.

We walked along pretty brisk for a ways, neither of us saying much of anything. Whatever there was I cal'late I said. By and by we come to the railroad crossing. And here Hartley stops short.

" Sol," says he, " I believe I'll go back by

train. I don't feel like a sea trip this afternoon. That—er—that crack on the head has shaken me up some, I guess. Explain to Van, will you? Tell him I'm all right, but that I've got a little headache. Understand?"

I presumed likely that I understood—more maybe than he thought I did. Headache is a fair to middling excuse, but I judged there was other things. I'd seen them two look at each other when they met, and—well, they say a nod's as good as a wink to a blind horse, and I ain't blind. I made a sort of note in my mind to get the pumps to working again on Lord James next time I got a chance at him alone.

Hartley left me and went over to the railroad depot and I kept on down the road to the shore. I was loafing along, going over to myself the doings of the afternoon and wondering what Van Brunt would say and so on, when I come out into the clear place at the top of Meeting House Hill. And the meeting house clock struck four.

I jumped like I'd set down on a hot stove. I hadn't no idea it was as late as that. The pig and the Page girl and the rest of the mix-up had put all notion of time out of my head. I yanked out my watch to make sure that that clock was right, and then I glanced at the sky. Over to the east'ard a big, fat, gray fog bank was piling up. 'Twas high water at two, Eastwich Port cove is a nasty place to get out of at low tide, and here was an easterly fog coming.

As a general thing I don't take anybody's wash when it comes to handling a boat, or looking out for weather and such, but now I was ready to sing small. A ten-year-old boy brought up along shore would have known better than to do as I'd done. Don't make no odds how good an excuse I had for forgetting; no excuse is good where it comes to sailboating. I went down that hill like the man in the tin coffin went to Tophet, "clinketty jingle." I jumped fences and cut across lots, and I'm ready to swear right now that there's more horse briars to the square inch in Eastwich Port than in any other place on the Lord's green earth. I bust through the pines and come out on the beach yelling, "Hi! Turn out, everybody! Get aboard now. Lively!"

And, by time! there wa'n't a soul in sight. For no less than twenty-two and a half minutes by my watch I walked up and down that beach, seeing the tide go out and bellering "Ahoy!" and "Where are you?" at the top of my lungs. And then, lo and behold you, here comes Van Brunt and Lord James, poking along as easy as if they had all the time there was. Van had been over behind the point taking a swim and his Lordship had gone along to set on his boss's trousers and keep the creases in, or some such mighty important job.

"All right, skipper; all *right*," drawls Van, cool as a Sunday school boy at an ice cream sociable. "You've got good lungs and you'd ought to be careful of 'em. I've heard you whooping for the last ten minutes. What did you and Martin have when you were up town? By the way, where *is* Martin?"

He was so everlasting comfortable and sassy and I was so biling hot and nervous that it made me mad.

"He's gone home on the train," I snapped out. "Got a headache."

"Headache, eh? Humph! What *did* you have up town and where did you get it?"

"Never mind where we got it," says I. "You'll get a headache from setting up stuck on a shoal all night if you don't get aboard that boat. Look at them clouds."

He looked at 'em. "Ah," he says; "very like a whale."

I didn't know what he meant and I didn't care.

"Whale!" says I. "Well, we'll be lucky if we ain't the Jonahs. Get aboard with that basket, you Opper what's-your-name, will you; if you want to fetch port to-night."

Lord James looked like he'd like to put another "'ead" on me, but his boss was round and he dassent talk back. Between us we loaded the dunnage. Then Van got aboard, deliberate enough to try a parson's patience, and I cast loose and got sail on the *Dora Bassett*. We'd made a start, anyhow.

But it turned out that was all we'd made. Van commenced to ask me more about Hartley, and afore I could tell him the news about the pig race and the rest, the *Dora Bassett* run her nose on a sand flat and there she stuck. I was afraid of that tide all along.

I tried to get her off with the oar, but 'twas no go. Then I pulled the skiff alongside—the one we'd been towing astern—and got into that and tried that way. But that wouldn't work either. Finally I jumped overboard up to my waist and then I got her off.

But she stuck again afore we got out of the cove.

I splashed and shoved and worked for another half hour or so, the wind dying out and the fog drifting in. Time I got her afloat this time and had listened to a steady stretch of Van Brunt's lazy sarcasms, my temper was worn to shoe-strings. Consarn the man! It didn't seem to make no difference to him whether he got home that night or a week from then.

We got out of that blessed cove and into the channel somewheres around six o'clock. Then 'twas a dead beat home and the breeze pretty nigh gone. A few minutes, and the fog shut down on us, wet and thick and heavy as ever I see it. We poked along for an hour or so more and then 'twas 'most dark and we wa'n't half way to Wellmouth. Lord James was in his usual position, hanging on to the centerboard and moving his head from one side to t'other as if he was afraid of being hit when he wa'n't looking. I'd pretty nigh scalped him with the boom once or twice and now he ducked whenever the tiller squeaked. He certainly looked like a statue of misery in a fountain, with the fog dripping off his side-whiskers.

Van was stretched out on the locker, blowing smoke rings and spouting poetry. I'd been too busy to tell him a word about his girl's being in the neighborhood. Fact is, I didn't like the feel of things. I believed there was wind coming.

"See here," says I, finally, "one of you fellers' 'll have to go for'ard and keep an eye out for shoals. We're on the edge of the channel here and I want to be in deep water afore a squall hits us. I cal'late there's one pretty nigh due."

His Lordship just stared at me fishy-eyed and pitiful. As for Van, he went on reciting something about being on the sea, "with the blue above and the blue below." *He* wa'n't going to stir—not him.

"Look here," I says. "If we strike a sand bar and a squall strikes us at the same time we'll *go* below, way down, where it's a big sight bluer than 'tis here, 'cording to the minister's tell. Go for'ard on lookout, won't you?"

So he went, though I doubt if he'd have known a bar when he see one—not that kind anyway.

Pretty soon the breeze give out altogether. And then, from off in the distance, I heard a noise, a rushing, roaring kind of noise.

"Hark!" I yells. "Do you hear that? Here she comes! Down with the jib. Haul on that rope, Mr. Van, will you? No, no! T'other one! *T'other* one! Godfrey scissors! Here you Opper; hang on to that tiller! Keep her just as she is."

I made a long arm, grabbed that valet man by the collar, yanked him into the sternsheets and jammed the tiller into his hand. Then I took a flying leap for'ard where the Twin was trying to cast loose the peak halliard, having a notion, it seemed, that it ought to belong to the jib.

The squall struck us. The fog split into pieces, same as a rotten tops'l. The *Dora Bassett* heeled over till I thought she was going on her beam ends. His Lordship turned loose a yell like a tugboat whistle, lets go the tiller and dives headfirst into the cockpit amidships. As for me, I was swinging out over the side with my whole weight on the jib downhaul, pawing air with my feet, and trying to get back my balance.

That downhaul was old and some rotten. It broke and I went overboard with a howl and a splash.

I went down far enough to begin to get glimpses of that blue place I was speaking of just now. Then I pawed up for air. When my head stuck out of water there was something big and black swooping past it. I made a grab and caught hold.

As luck would have it 'twas the skiff we was towing astern.

I climbed into that skiff like a cat up a tree. I was full of salt water—eyes and all—but I could see the *Dora Bassett* flopping ahead of me with her gaff halfway down her mast. Seems the halliard had broken just after the downhaul did.

I roared, a sputtering kind of roar. And then Van's head stuck out over the sloop's stern.

"God sakes!" says he. "Are you drowned?"

"Drowned!" I hollers. "Think I'm a pesky lubber just cause you—" I had to stop here to cough. I was a regular tank, as you might say, of salt water.

"Good heavens!" says Van. "Do they always do that—boats, I mean?"

"Always do—" I was so mad at myself and all creation that I could scarcely answer. "Oh, suffering mighty! if ever I go to sea again with a parcel of— Catch a hold of that tiller! Bring her into the wind! Cast off that mainsheet! *Cast it off! Here comes another one!*"

I suppose mainsheets are kind of scarce on the "Street." Anyhow I see that he didn't know what I meant

"That rope at the stern," I hollers, dancing around in the skiff. "Cast it off! *Lively!*"

The second squall struck us. I see the *Dora Bassett* drive off in a sweeping half circle, the end of the boom knocking the tops of the waves to pieces and the spray flying like a waterfall. And, louder than the wind or anything else, I could hear Lord James bellering for home and mother.

But 'twan't till afterwards that I remembered any of this. Just then I had other fish to fry. There was two or three ropes at the sailboat's stern and Van had cast off one of 'em, same as I ordered.

Only, as it happened, instead of the mainsheet he'd cast off the skiff's painter. Me and the *Dora Bassett* was parting company fast.

From out of the dark ahead of me come a yell, louder even than Lord James' distress signals.

"Sol!" hollers Van Brunt. "Sol Pratt!"

"Ay, ay!" I screams. "I'm all right. Never mind me. Put your helm over to port."

"Put what?"

"Put—your—helm—over—to—port! Port! you lubber! PORT!" My manners had gone overboard when I did and *they'd* missed the skiff.

'Twas quiet for a minute. Then, from further off comes the screech:

"What — part — of—the — damn—thing—is—port?"

"Never mind!" I yells. "Keep—her—just—as — she — is. You'll — fetch — up — all — right. Better—take—reef. Slack—that—main—sheet!"

Then I had to quit and grab up the oars and bring the skiff bow on to the seas. When I got her headed right I couldn't see nor hear nothing of the *Dora Bassett*. As Major Philander Phinney says when he gets to telling how much better General Grant would have done if he'd took his advice. I was "disconnected with my base of supplies."

CHAPTER VI

OZONE ISLAND

I WAS pretty busy for the next good while 'tending to that skiff. And scared, don't say a word. Not scared for myself, you understand—no indeed. When I get drowned, with a tight plank under me and a pair of oars in my hand, 'twon't be in the bay, I'll tell you that. But I was scared for Van Brunt and His Lordship in the *Dora Bassett*. They didn't either of 'em know the jib boom from the rudder, and the valet was too crazy frightened to be of any use if he had.

But Van was sure to be cool enough, and the broken gaff would act like a double reef, so that was some comfort. And the squall wa'n't going to amount to nothing—'twas only a fair breeze even now—so if Van had sense enough to keep the tiller straight and let her run they'd fetch up somewheres alongshore, I judged. And, to make me hope still more, the squall had brought a complete change of wind with it; now 'twas blowing back up the bay instead of out to sea.

So I squared my shoulders and laid to the oars, heading for where, judging by the wind, the land ought to be. 'Twas darker than a black kitten in a nigger's pocket, but I cal'lated to be able to hit the broadside of the United States somewheres. I got aground on the flats five or six times, but along towards midnight I butted ashore at the little end of nowhere where there was nothing but bushes and sand and pines, no sign of civilization. And by this time 'twas pouring rain.

After a couple of years of scratching and swearing and falling down I come out of the scrub into a kind of clearing. Then I discovered a barbed wire fence by hanging up on it like a sheet on a line and located the back of a barn by banging into it with my head. Then a nice talkative dog come out of the barn and located me, and things commenced to liven up.

While me and the dog was conducting our experience meeting a light showed in an upstairs window a little ways off and somebody sticks their head out and wants to know what's the matter.

"Who are you?" he says.

"My name's Pratt," says I.

"*Where* are you?"

"Well," I says, "judging by the feel and smell I'm on the top of the pig-sty. But I ain't real sure. I can tell you where your dog is, if you want to know."

"What are you doing round here this time of night?" he says.

I told him as well as I could. The dog was having a conniption fit, trying to bark itself inside out, and I had to say things over three or four times so's a body could hear. But the feller at the window wa'n't satisfied even then. I never see such a wooden-head.

"*What* Pratt did you say you was?" he hollers.

I told him my name and where I hailed from.

"Sol Pratt?" says he. "Of Wellmouth? What are you doing way over here?"

"Blast it all!" I yells. "If I wa'n't half drowned already I should say I was getting wet. Turn out and let a feller into the kitchen or somewheres, won't you? And tie up this everlasting dog."

That seemed to wake him up some and in ten minutes or so he comes poking out with a lantern. I knew him then. 'Twas Ebenezer Holbrook, Huldy Ann Scudder's sister's husband, who lives over in the woods on the line between South Eastwich and West Ostable. There was another man with him and blest if it didn't turn out to be Nate Scudder himself. Him and Huldy was visiting over there, same as he said they was going to.

Nate had more than a million questions to ask. Ebenezer tied up the dog—the critter pretty nigh broke down and sobbed when he found I wa'n't to be fed to him—and we went into the kitchen. Then Mrs. Holbrook and Huldy Ann, rigged up tasty and becoming in curl papers and bedquilts, floated downstairs and there was more questions.

When Nate found out that one of his lodgers was cast adrift in the bay he was almost as worried and upset as I was. But Ebenezer agreed with us that there was a good chance of the sloop's getting ashore safe. He said why didn't I turn in on his setting-room lounge for the few hours between then and sun-up, and in the morning me and Nate could take his yawl dory and cruise alongshore and hunt. So I done it, though 'twas precious little sleep I got.

About six o'clock we started. I thought first I'd go up to Eastwich village and telegraph to Hartley. Then I thought I'd better not; no use to scare him till I had to. Nate had heard about the pig chase and Hartley's doings over there and he pestered the life out of me with questions about that.

"Queer that boy should turn out to be his brother, wa'n't it?" he says.

"Whose brother?" says I, leaning out over the yawl's side and watching for signs of the *Dora Bassett*.

"Why, Hartley's," says he.

"Brother!" says I. "'Twan't his brother. No relation to him."

"I heard different," he says. "I heard 'twas his brother, name of Oscar Dennis. And that woman from the school was his brother's wife. Some says she ain't living with her husband and some say Hartley's right name is Dennis and that she's his wife and he was down here hiding from her. Seems when that boy first dove into the crowd 'twas because he'd seen Hartley. They say that when that woman and this Hartley met, she sings out, 'My God! my husband!' That's what some says she said, and others says——"

"She never said no such thing," I says. "She wouldn't swear if he was her husband four times over; she ain't that kind. And she ain't his wife nor his sister nor his sister-in-law nor his grandmother's cat's aunt, neither. She's no relation to him and neither's the boy. Who's been giving you all this rigmarole?"

It seems he'd heard it from a feller that lived next door to Ebenezer; and the feller had heard it from somebody else that had got it from somebody else and so on and so on and so on. Nigh's I could find out it had started from Hartley's telling me that the boy was a "brother outcast." Some idiot with poor ears and worse brains had thought he said "brother Oscar," and the whole string of yarns had sprouted from that. Shows you what good soil there is for planting lies down our way. If lies was fetching ten cents a barrel the whole neighborhood would have been rich years ago.

All the time me and Nate was pow-wowing this way the yawl was sailing up the bay towing my skiff behind her. There was a nice fair wind and a smooth sea and 'twas so clear after the rain, that we could see the hills across the bay. But no sign could we see of the *Dora Bassett* nor her passengers. I was getting more worried every minute.

We cruised along till we got abreast of the point from where the Old Home pier was in sight. But the sloop wa'n't at the pier. No use going any farther, so we come about and begun to beat back again the way we'd come. Scudder was worried too, but his worriment had caught him in the pocketbook; proves how disease will always get hold of a feller's tenderest place.

"Look here, Sol," says he; "do you cal'late Hartley 'll want to stay to my house if his chum's drowned?"

"I don't know," I says, impatient. "No, I guess not."

"Well now, he agreed to take it for a month and there's five days to run yet. Ain't he liable for them days?" he says.

I was feeling just mean enough to want somebody else to feel that way, so I answers,

"Well, you can't hold a lunatic, 'cording to law. And you and Huldy Ann have agreed that he's crazy."

He thumped the boat's rail. "Crazy or not," says he, "I can't afford to lose them days. I shan't give him back none of his money." Then he thought a minute and begun to see a speck of comfort. "Maybe the shock of t'other feller's drowning 'll make him sick," he says. "Then he'll have to stay *longer* than the month."

Trust Nate Scudder to see a silver lining to any

cloud—and then rip out the lining and put it in his pocket.

By this time we was beating in towards where the Neck Road comes down to the beach. And there on the shore was a feller hailing us. And when we got close in it turned out to be Hartley himself.

He was glad enough to see me, but when he found that Van and Lord James had turned up missing he was in a state. He'd been kind of scared when we didn't come back during the night and had walked down to the beach in the morning to see if he could sight us.

We headed off shore again. Nate watched Hartley pretty close and I suppose when he seen that the Twin didn't show any symptoms of getting sick, he begun to worry again. He got out a piece of pencil and an old envelope and commenced to figure.

"Mr. Hartley," says he, after awhile; "about them lady friends of yours over to Eastwich. Do you cal'late they're going to like where they are? Seems to me a place that's as easy to run away from as that ain't the best place for a boy's school. If they was on an island now, the scholars couldn't run off. I know a nice island they could have cheap. Fact is, I own it—that is, Huldy owns it; it's in her name. That's it over there."

Hartley didn't answer. I looked where Nate was pointing.

"Oh!" says I. "Horsefoot Bar. That's a healthy place for a school. Might do for a reform school maybe, if you wa'n't particular how the reforming was done."

Horsefoot Bar is a little island about five mile from the Old Home House, a mile and a half from the mainland, and two foot from the jumping-off place. By the help of Providence, decent weather, a horse, two whips, and a boat, you can make it from Wellmouth depot in three hours. And when you have made it, you can set in the sand and hang on to your hat and listen to the lonesomeness. I'd forgot that Scudder owned it. When him and I had sailed up that morning we'd passed it on the outside; now we was between it and the beach.

"It's a nice dry place," says Nate, arguing, "and you might live there forever and nobody could run away."

"Humph!" says I, thinking of something I'd seen in a newspaper; "Hell's got all *them* recommendations."

Hartley was looking at the Bar now. All to once he grabbed me by the arm and pointed.

"Sol," he says, "what's that sticking up over the point there? There, behind those trees? Isn't it a boat's mast?"

I looked, and looked once more. From where we was you could see a part of Horsefoot Bar that was out of sight from the rest of the bay. As I say, I looked. Then I gave the tiller a shove that brought the boom across with a slat. It took Nate's hat with it and cracked him on the bald spot like thumping a ripe watermelon. Nate grabbed for the hat and I drove the yawl for Horsefoot Bar. I'd spied the *Dora Bassett's* mast over the sandspit.

In a jiffy we see her plain. She was lying on her side in a little cove, just as the tide had left her. Her canvas was down in a heap, partly on deck and partly overboard, but she didn't seem to be hurt none. I beached the yawl just alongside of her, dropped the sail, chucked over the anchor and jumped over myself. Hartley and Scudder followed. We was yelling like loons.

Up through the bunch of scrub pines we tore, still hollering. And then, from away off ahead somewheres, come the answer. I was so tickled I could have stood on my head.

In a minute here comes Lord James to meet us. His Lordship looked yellow and faded, like a wilted sunflower, and his whiskers seemed to be running to seed. But his dignity was on deck all right.

"Mr. 'Artley," says he, touching what was left of his hat; "'ope you're well, sir."

"Where's Van?" asked Hartley, brisk.

"Mr. Van Brunt, sir? Up at the 'ouse, waiting for you, sir."

"The house?" says Hartley.

"The *house*?" says I. Then I remembered.

There is a house on Horsefoot Bar. It was built by old man Marcellus Berry, and in Marcellus's day they *built* houses, didn't stick 'em together with wall paper and a mortgage, like they do now. Consequence is that, though the winter weather on Horsefoot made Marcellus lay down a considerable spell ago, his house still stands, as pert and sassy an old gable-ended jail as ever was. The house was there, and Scudder owned it. Likewise he owned the sheds and barn in back, and the sickly bunch of scrub pines, and the beach plum bushes, and the beach grass and the poverty grass, and the world-without-end of sand that all these things was stuck up in. As for the live stock, that was seven thousand hop-toads, twenty million sand fleas, and green-heads and mosquitoes forever and ever, amen.

We fell into the valet's wake and waded through the sand hummocks up to the house. And there on the piazza, sitting in a busted cane-seat chair with his feet cocked up on the railing and the regulation cigar in his mouth, was Van Brunt, kind of damp and wrinkled so far as clothes went, but otherwise as serene and chipper a Robinson Crusoe as the average man is likely to strike in one life time.

Wa'n't we glad to see him! And he was just as glad to see us.

"Hello, skipper," says he, reaching out his hand. "So you got ashore all right. Good enough. I was a bit fearful for you after you left us last night."

After I left *him!* I liked that. And he was fearful for *me*.

"Humph!" says I, "I had a notion that 'twas you that did the leaving. Talk about dropping an acquaintance! I never was dropped like that afore! Look here, Mr. Van Brunt, afore you and me go to sea together again we'll have a little lesson in running rigging. I want to learn you what a mainsheet is."

"Oh," he says, careless like, "I guess I found it, after a while. At any rate if it's a rope I cut it. I cut all the ropes in sight."

"You *did?*" says I, with my mouth open.

"Yes. That's an acrobatic boat of yours; it seemed to want to turn somersets. I judged that that sail made it top-heavy so I told James to take the sail down. He didn't know how but we decided that the ropes must have something to do with it. So I cut 'em, one after the other, and the sail came down."

"Sudden?" says I.

"Well, fairly so. Some of it was in the water and the rest of it on James. I resurrected him finally and we pulled most of it into the boat. It went better then."

"Did, hey?" says I. I was learning seamanship fast.

"Yes," says he. "If I were you I wouldn't have any sail on that boat. She does much better without one. Then it began to rain and I got some of the dry sail over me. I believe I went to sleep then—or soon after."

Nate Scudder's eyes was big as preserve dishes. I guess mine was bigger still.

"Good Lord!" says I. "Did his—did James go to sleep too?"

"No," says Van. "I think not. I believe James was holding some sort of religious service. How about it, James?"

His Lordship looked sheepish. "Well, sir," he says. "I don't know sir. I may 'ave been a bit nervous; I'm not used to a boat, sir."

"I shouldn't mind your praying, James," Van says, sober as a deacon; "if you didn't yell so. However, we got here on this island about five o'clock, I believe. Rather, the boat came here herself; we didn't have anything to do with it."

I never in *my* life! They say the Almighty looks out for the lame and the lazy. Van Brunt wa'n't lame, but——

"Well," says I. "I'll believe in special Providences after this."

Van jumped out of the chair.

"By George!" he sings out. "Talking of special Providences; Martin, come here."

He grabbed t'other Twin by the arm and led him down off the piazza and up to the top of a little hill near the house. The rest of us followed without being invited. I know you couldn't have kept me back with a chain cable. I haven't visited many asylums and I wanted to see the patients perform.

"Look here, Martin," says Van, when we got to the top of the hill. "Look around you."

We all looked, I guess; I know I did. There was the old Berry house, square and weather-beat and gray. And there was a derelict barn and a half dozen pig pens and hen houses stranded alongside of it. And there was Horsefoot Bar all around us for a half mile or so, sand and beach grass and hop-toads, all complete. And beyond on one side was the bay, with the water looking blue and pretty in the forenoon sunshine. And on t'other side was the mile and a half strip we'd just sailed across, with the beach and mainland over yonder. Not a soul but us in sight anywheres. The whole lay-out would have made a first-rate photograph of the last place the Lord made; the one He forgot to finish.

"Look at it!" hollers Van. "Look at it! Now what is it?"

I begun to be sorry the keeper hadn't arrived that time when I thought he was coming. I cal'-

lated he was needed right now. Martin seemed to think so, too. He looked puzzled.

"What is it?" he says. "What's what? What do you mean?"

"Why this whole business. Island and house and scenery and quiet and all. You old blockhead!" hollers Van, giving the other Twin an everlasting bang on the back; "Don't you *see?* It's what we've been looking for all these weeks—it's the pure, unadulterated, accept-no-imitations *Natural Life!*"

I set down in the sand. Things were coming too fast for *me*. If this kept on I'd be counting my fingers and playing cat's cradle along with the rest of the loons pretty soon. I knew it.

But, would you believe it, Martin Hartley didn't seem to think his chum was out of his mind. He fetched a long breath.

"By Jove!" he says, slow; "I don't know but you're right."

"Right? You bet I'm right! It's been growing on me ever since I landed. We'll be alone; no females, native or imported, to bother us. Here's a bully old house with some furniture, bedsteads and so on, already in it. I broke a window and climbed in for a rummage. Jolliest old ark you ever saw. Here's a veranda to sit on, and air to breathe, and a barn for a cow, and plenty of room for a garden and chickens—whew! Man alive, it's Paradise! And I want to locate the man that owns it. I want to find him *quick.*"

He didn't have to say it but once. Nate Scudder was so full of joy that he had to shove his hands in his pockets to keep from hugging himself.

"*I* own it," he says.

"You *do!* Scudder, you're a gem. I begin to love you like a brother. Martin and I hire this place; do you understand? It's ours from this minute, for as long as we want it."

Nate commenced to hem and haw. "Well, I don't know," he says. "I don't know's I ought to let you have it. There's been considerable many folks after it, and——"

"Never mind. They can't have it. We outbid 'em. See?"

"What will we do for groceries?" asks Hartley considering.

"Scudder 'll bring 'em to us," says Van. "Won't you, Scudder?"

"Well, I don't know, Mr. Van Brunt. I'm pretty busy now, and——"

"We'll pay you for your time, of course."

"What about beds and cooking utensils and so on?" asks Hartley, considering some more.

"Scudder'll buy 'em for us somewheres."

"And milk, and eggs, and butter?"

"Scudder—till we get our own chickens and cow."

"And—er—well, a cook? Who'll do the cooking?"

Van Brunt stoops down and slaps me on the shoulder.

"Pratt," says he. "Pratt will come here and cook for us, and navigate us, and be our general manager. Pratt's the boy!"

"Hold on there!" I sings out. "Avast heaving, will you. If you think for one minute that I'm going to quit my summer job to come to this hole and live, you're——"

"You're coming," says Van. "Never mind the price; we'll pay it. Now shut up! you're coming."

What can you say to a chap like that? I groaned.

"Live on Horsefoot Bar," I says. "*Live* on it!"

"Horsefoot Bar?" says Van. "Is that its name? Well, it's Horsefoot Bar no more. I've been evolving a name ever since I began to breathe here. Breathe, Martin," he says. "Draw a good breath. That's it. That's pure ozone. Gentlemen, permit me to introduce to you, *Ozone Island.*"

Scudder grinned. He was feeling ready to grin at most anything just then.

"Ozone Island?" says Hartley. "Ozone Island. A restful name. Well, it's a restful spot. Isn't it, skipper?"

"Yes," says I. "As restful as being buried alive; and pretty nigh as pleasant."

CHAPTER VII

SWEET SIMPLICITY

AND so that's how they begun to live the Natural Life, what Van called the "accept-no-imitations" kind. I say "they" but I ought to have said "we" for I was in it. I was in it over head and hands from that time on. I didn't mean to be. When I said I wouldn't emigrate to Horsefoot Ozone and be cook and general roustabout for the Heavenly Twins I was just as certain I meant what I said as a body could be.

"No," says I.

"Yes," says Van.

"How can I leave the Old Home folks?" I says.

"How can you leave us?" he says.

"But you've got James."

"Yes, but James hasn't got us."

"But I can't *afford* to come," says I.

"You can't afford to do anything else," says he.

And that's about what it amounted to—I

couldn't afford to do nothing else. The wages kept jumping like summer folks' bids at one of them auction sales of "antiques." I seemed to be as valuable as grandmother's busted hair cloth sofa. If I'd hung out long enough I cal'late the Heavenlies would have fixed me so I'd have begun to feel 'twas a crime to die rich. *I* give in first; I want everybody to understand that.

"All right," says I. "That'll do; I'll come. But I hope you'll pay me in a dark room. I'll be ashamed to look you in the face and take that much money."

They said they was satisfied if I was. I was satisfied, all but my conscience. Made me wish I could swop consciences with Scudder.

Nate's conscience wasn't worrying him any; you can bet on that. I wa'n't around when he made the deal for renting 'em the island, but, from what I heard afterwards, the price would have been high if he'd been selling it to 'em by the pound to scour knives with. He agreed to get bedding for 'em and tin things, and a pig, and crockery, and hens, and groceries, and boards to tinker up the barn with, and anything else that might come in handy. Likewise he was to fetch and carry for 'em between the village and the island; so much to fetch and twice that to carry. And Huldy Ann was to do the washing.

When the Twins told me about it you'd think they'd just pulled through one of them stock "deals" of theirs, and come out on top.

"Isn't it great?" crows Van, happy as a clam at high water. "We've arranged it all. Everything is provided for and will be done."

I could see *two* things that was going to be done—brown; but I didn't say nothing.

"It's mighty good of Scudder to accommodate us this way," says Hartley. "He's a gem, a rough diamond."

"Scudder," says Van, "is one of Nature's noblemen."

Of course 'twa'n't none of my funeral; I couldn't interfere. But I'm a democrat myself, so the nobility don't appeal to me much, and if Nate Scudder's a diamond I'm glad I can't afford jewelry.

The next day was a busy one for all hands, each in his own particular line. Nate commenced running "accommodation" trains, so to speak, between his house and the village and Horsefoot Bar—Ozone Island, I should say. As for me, I went up to the Old Home House right off, explained matters to the manager, and cleared out for my new job. The Heavenlies moved over to Ozone that very morning. Lord James went with 'em and the simple naturalness commenced.

Fast as Nate would arrive in his dory with a cargo of dunnage I'd cart it up to the Berry house and dump it on the piazza. Lord James was flying around, with a face on him as sour as a cranberry pie, opening windows and airing rooms and sweeping out, and the like of that. The old shebang had been shut up for a couple of years and was as musty and damp as a receiving tomb. His Lordship looked like the head mourner; this kind of work jarred his dignity.

"Look a-'ere, Pratt," says he to me. "'Ow long do you think we're going to stay 'ere?"

"Where?" says I, sliding a trunk and a coal hod off my shoulders, and mopping my forehead with my shirt-sleeve.

"Why 'ere, on this 'orrible sand 'eap."

"You want to be careful," says I, "how you call names. This is Ozone Horsefoot Island, and it's a branch station of Paradise. Didn't you hear the boss say so?"

"But 'ow long are we going to stay 'ere?" he says again.

"Well," says I, "when a feller gets to Paradise it's the general idea that he's there for keeps. What are you growling about? Such a nice restful spot, too. Don't you like to be restful?"

He looked at his hands, they was all over blisters from the broom.

"Restful!" he groans. "Good 'eavens!"

"Come, James," says Hartley, loafing around the corner, with his hands in his pockets. "Get a move on. We must have this house in order by to-night."

The Twins was awful busy, too. They done the heavy superintending. Hartley superintended the house and piazza and Van Brunt bossed the unloading and trucking of the dunnage from the dory. As for me, I was the truck. After the first day was over I could see that all the natural living I'd done in my time wa'n't the real thing at all. Not a circumstance to it.

I carted dunnage all the forenoon. Then I cooked dinner and washed dishes. James was going to help me wipe 'em but Van's clothes had got wet when he was adrift in the *Dora Bassett* and they had to be pressed. So I wiped and cleaned up and carted more dunnage, including stove pipe and blankets and flour and quilts and nails and pork and pillows and a rake and sugar, and the land knows what. Then I cooked supper. And *how* them Paradise tenants did eat!

"By gad, you know!" busts out Van Brunt, with his mouth full; "this is what we've been looking for, Martin. *This* is getting back to nature."

Hartley grunted, being too busy with a fried mackerel to talk with comfort. But it was easy to see he was satisfied.

They went on, bragging about how good it was to cut loose from the fight and worry of the Street. At last, according to Van, they realized that life was worth living.

"No more speculation for me," he says, joyful. "No more fretting about margins. I don't give a continental if the bottom drops out of the market and carries the sides with it. I hereby solemnly swear for the fifth time never to buy another share of stock."

Then he reaches after another half-acre slab of my johnny-cake.

Lord James was upstairs in the sleeping vaults sorting out bed clothes. The sheets and blankets and things was more or less mixed up with the hardware and groceries. I was out in the kitchen getting ready a second relay of mackerel. The dining-room door was open, so I could see and hear everything.

" By the way, Martin," says Van, buttering the johnny-cake, " how did Agnes look? Well?"

" Yes," says Hartley, short.

" She must have been surprised to see you. Did you tell her we were naturalized citizens, or on the road to it?"

" No."

" No? Why not? She probably thinks that we're down here organizing another syndicate. For a girl whose mother is of the world worldly, Agnes has developed queer ideas. I suppose I ought to go over and see her," he went on. " You said she had another girl with her. Who is it?"

" Margaret Talford."

" Talford—Talford? One of the Newport Talfords? Oh, I know. Pretty little girl, dark hair and brown eyes, and—and a *way* with her?"

" I guess so. Very likely. I haven't seen her."

Van seemed to be thinking. " I'll go over to-morrow," he says.

Then he commenced to whoop for more mackerel and 'twas time for me to load up the platter.

I thought I'd cooked supper enough for six men, but when the Twins got through I had to fry another ration for me and Lord James. Eat! I never see such sharks in *my* life.

When they'd finished everything on the table, except the knives and forks and the dishes, the Heavenlies went outside to smoke cigars and promenade up and down the beach. His Lordship and I set down to have a bite ourselves.

"Say," says I, "that Page girl is a good looker, ain't she?"

He was horrified, same as he always was when you mentioned the New York big bugs without getting up and bowing.

"Miss Page," says he, "is a member of one of our first families."

"Want to know," says I. "First in what?"

"First in everything," he says. "Her father was one of our oldest residents."

"So?" says I. "Oldest inhabitant, hey? I suppose he could remember way back afore the town hall was built, and about the hard winter of '38, and how his ma's cousin used to do chores for George Washington."

I knew pretty well what he meant, but, you see, I liked to stir him up. He was such an innocent critter; always swallowed hook, line and sinker. It done me good to see him stare at me after I said things like this.

All he said now though was " 'Orrors! "

" How about your boss, this Van Brunt? " says I. " He's another first rater, hey? "

The Van Brunts was even more " first families " than the Pages, so the valet said. They'd been there ever since New York was built. 'Twas their ancestors that got up the first barn-raising, or words to that effect.

" And Hartley? " says I.

That was different. The Hartleys was another breed of cats. Martin's dad was born in Chicago or somewheres outside of New York. He'd repented of it, of course, and tried to live it down, but he never had been quite the big apples on the top layer, like the Van Brunts. He was dead now, old man Hartley was; been dead three or four years.

" How about ma? " says I.

She was dead, too; died a year or more ago. Martin was an orphan.

And then I cal'lated it was about time to heave out the question that I'd been leading up to all along.

"What made the Page girl cut loose from him and take up with Van?" I says. "She don't look like the kind that would be too hard on a chap just because his dad made the mistake of being born out of township limits."

Lord James fidgeted some over that. First he said he didn't know.

"Well," says I, "let's guess then. Guessing's a good Yankee trick and you'd ought to have picked it up by this time. You guess first."

He didn't want to guess, but I kept at him, throwing out all sorts of foolish maybes and perhapses. Finally he got tired of saying "No."

"Oh, I don't know," says he. "I 'eard as 'ow 'twas because 'e was too mercenary. 'E was an awful chap in the Street after 'is old man died. 'E was there night and day. 'Ardly came 'ome at all."

"Humph!" says I. "I'd never suspicioned it to look at him. Wa'n't he doing well at his job?"

Lord James said it wa'n't that. Said he was doing mighty well. Folks was calling him a "born financier" and all sorts of names.

"So?" says I. "Then I don't see that Miss Page had any complaints. 'Tain't usual for a young woman to kick because her steady company is making too much money. There's something else. Out with it. I'll keep my mouth shut."

So then he told me a little—much as he knew, I guess likely. Seems that he was acquainted with the feller they call the butler—sort of a steward, I judged he was—over at the Page girl's house. And this butler was sweet on the "maid"—the young woman valet who took care of Agnes's duds and spare rigging. And one night this maid happened to be in the "conservatory"—which I presumed likely was the high-toned name for the preserve closet—and Miss Page and Hartley was in the setting room. And Agnes was laying into Martin for staying down town and neglecting her.

The maid said she could hear only part of the talk, but 'twas more than average sharp and vinegarry. Agnes told Martin he was getting more mercenary every day he lived. That all he thought of was the office and making money. She detested a mercenary, hard, money-grasping man. Said money-loving was the worst vice there was, and she thanked God she had none of it, meaning vice, of course—she had money enough to sink a ship.

Then Martin he speaks up proud and short and says he *has* been working hard and had been trying to make money. Said he had a good reason for it, and some day he would tell her what it was. She said he could tell her now or hang his May-baskets on somebody else's door—or words to that effect. He says " Very well," and she says something else, but the maid didn't hear it because just then old lady Page come in and give her her walking papers for listening.

" And so," says Lord James, " the engagement was broke off. And a good thing too, I say. W'at's the use of 'er lowering 'erself to marry a man whose father got 'is money in trade? "

" How did Van's dad get his money? " I asks.

" By in'eritance," says he. " Of course Mr. Edward dabbles in shares, but, Lord love you, only for the fun of it."

" How was the inheritance come by in the first place? " says I. He didn't know, but I found out afterwards. Grandpa Van Brunt was an alderman.

The Twins come back into the house then. They come in slapping and jawing. I judged that the mosquitoes was living the Natural Life too. The Heavenlies set down on each side of the fireplace—I had a wood fire going, just for sociableness—and smoked and talked.

By and by Van rummages out that Natural book and spreads it open.

"Martin," says he, "hark to the voice of the oracle. Come in here, skipper, and improve your mind."

But me and his Lordship was improving the dishes just then, and, when that was done, he had beds to make and I had bread to mix and fires to lay and wood to chop and a couple of million other chores to do. The Twins read and talked until they got sleepy, which was about half past nine or so; earlier than usual, but neither of 'em had rested well the night afore, I guess. Anyhow they went upstairs to turn in and I kept on with my work. Lord James turned in too. He had the back bedroom, the one over the kitchen.

'Twas still as still could be. The door and windows was open and there wa'n't a sound except the mosquitoes humming glad and thankful, and the breeze whining in the pines outside and the waves moaning along the bay shore of the island. Once in awhile I'd hear his Lordship thrash over in bed and fetch a grunt or a groan in his sleep. He had one of the late Marcellus's cornhusk mattresses and I wouldn't wonder if there was a cob end or two in with the husks. A rake across the back from a corn cob ain't the most comforting thing in the world even when a feller is used to it, and Lord James had been brought up tender.

Pretty soon I went to the back door to throw out some fish-bones and things and then I heard somebody tramping through the sand up to the house. Neighbors are scarcer than snake's finger-nails 'round Horsefoot Ozone and I couldn't think who was coming at this time of night. I ain't a nervous chap, generally speaking, but I remembered how old Marcellus had died in this very house all sole alone, and the short hairs at the back of my neck begun to bristle up. I cal'lated if anything would fetch a sot old codger like Marcellus out of his grave, the doings of the Heavenlies was that thing.

But in a minute more the walker got into the light from the door and I could see him. And I was 'most as much surprised as if he *had* been Marcellus himself. 'Twas Nate Scudder, with his arms full of bundles.

"What in the nation?" says I.

"Hello, Sol," says he. "Where's the folks?"

"Turned in," says I. "What's up?"

He seemed real disappointed. Set the bundles down on the kitchen table and puffed. That sand is hard walking, and nobody knows it better than I do.

"Turned in so early, have they?" he says. "That's too bad. I wanted to see 'em."

"Want me to roust 'em out?" I asks.

"No, I guess not. But they're nice folks as ever I see and I've fetched 'em a few presents."

I flopped into a chair. I was getting used to surprises, but Nate's giving anybody a present was the biggest wonder yet. I figured that lunacy was catching and we was all going crazy together.

"Yes," says he. "Me and Huldy Ann's been talking it over. They've hired this house and—and—all the rest of it and we want 'em to like it. Don't want 'em to get tired and leave, you see."

I see all right. When the melon's getting ripe that's the time to watch it.

"Yes," he says. "I like them young feller's well's anybody I ever see and so does Huldy. We got to thinking of 'em over here in this big house and we wanted 'em to feel at home; just as if *'twas* home. Now there's nothing like pictures and such on the walls to make a place homey. So Huldy and me has sent 'em these few things to hang up 'round."

He commenced to undo the bundles.

"'Twas Huldy Ann's notion," he went on. "When she bought this place at auction there was the furniture and fixings in it that belonged to Marcellus. Some of 'em we left here, beds and chairs and the like of that, and some we took over to our house. There was more than we needed and these is some we had in the attic."

He'd got the newspapers and strings off by this time and he spread the presents out on the floor. There was a wax wreath, from old Mrs. Berry's funeral, in a round case; and a crayon enlargement of a daguerreotype of Marcellus when he was thirty or so; he had a fancy vest on and a choker and a fringed-end necktie, and looked like he was freezing to death fast and knew it. Likewise there was a shell work basket in a shell frame with about a third of the shells missing; and two silver coffin plates on black velvet; and a worsted motto thing with "What is Home Without a Mother" on it.

"There!" says Nate, happy and generous. "We'll give 'em them things, Huldy and me. Leastways they can have 'em to look at while they're here. Have 'em strung around on the setting-room walls and it kind of takes off the bare look. Gives 'em something to think about too, don't it?"

"Yes," says I; "I should think 'twould. I wouldn't think of much else, seems to me."

"Yes," says he. "Well, I hoped they could have 'em to-night afore they went to bed. But you explain about 'em in the morning. Tell 'em they're from me and Huldy. I'll be around after breakfast anyhow to fetch some more things from the store and see if there ain't something else I can do. Good night."

"Good night," says I, absent-minded. *I* couldn't get my mind off them coffin plates.

He kind of hesitated.

"Oh say," he says. "Did you eat all of them mackerel you had? If you didn't, and they're likely to spoil, why, I'll take a couple along home with me. Huldy's dreadful fond of mackerel."

"There ain't but one left," says I, "and——"

"Oh well," he says; "one 'll be enough for us. We're awful small eaters."

So I trotted out the mackerel and he done it up in a piece of the newspaper and went away to his dory. I lugged in the presents and laid 'em away in the old chest of drawers in the dining room. Felt like an undertaker, too, I did, all the time I was doing it. I didn't want the Heavenlies to see them relics till they'd ate a good breakfast—they was too much for an empty stomach. Then I locked up and took the lamp and went to my room.

After I got undressed I opened the window and leaned on the sill and thought. I thought about my new job and what I could see was coming to me in the way of work, and about Lord James and Nate and all. And then I thought of Hartley and that Page girl. Martin didn't act to me like a money-grabber. I couldn't understand it. One thing I was sure of, them two was meant for each other and it seemed to me that they still liked each other. But there was Van Brunt—I liked him too.

Just then a thundering great greenhead bit me on the back of the neck and I slammed down the sash and turned in on my bale of corncobs. Tired! don't talk!

CHAPTER VIII

MR. SCUDDER'S PRESENTS

I WAS up the next morning about five and pitched in making biscuit and lugging water and so on. Lord James comes poking down after a while. He looked pretty well used up.

"See 'ere, Pratt," says he. "W'at they got in them blooming beds—bricks?"

"Why?" says I. "Was yours hard?"

"'Ard? Upon me word I'm all full of 'oles, like a grater. My back is that sore you wouldn't believe it. And w'at makes 'em so noisy?"

"That's the husks," says I. "They do rustle when a feller ain't used to 'em."

"Rustle! When I'd go to roll over, upon me word the sounds was 'orrifying. Like the water washing around that boat of yours, it was. I dreamed about being adrift in that awful boat all night. About that and ghosts."

"Ghosts, hey? Did you dream of ghosts?"

"That I did. I could 'ear 'em groaning."

" 'Twas yourself that was groaning," says I. "A feller that took aboard the cargo of supper that you did hadn't ought to sleep on cornhusks."

"I didn't sleep; not a 'ealthy Christian sleep, I didn't. I say, Pratt, did you ever 'ear that this old 'ouse was 'aunted?"

"Well," says I, "I don't know as I ever heard that exactly. But old Mrs. Berry died in it and then Marcellus lived here alone till *he* died. Seems to me he died in that room of yours, come to think of it," says I, cheering him up.

He turned pale, instead of the yellow he'd been lately.

" 'Oly Moses!" says he. "You can't mean it."

"I can mean more than that without half trying," I says. "Yes, I remember now. He *did* die there and they say he died hard. Maybe that was on account of the bed though."

He was mighty upset. Commenced to tell about a friend of his over in "the old country" who had been butler at a place that was haunted. I asked if his friend had ever seen any of the spooks.

"No," says he, " 'e never saw 'em 'imself, but it was a tradition in the family. Everybody knew it. It was a white lady, and she used to trip about the 'ouse and over the lawns nights," he says.

"White, was she?" says I. "Well, I suppose if she'd been black they wouldn't have been able to see her in the night. Never heard of a colored ghost anyway, did you?"

"I mean she was all dressed in white," he says, scornful. "And they say 'twas 'orrid to see her a-gliding around over the grass."

"Want to know!" says I. "Well, if you see old Marcellus gliding around the hummocks outside, call me, will you? I'd like to see how he manages to navigate through the sand. That's a job for a strong, healthy man, let alone a dead one."

I guess he see I didn't take much stock in his ghost yarns, so he quit and went to getting the things on the breakfast table. But he was nervous and broke a dish and sprinkled forks and spoons over the floor like he was sowing 'em. Pretty soon he had to stop and hustle upstairs, for the Twins was shouting for their duds. For grown men they was the most helpless critters; His Lordship was a sort of nurse to 'em, as you might say.

After a while he had 'em dressed and ready and

they come down to breakfast. Nate had brought over feather beds for them, so they had slept pretty well. Van Brunt was rigged up special because he was going to Eastwich that forenoon to see his girl.

I'd cooked a whopping big breakfast but 'twas only just enough. Van was a regular famine breeder and Hartley wa'n't far astern of him. The Natural Life was agreeing with both of 'em fine so far. Martin's cheeks was filling out and him and his chum was sun-burned to brick red.

After breakfast they went out for their usual promenade. By and by I heard 'em hailing me from the back of the house. When I reached 'em they was standing by the barn, with their hands in their pockets, and looking as happy and proud as if they'd discovered America.

"Come here, skipper," says Van. "Do you see this?"

He was pointing at a kind of flat place in the lee of the pig sties. 'Twas a sort of small desert, as you might say: a bunch or two of beachgrass in the middle of it and the rest poverty grass and sand.

"I don't see much," says I. "What do you mean?"

"I mean the location," says he. "Here's where we'll have our garden."

I looked at him to see if he was joking. But it appeared he wa'n't.

"*Garden?*" says I.

"Sure," he says. "It's an ideal spot. Sun all day long."

"You could make a garden here, couldn't you, Sol?" asks Hartley.

"Maybe I could," says I, "if I dug through to Chiny and hit loam on t'other side. Otherwise you couldn't raise nothing in this sand but blisters."

"Scudder could bring us loam," says Van. "We've thought of that."

"Starting a garden in July!" says I. "What do you cal'late to raise—Christmas trees?"

"Late vegetables, of course," says Van. "Martin and I intend to stay all through September. Think of it, Martin; green corn from our own plantation. And cucumbers in the morning, with the dew on 'em."

"And tomatters already baked in the sun," I says, disgusted. "You take my advice and buy your green stuff off Scudder."

But they wouldn't hear of it. Called me a Jeremiah and so on.

"All right," says I, finally. "Have it your own way. But who's going to *work* this cucumbers and dew farm?"

"Why, we are, of course," says Van. "That's part of the game, isn't it, Martin? Nothing so healthful as outdoor work for caged birds like us. Maybe we'll have two gardens, one apiece. Then we'll see who raises the first crop."

I could see 'em doing it! But there was no use arguing then. I put my trust in Scudder's not being able to fetch the loam.

Pretty soon Nate heaves in sight in the dory with a cargo of skim milk and store eggs and butter. Van Brunt and I went down to meet him. Van didn't give him a chance to talk; just as soon as the stuff was put on shore he announces that Scudder must go right back and drive him over to Eastwich. Nate backed and filled, as usual, telling how busy he was, and how he hadn't ought to leave, and so on. But Van corks him right up with a five-dollar bill and off they went.

I lugged the milk and butter and the rest of the truck up to the house and started in on another stretch of work. I'd had a vacation of ten minutes or so; now 'twas time to begin again. After I'd cleared up round the kitchen and the like of that, I went off down to the *Dora Bassett* and tackled her. Van Brunt had cut away about everything but the mast, and I had to rig new halliards and sheets and downhauls and land knows what. Drat that Heavenly! 'twas a two days' job.

While I was making a start on it Hartley comes loafing down from the house.

"Skipper," he says, "let's have another one of your chowders for lunch, will you? They're the real thing."

"Well, I tell you, Mr. Hartley," says I, "if we have chowder I'd ought to go and dig the clams right now, on account of the tide. And, honest, I hate to leave this work I'm on. Still, of course, if you say so, why——"

"What's the matter with my digging 'em?" he says.

I grinned. "Why, nothing," I says, "so far as I know, except that it's something of a job."

"Job!" he says. "It'll be fun. Tell me where to go—and what to dig 'em with, and—and how to do it."

I told him to take the skiff and a clam hoe and a couple of buckets and row across to the mainland. There was clams all alongshore there, I knew.

"You go along till you see a lot of little holes in the sand," I says, "then you dig. Want to look out that they ain't sand-worm holes, nor razor fish. And when you begin to dig," I says, "you want to lay right into it, 'cause the clams are likely to be 'run-downs' and they get under fast. So——"

"Hold on a minute," says he. "How am I going to tell a worm-hole from a clam-hole, or a clam-hole from a—what was it?—barber fish hole?"

"Razor fish," says I. "Not barber. Well, I don't know how to tell you, exactly. If it's a sand-worm there's likely to be a little tiny hole alongside the regular one; that is, there is sometimes and sometimes there ain't. And if it's razor fish—well, *I* can tell 'em, but I cal'late you'll have to use your own judgment."

He said all right, he guessed he'd get along. So off he went, and pretty soon him and Lord James comes down and gets aboard the skiff. His Lordship was loaded with no less than four buckets, besides a clam hoe and the garden hoe and the stove shovel. 'Twas the most imposing clam hunt outfit ever I see. If I'd been a clam and see that battery coming my way I'd have took to tall timber.

"Sure you've got hoes and buckets enough?" I asks, sarcastic.

"I guess so," says he, looking around at the weapons. "We might need another pail perhaps, but if we do I'll send James after it."

His Lordship started rowing, taking strokes first with one hand and then with the other, and the fleet got under way and waltzed, as you might say, zigzag across to the main. 'Twas as calm as a millpond and they hit land up towards the point by the Neck Road. Then the clam slaughterers got out and disappeared round behind the point. I went on with my rigging.

It got to be eleven o'clock and no signs of 'em. Then twelve; lunch time. Tide was coming in fast, you couldn't have got a clam now without a diving outfit. But still all quiet on the Potomac. I went up to the house and commenced to slice ham and fry potatoes. I had my doubts about that chowder.

Everything was ready by and by and I stepped to the door to take an observation. And then I see 'em coming, rowing more crab fashion than ever. I walked down to the inlet to meet 'em. And such sights as they was. Blessed if they didn't look like they'd been through the war—Lord James especial.

"Hi, Sol!" sings out Hartley, as the skiff floats in, broadside on. "My! but I'm glad to see you. Give James a lift with the clams and things, will you? I'm done up."

He looked it. He was barefoot and bare-armed, with his trousers rolled up above his knees and his shirt sleeves above his elbows. And the valet was the same, and both of 'em soaking wet and just plastered with wet sand and clay.

I give one glance at them bare legs and arms.

"For the land sakes!" I sings out. "Pull down your pants and your sleeves. You're burned to a blister already."

And so they was. Tender white skins like theirs, wet with salt water and out in that sun!

They pulled 'em down looking like they didn't know what for, and come hopping and groaning ashore. His Lordship's back was so lame from bending over that he couldn't hardly straighten up without howling.

"Did you need the extra bucket?" I asks.

"Why no, I believe not," says Hartley. "You

see I dug for a while and then I went to look for better places, and James did the digging. We found holes enough, but they didn't seem to be the right kind. Worms, did you call those things? Sea serpents, you meant, I guess. I never saw such creatures. And there was one place where there were millions of holes, but chockful of crabs."

"Um-hum," says I. "Fiddlers. You must have gone plumb up into the march bank to run into *them*."

"They was 'orrid things," says Lord James, rolling his eyes. "And they 'ad claws and swarmed over my feet. I give you me word I was that——"

"That'll do, James," says Hartley. "Well, I was successful at last, skipper. Struck a place where clams were actually in layers just under the sand. We turned 'em over with the hoes like winking. I pointed 'em out and James picked 'em up. Just look at those buckets, will you?"

I looked at 'em. There was three buckets chock, brimming full.

"Good land of love!" says I. "Them ain't clams—they're quahaugs."

"They're clams in New York," he says.

"Maybe so," says I. "We call 'em quahaugs here. And there's no quahaugs in this part of the bay unless they've been bedded. Was there any marks around 'em?"

"There was a lot of sticks stuck up around," he says, "but we knocked those out of the way."

"You *did?*" says I. "Did you leave any of the—what you call clams?"

"You bet we didn't, says he. "We took the last one. Had too much trouble finding 'em to leave any."

"Humph!" says I. "That's nice. You've cleaned out somebody's private quahaug bed. Them quahaugs was all brought over by somebody and planted where you found 'em. The sticks was to mark the place."

"You don't mean it?" he says.

"Yes, I do," says I. "I cal'late we'll hear from them quahaugs afore long."

And sure enough we did, but that comes later. On the way up to the house I turns to his Lordship, who was limping barefoot over the beach-grass stubbles, and says I:

"Ain't clamming fun?" I says.

"My word!" says he, but it expressed his feelings all right.

All the afternoon the clam hunters kept getting lamer and lamer and sorer and sorer. Their sunburnt legs and arms was hurting 'em scandalous. Hartley flopped into a piazza chair and stayed there, and Lord James crept around with his limbs spread out like windmill sails. And every time he'd bump into a chair or anything you could hear him whoop to glory.

Van Brunt got home about supper time. Scudder rowed him over. I had the quahaug chowder made and he ate enough for all hands. Hartley was feeling too used up to relish it much, and his Lordship didn't eat nothing. I let him off on the dish washing and he went off to the tail end of the veranda and went to sleep in a chair.

After supper Van told about his trip to Eastwich. Agnes and the Talford girl was well, he said, and they and their Fresh Air tribe was coming to the Island next day for a picnic.

"By the way, skipper," says Van; "Scudder says he brought some presents for us last night after we went to bed. Where are they?"

Thunderation! I'd forgot all about them "presents." I'd felt like an undertaker when I laid 'em away in that drawer, and now I felt like a grave robber as I dug 'em up again. I spread 'em out on the table, coffin plates in the middle and wreath on one end and "What is Home Without a Mother" on t'other.

You'd ought to have heard them Heavenlies laugh! Nate's presents certainly made a hit. Van he just laid back and roared.

"Oh, by Jove!" he says, panting. "This is *too* good! This is lovely. Shades of Hannah Jane Purvis! Martin, how the widow of the man that didn't feel like beans would have appreciated these, hey? This—*this* would have been her idea of an art gallery."

"Pack 'em away again, Sol," says Hartley. "Now that the relatives have had an opportunity to view the remains, the funeral may go on. Bury 'em quick."

"*Bury* 'em?" says Van. "Not much. They're too dreamily beautiful. Martin, I'm surprised at you. What *is* home without a family vault, anyway? And yet— Hold on!" he says, holding up his hand. "I have an idea. We'll give them to James."

"To James?" says me and Martin together.

"Of course, to James. James is funereal and solemn and dignified. They ought to appeal to his taste. They're right in his line. We will decorate James' room with 'em. What is it they were warranted to do, skipper, when 'strung up around?' Oh yes! to be sure. 'Take away the bare look.' James' room *is* bare, now that I think of it. Come and join the Memorial Day parade, Martin."

He was out in the kitchen, getting the hammer and nails and string. Going to decorate the valet's bedroom right off. Hartley laughed and said, "Oh, let the poor devil alone, Van. He's had troubles enough for one day." But you couldn't stop that Van Brunt critter when he got started.

He makes me load the presents in my arms and takes the lamp and leads the way upstairs. And then he sets to work and hangs them presents round Lord James' room. He put the coffin plates over the washstand at the foot of the bed, and the wreath over the head, and hung the picture of Marcellus over the looking-glass and the shell work by the closet door.

"Now," says he, "for the motto—the crowning touch. Where? Where?"

Finally he hung it on top of the bureau.

"Perhaps," says he, "its influence may make James more motherly; who knows?"

Then we went down stairs and he made me

promise to say nothing. Then he was for waking his Lordship up and ordering him to bed right then, but his chum wouldn't hear of it. Martin said let the poor fellow have his nap out. *He* knew how he felt. So Van give in after awhile.

Pretty soon Hartley got tired of waiting and said he was going to turn in; he was played out, he said. Van wanted to wait longer, but he didn't. He went to bed too. At half-past ten or so my round of chores was done and I sung out to Lord James to wake up and come in because I wanted to lock up. But he wouldn't.

"Let me alone," he says, pleading. "I'm 'appy for the first time in 'ours. I'll lock up, myself, by and by," he says. So I left him out on the piazza and went aloft and turned in. And it didn't take me long to get to sleep, I tell you.

What woke me up was a howl like an engyne tooting. I bounced out of bed like I had springs under me, instead of corncobs and ropes.

Then comes another screech. Then a *smashity —bang*—SMASH! Then more yells, and feet going down the hall and falling down stairs. Then a door banging and sounds like all the furniture on the island was being upset.

I lit a lamp and got out into the hall. There I

met the Heavenly Twins just coming from their room. They was dressed light and gauzy, same as me, but Van had a revolver in his hand and Hartley was swinging a chair by the back.

"What on earth?" says Van.

"It's in the dining room, whatever it is," says I.

I grabbed up something to use for a club—it turned out later to be the littlest joint of Hartley's fish pole—and we tip-toed down stairs to the dining room door. And that door was locked fast.

CHAPTER IX

THE "FRESH-AIRERS"

FIRST I tried that door, then Hartley tried it, and then Van; each of us just as soft and quiet as possible. Then we listened. Not a sound.

Then Van catches me by the arm and begins to pull me and Martin back along the hall. When we got to the end, by the parlor door, he whispers, low and cautious:

"We must break the door down. It's locked on the inside. Sol, you put that lamp on the stairs. Better turn it down, too. A light gives the other man all the advantage if it comes to shooting. Now ready, when I say the word. All rush together. One—two——"

"Wait a minute," whispers Hartley—he was always cool-headed. "Where's James?"

"James?" repeats Van. "What? James?"

"James?" says I. And then I begun to get my senses back. Wake a feller up out of a sound sleep the way we was and it takes a few minutes for him to get on earth again.

"James!" says I. "I'll bet——"

"Idiot!" says Van, speaking about himself I judge. Then he walks down the hall and gives that door a kick.

"James," he sings out. "Is that you? Open this door."

For a second or two there wa'n't a sound. Then a voice says, weak and chattery, "O-o-h, my soul!"

"What's the matter with him?" says Van. "Is he hurt? Where's the key, skipper? Inside, of course. But—but where's the key-hole?"

Then I remembered. "There ain't any key-hole," I says. "There's no lock *on* the door."

"Then what—? Come on, Martin."

He set his shoulder to the door and commenced to shove. Me and Hartley helped, and the door begun to open. It opened slow, because the dining table and two or three chairs and the chest of drawers was braced against it. We got in finally.

"Bring the lamp," says Hartley. I done it. The room was empty.

"James!" hollers Van. "James!"

The closet door opens just a crack. Then it swung wide and his Lordship, half dressed and white as an old clamshell, staggers into the room.

"Oh!" says he. "Oh, Mr. Van Brunt, sir!"

He was shaking like a palsy.

"What ails you, man?" says Hartley. "Speak up."

The valet rolls his eyes around to me.

"I seen it," he says. "I seen it plain. It's 'im!"

"Him? Who?" says I.

"The ghost. The old cove as owned this 'ouse. 'E was up in my room a-waiting for me."

"What are you talking about?" asks Van, impatient. I begun to see light, but the Heavenlies didn't—not yet.

"'E was up in my room, sir," said Lord James, wild-like. "I 'ad me coat and waistcoat off, sir, and then I goes over to the mirror intending to see if me face looked as 'ot as it felt. And I lights my lamp and there 'e was a-glaring at me. 'E 'ad 'is 'ead through the mirror, sir. And there was coffins around, and wreaths. It's a warning to me, sir. I'm a dead man."

And then we began to laugh.

"The presents!" says Van, between roars. "Scudder's heirlooms. Ho! ho!"

His Lordship stared at us like he thought we was crazy. I more than half pitied him. Martin did too, I guess, for he says:

"It's all right, James. Just one of Mr. Van Brunt's jokes. You see——"

"But I *saw* 'im, sir. 'E was there, and there was wreaths and coffins 'ung about, and——"

"It's all right," says I. "Here! come along and I'll show you."

But not one step would he stir. A derrick wouldn't have lifted him up them stairs. So I quit trying and went aloft and fetched down the crayon enlargement and the wreath. Then I set out to explain.

"Why, you imbecile!" says Van. "Where's your taste for art? We were beautifying your room. Taking off the bare look, as per Scudder."

James' color begun to come back. And when it come it come thick. He reddened up so you could see it even through the sun-burn.

"Mr. Van Brunt," he says, getting madder every minute, "I give you notice. I leave to-morrow morning."

"Don't be an idiot—" begins Van, but his Lordship cut him short.

"I leave to-morrow morning," he shouts. "Ain't it enough to bring me to this Gawd-forsaken 'ole and work me 'alf to death and blister me from 'ead to foot, without this? I give you warning now. I'm going 'ome. And you be glad I ain't 'aving the law on you for this outrage. Us poor servants 'as rights, and——"

There was more, plenty more. We couldn't shut him up. And the Heavenlies' explanations didn't count either. He was dead set on leaving in the morning.

Finally, we give it up and went back to bed. Lord James said he was going to stay in the kitchen all night. Nothing would hire him to sleep in Marcellus' receiving tomb again.

"Humph!" says Hartley, as the Twins went upstairs, "it looks to me as if your joke had lost us the best valet you ever had, Van."

Van cussed under his breath. "He shan't leave," he said. "I must keep him somehow. He's invaluable in the city, and we may go back there some time. Not for months, though, of course," he adds.

But in the morning James was worse set than

ever. He wouldn't help with breakfast nor nothing; went aloft at daylight and begun to pack his trunk. He was going to leave, that's all there was about it.

The Twins was pretty blue during breakfast, Van about losing his Lordship, and Hartley on account of sun-burn, I cal'late. 'Twas another elegant day and there was wind enough to keep the flies and mosquitoes away from the house. If you got in the lee anywheres, though, they was laying for you in droves. They didn't bother me much, 'count of my hide being tough and leathery and my flavor too salt maybe; but they was fattening up fast on the Heavenlies and James.

About ten o'clock Scudder shows up with the first dory-load of Fresh Airers from the Eastwich place. Miss Agnes come along with 'em. Then the second load come, cap'ned by the Talford girl. And then there was doings.

Them Fresh Air young ones wa'n't all of a piece with Redny, which was a mercy. He was a handful in himself, that little sorrel-top was—but there was enough like him to keep things stirred up. Marcellus' old shingled prison had to take it that day. There must have been some stewing in Heaven if old Lady Berry could look down and see them youngsters whooping and carrying-on in the front parlor. In Mrs. B's day that parlor was a kind of saint's rest, as you might say, and the only time anybody opened its door was when she sailed in with the broom and feather duster. And then she must have had to navigate by compass, because the blinds was always shut tight and the curtains drawn and 'twas too dark to see anything.

Hartley looked out for the children and Van Brunt piloted the two girls over the place, pointing out where the garden was going to be some day, and where the hens was likely to roost and the pig to board. They seemed to be as pleased and tickled as he was and thought everything was "lovely" and "just too quaint and dear." I was busy cooking and Lord James sulked out in the barn. He couldn't get away until late afternoon on account of the train.

Redny stuck to Hartley like a mud-turtle to a big toe. He was right at his heels all the time. By and by the pair of 'em come out in the kitchen to see me.

"Hello, Andrew Jackson," says I to the boy. "How do you like this part of the country?"

"Great!" says he, his eyes snapping. "Gee, ain't we having the peach of a time!"

"Must feed you well over there," I says. "Seems to me you're getting fat already. Board's up to the mark of the Newsboys' Home, ain't it?"

"Bet you!" says he. "Chicken, and pie, and all the milk you want. And cream—aw say!" and he smacked his lips.

"How'd you like to live here all the time?"

He shook his head. "Naw," he says. "Too still. Sometimes I can't sleep good 'cause it's so still. No El, nor whistles nor fights nor nothing. And no Chinks to chuck rocks at. Miss Agony won't let you chuck rocks at folks anyhow."

"Don't you wish you was back to New York with your dad?" I says.

"Not much," he says. "The old man used to club me too good. When he was full I'd get a belting most every day."

I looked at Hartley and he at me. Poor little shaver! It's when I see how some folks treat children that I get to thinking I could make a better world than this is.

"Going to run away again?" I asks, after a minute.

"Naw," says Redny. "Not while I'm down here. Miss Agony cries over me and I'd rather be licked any time than that."

Hartley rumpled the youngster's hair with his fingers.

"Sol," he says, "there's good here if you can get at it. Too much good to be running to waste. Ah hum! Must be rather pleasant to have one or two of your own; must make life almost worth living. That's where you and I have missed it."

"You've got plenty of time yet," says I. "Maybe you'll be down in these diggings nine or ten year from now with a family of your own."

He smiled, kind of sad and one-sided. Then he got up and walked out to the piazza. Redny hung around a spell, long enough to ask a couple million questions. Then he went into the parlor with the rest of the young Injuns.

Pretty soon I heard some one speak. I looked through the door way and see the Page girl coming up the porch steps alone. Hartley stood up and lifted his cap.

"Where's Van?" he asked.

"He's down on the beach with Margaret. I came back to look after the children."

"They're all right," says Martin. "Playing games in the front room."

Agnes stopped for a second in the doorway.

"I don't just understand," she said, hesitating, "why you are here. Is it true that your health is bad?"

"No," he said, with a little laugh. "I did feel rather gone to seed before I left town, but now I'm having the time of my life."

"Indeed?" says she. "So far from Wall Street? I'm surprised."

He didn't seem to answer—leastways I didn't hear him. Next thing I knew he was standing on the top step.

"Please excuse me," he says, pretty frosty. "I must speak to James."

He went off down the steps and out of sight. She stood and watched him a minute, and I thought she looked puzzled—and solemn. Then she went into the parlor.

We had dinner out doors on the piazza. While it was going on the grown-ups didn't do much talking. It's precious little fun trying to talk against a typhoon and an earthquake mixed, and that's what them Fresh Air young ones turned that meal into. 'Twas "Hurrah boys! Stand from under!" from the beginning. When I wa'n't filling up fish plates I was dodging potato skins and similar bouquets. They didn't fire 'em at me, you understand, but it's always the feller that's looking on at the row who gets hit. Redny was cap'n of the gun crew. He could chuck a potato skin with his left hand and eat with his right and look pious and shocked, all at the same time.

When the Juniors was filled up—and it wa'n't no slouch of a job to *get* 'em filled—they went off to start a riot somewheres else, and the Twins and the girls had a chance. Van got to telling about Scudder's presents, and he was funny as usual. That Margaret Talford would laugh until I had to join in just out of sympathy, even though I *was* up to my eyes in soapsuds and dishwashing. She was a jolly girl, that one; pretty and full of snap and go.

Nothing would do but them "presents" must go on exhibition. So Van lugged 'em down from James' room and lined 'em up on the piazza for inspection. He took a stick for a pointer and give a lecture about 'em, same as if they was a panorama, pointing out what he called the "feeling" and "atmosphere" of the shell basket and the "perspective" of Marcellus in the crayon enlargement. He had a good time and so did everybody else, especially Miss Talford.

By and by she clapped her hands. "Oh!" says

she, "I've got an idea. Did you say your man was going to leave you, Mr. Van Brunt?"

Van heaved a sigh. "Yes," he says. "I believe he is. I fear that James hasn't the artistic temperament. I confess I'm disappointed. He certainly looked as if he had it; he was sad and soulful and—and—dyspeptic. But no; even the 'Motherless Home' didn't appeal to him. He *says* he's going to-night."

"I wonder if he would come over to the school?" says she. "We need a man there, don't we, Agnes? To help about the place, and look out for the boys, and to—well, to protect us."

"Lucky James!" says Van. "But *why* James? Won't Martin here do—or—excuse my blushes—myself?"

But the Talford girl laughed and said he wouldn't do at all. He lacked dignity, she said, and didn't look the part. She asked Miss Page if she really didn't think that James would be just the man for them. Agnes said perhaps he would. So the four of 'em went away for a walk on the beach and to talk it over.

I'll bet I called that valet anything but a church member and a good feller a dozen times over while I was diving into them dishes. I washed and washed till, seemed to me, I was soaked out fresh enough to bile, like a pickled codfish. And when the washing was done there was the wiping. I laid out a bale or so of dish towels and pitched in.

Pretty soon somebody says, "Mayn't I help?"

I swung around and there was Agnes Page. Nice to look at, she was, too.

"Can't I help you, please?" says she, picking up a towel.

"Land sakes, no!" says I. "You'll spoil your fine clothes. Besides I've got sort of used to it by this time; my arm goes round of itself, like a paddle wheel."

She laughed and grabbed a chowder plate and commenced to wipe. She done fairly well for anybody who hadn't practiced much, but she never would have won the cup for speed. One dish every five minutes is all right, maybe, if you're getting paid by the year, but— However, I judged her ma kept hired help to home. I wondered what she'd done with Hartley.

By and by she says, "Mr. Pratt, how long do you expect to stay here?"

"Here?" says I. "On Horsefoot—on Ozone Island? Land knows. Long's the Heavenlies—that is, long's Mr. Van Brunt and Mr. Hartley stay here, I guess. It's a restful place, ain't it?" says I, reaching for the next stack of dishes.

She smiled. "No doubt they find it so," she says. "How do *you* like the Natural Life?"

"Who—me? Oh, I cal'late I shall like it tip-top when I get a little more used to it—that is, if I last. I was oldest boy in a family of nine, and dad died young, so I was brought up Natural, as you might say. It's been some time, though, since I had so many hours of straight-along, pitch-in-and-hustle Naturalness in the day's run; been getting artificial and lazy of late years, I guess. But I'm tough, and I'll be all right and used to it pretty soon—getting lots of practice. By the way," I says, "who was it that sent 'em here?"

"Who?" says she, looking surprised. "Sent? I don't understand."

"Was Mr. Van Brunt and his chum sent here by the doctor, or who?"

"Why, I didn't know they were sent at all. I think they came here of their own accord."

"Humph!" says I, considering. "Was any of their folks ever took this way? Does it run in the families?"

That seemed to tickle her and I guess she understood what I meant. But she didn't answer the question; went on dry-polishing the pickle dish. Then says she, kind of accidental on purpose:

"Is Mr. Hartley's health improving?"

"Oh yes!" says I. "He's picking up some, 'specially in his appetite. He ain't up to Van Brunt in that line yet, though. Van eats for three; Hartley's only up to the one-man-and-a-boy mark so far. He'd do better if he didn't have them blue streaks of his. Seems to have something on his mind."

"Perhaps he's troubled about leaving his business," she suggests, looking sideways at the pickle dish.

"Guess not," says I, looking sideways at her. "I don't think I've heard him mention business since he's been down. No, 'tain't that, according to my notion. He ain't in love, is he?"

She looked at me then pretty hard; but I was as wooden-faced as a cigar sign.

"Dear me, no," she laughs, brisk. "I guess not. What made you think that?"

"Oh, nothing," says I. "I ain't ever been took that way myself, but it seemed to me he had all the symptoms. Didn't know but he was fretting about some young woman. He's a fine chap, that young Hartley. It 'll be a lucky girl that gets him."

She didn't say much more, but she looked at me every once in a while as if she was wondering. I never let on. I was as innocent and easy as the cat with the cream on its whiskers. I had a sneaking hope that I might have boosted Hartley a little mite, and I felt good down one side. Then I thought of Van, and I felt mean all up the other.

After a spell the Twins and Miss Talford happened along, and what a time Van Brunt made when he see his girl helping me wipe dishes.

"Well, well!" he says. "Is this the way you hurry back to 'see what the dear children are doing?' Sol, you old fascinator, how do you do it? Martin and I fell in love with him at first sight, Miss Talford; and now look at Agnes."

"Hold on there," says I. "Don't spread it to thick. I ain't got but one hat that 'll do for Sunday, and I want that to fit me. I was giving Miss Page a few lessons in housekeeping, and you'd ought to thank me for that, Mr. Van Brunt."

It seems the Talford girl had seen James and he had agreed to go to Eastwich with 'em. 'Twas a good chance for him, a soft job and all that. Truth to tell, I guess he was kind of sorry about parting from Van altogether, the gleaning might not be so good in his next boss's berry pasture.

So about six o'clock Scudder come with his dory and the picnic broke up. The Fresh-Airers were pretty nigh played out by this time. The smaller children was nodding with their heads on the shoulders of the bigger ones, and I even had to tote two of the littlest in my arms down to the beach. But they was all full fed and sun-burned and dirty and happy, and they'd had the bulliest time in their poor, pinched-up little lives.

"Well, good-by, Andrew Jackson," says I to Redny. "Had good time enough to want to come again, have you?"

"Sure thing," says he.

"Like it as well here as you do over at the school?"

"Yup," he says. "Ain't nobody to plug potato skins at over there."

He was a smart little coot. Had the makings of a man in him if you dug down far enough to get at it.

Lord James comes down to the shore tugging his trunk behind him.

"So long, Hopper," says I. "Shall I give

your love to Marcellus' spook if it comes gliding again?"

He looked at me very solemn. "You'd better come too," he says. "You take my advice and leave this blooming island now w'ile you 'ave the chance. There'll come a time," says he, "when you won't 'ave it."

He climbed into the dory and set down all huddled up in the stern with his trunk between his knees. Scudder begins rowing and they moved off.

"There," says Van, referring to his Lordship, "goes the final tie that binds us to a sordid past. Shall we sing 'The Last Link is Broken,' Martin? Or have you something more appropriate to suggest, skipper?"

"I have for myself," says I. "It's 'Work for the Night is Coming.'"

And I hurried up to the house to get supper.

CHAPTER X

THE VOYAGE OF THE ARK

THE Heavenlies was late down to breakfast next morning, owing, I cal'late, to the loss of Lord James. I could hear 'em hailing each other, asking, " What's become of my golf stockings? " and the like of that. Trouble seemed to be that they had too *many* clothes. If they'd been limited to one suit for Sunday and a pair of overalls to cover up the ruins the rest of the week, like I was, they'd have got along better.

But they was rigged at last and at breakfast was chipper as a pair of mackerel gulls. They commenced to talk garden. Consarn 'em, I hoped they'd forgot that.

" The loam business is all right, Sol," says Van. " Scudder will bring us loam at three dollars a boat load. He says it 'll take about fifteen boat loads."

" He does, hey? " says I. " At three dollars per? That's generous of him. Anything else? "

" Yes. He is to continue to bring us milk. We

have decided that perhaps for the present we had better not keep a cow."

Small favors thankfully received. I was glad that milking wa'n't going to be added to the general joyfulness.

"I think that's a nice far-sighted decision," says I. "Unless you could learn your cow to eat seaweed, I don't see——"

"Oh, Scudder could bring us hay," says Van. "And we could give the animal the spare vegetables from the garden."

"Twould be a long time between meals for the poor critter, I'm afraid," says I. "How much is Nate charging for the milk?"

"Nine cents a quart. That's only one cent more than you have to pay in New York, and, when you consider how far he has to bring it, *I* call it dirt cheap."

Well, 'twas about as cheap as the garden dirt, but I didn't say nothing.

"We're going to raise chickens too," says Hartley. "Scudder, so Van says, will sell us live Plymouth Rocks at thirty cents a pound. Skipper, you might fix up the poultry yard in your spare time."

In my *spare* time. There was a joke in that, but it wa'n't so intended.

Then Van Brunt began to preach "pig." Seems Nate had told him that the one thing needful to turn Ozone Island into a genuine Natural Life heaven was a pig, and of course he, Nate, had the only pig in creation that was worth buying.

"He showed it to me the other morning," says Van. "The prettiest little black and white fellow you ever saw, Martin. Miss Talford saw him yesterday because she came over, and she said he was a dear. You might be repairing a sty for him in your odd moments, Sol."

My odd moments, and my even ones too, was pretty well filled up for the next few days. The Heavenlies loafed and superintended and smoked and fished and ate. All I had to do was to turn out with the gulls, and cook breakfast, and clear away, and wash dishes, and build hen yards, and fix up a leaky pig pen, and get ready them blessed gardens, and sweep and dust, and dig clams, and make beds, and get dinner, and sail a boat, and chop wood, and bundle up washing for Nate to take to Huldy Ann, and scour knives, and—and—well, there was plenty more. Seven or eight hundred odd jobs have slipped my memory.

The gardens was ready for planting on a

Wednesday. Nate fetched over the last dory load of loam the night afore and I spread it afore I got supper. The chickens and the hog was to come on Thursday. I was to take the skiff and go after 'em, Nate being engaged to cart a carry-all load of boarders to Ostable. Huldy Ann was to have the live stock at the shore ready for me.

"How's the menagerie coming, Nate?" I asked. "In cages or on the hoof?"

"Oh, I'll box 'em for you, Sol," he says. "The hens in one box and the pig in another. The pig's pretty thin—I mean young, so he won't be no heft to you."

Wednesday morning the Heavenly gardening begun. One patch was for Van Brunt and the other for Hartley. They had seeds by the peck, more or less, brought over by Scudder's express and charged for at undertaker's prices. The Twins started in with a vengeance. I showed 'em how. For once I was superintendent and the job suited me fine—nothing would have tickled me more, unless 'twas to turn in and take a nap.

Van takes one hoe and Hartley the other. Each of 'em was actually round-shouldered from the weight of the seeds in their pockets. They had cucumber seeds, and melon seeds, and land knows what. Wonder to me was they didn't try oranges and pineapples. And it the middle of July!

"Now Martin," says Van. "Here goes! Bet you fifty I get the first cucumber."

"I'll go you," says Martin, shucking his jacket. "Sol, what do I do next?"

I showed him. I started 'em even on cucumber beds. They hoed like they went by steam. You never see such ambitious farmers in your life as they was—just then.

"Kind of hard work, ain't it?" says I, watching their front hair get damp and stick to their foreheads.

"*Work?*" says Van. "This is recreation, man!"

"All right," I says. "Heave ahead and recreate. I've got to work, myself."

So I went in and swept out the dining room. Once in a while, through the open window, I'd get a sight of 'em laying into the cucumber beds, with the sun blazing down. I grinned. When the boot's been on one leg too long it's kind of nice to see somebody else's corns get pinched.

When they come into dinner they was just slopping over with joy. Gardening was more fun than a barrel of monkeys. But I noticed that when

Van got up from the table he riz kind of "steady by jerks" as if he had kinks in his back, and Martin moved his shoulders slow and easy and said "Ouch!" under his breath when he reached too far.

They didn't seem to be in any real hurry to get back to work, either. Stayed on the porch, and smoked two cigars instead of one. I had to chuck out a hint about getting them seeds covered up quick afore they'd leave their chairs. Then they went, and I could see the hoes moving; but they moved slower.

They turned in right after supper, which was unusual. Next morning I didn't hear a word about gardens. The conversation was pretty limited and doleful, being separated with grunts and groans, so to speak. When Van Brunt dropped his napkin he hollered to me to come and pick it up, and Hartley fed with his left hand and kept the right in his jacket side pocket. They didn't seem to enjoy that meal half so much as I did.

"Well," says I, to brighten things up; "I cal'late them cucumbers is ready to eat, pretty nigh, by this time. Started on your corn yet? No? Well, you mustn't lose no time. It's late in the season now. Come along with me and I'll get you going."

I headed for the door as I spoke. They looked at each other again.

"It's pretty cloudy for planting, isn't it?" asks Hartley. "We might be caught in the rain, you know."

"Rain your granny!" says I. "Them clouds is nothing but heat fog. It'll burn right off."

"Wait till we finish our cigars, skipper," says Van.

"No," says I. "You can smoke and plant at the same time. Smoke 'll drive away the mosquitoes."

They got up then and followed me out. The hoes was laying by the beds and I handed 'em one apiece. They took 'em, not with what you'd call enthusiasm, but more the way the boy took the licking—believing 'twas more blessed to give than to receive. The cucumber beds was begun beautiful, the first hills rounded up fine and lovely. But the tail end ones looked like the pauper section of the burying ground, more useful than ornamental. I showed 'em how to plant the corn and went away, leaving 'em leaning on their hoes, with a kind of halo of mosquitoes around their heads.

My talk about smoke was more or less sarcastic; the mosquitoes on Horsefoot Ozone was smoke-cured and fire-proof.

I got the breakfast work done about ten o'clock and then 'twas time to go after the pig and the hens. I took the skiff oars out of the barn and then walked around by the gardens to see how things was getting on. There laid the hoes by the places where the corn-hills was intended to be, but there wa'n't any corn-hills nor any Heavenly gardeners either; not a sign of 'em. I hailed once or twice but didn't get any answer. Then I went on down to the skiff. And there they was, sprawled out in the shade of the pines, as comfortable as you please.

"Hello, skipper," says Van Brunt, turning over on one elbow. "We've been waiting for you. We're going with you after the livestock."

"You are?" says I. "Got your farming done so early?"

"No-o," he drawls. "Not precisely. The fact is, Sol, Hartley and I have decided that agricultural labors are not——"

"Labors?" says I, shoving the skiff into the water. "Thought 'twas recreation."

"For definition see dictionary," he says. "It's

a painful condition, not a theory, with us, just now. Martin and I are convinced that what we need is a sea voyage. Come on, Martin."

Hartley got up, pretty average gingerly, and they climbed into the skiff. I pushed off and begun to row.

"Well," I says, after a minute or two, "it ain't for me to suggest anything, but, just for greens—like the old woman stewed the burdock leaves—I'd like to mention that if you *want* vegetables with the dew, and not icicles on 'em, you'd better be getting the rest of them seeds into the ground. What's the present standing of that cucumber bet?"

Van didn't open his eyes. "You win it," he says, lazy.

I stopped rowing and looked at him over my shoulder.

"Meaning—what?" says I.

"Just that. You win the bet. Likewise you cultivate the cucumbers. Martin and I, in convention assembled, have nominated you for Secretary of Agriculture. We resign."

I'd been expecting it. And I'd made up my mind what to say. But I hated to say it. Thinks I, "I'll wait till I get back to Ozone."

So I didn't answer, but went to rowing again. The tide was going out fast and 'twas a hard pull, three of us in that little skiff, but by and by we reached the main. And there was Scudder's hired boy waiting for us.

"Hello," says I. "Where's Huldy Ann—Mrs. Scudder, I mean?"

"She couldn't come," said the boy. "But I fetched the hens and things. Here they be."

He had the hens—a dozen of 'em—jammed into one lath coop. The door of it was fastened with a shaky wood button.

"Handle 'em kind of careful," says he. "That button undoes itself sometimes."

"Where's the pig?" says Hartley.

"Here he is."

We could hear him. He wa'n't in a box at all, as he'd ought to have been according to contract, but setting in the sand with his hind legs tied together with string. He was whirling in circles with his tail for a pivot, so to speak, and he seemed to be mainly squeal. Little he was, and thin—'peared to me to be thin as Nate's milk of human kindness—but the Heavenlies fell down and worshipped him like he was a hog angel.

"Humph!" says I. "Is that the 'dear'?"

"That's the dear," says Van, patting him at long distance.

Well, he weighed four pound and cost six dollars, so that's dear enough for anybody.

I loaded the critters into the skiff—the pig fairly sung psalms while I was doing it—and then the Twins climbed aboard.

"All right, skipper," says Van. "Shove off."

"Just a minute," says I. "What am *I* going to do—take the next train? This transport seems to be pretty well loaded."

It was. Van Brunt was on the amidships thwart. Hartley was up in the bow, with the pig between his knees. The chicken coop was piled in the stern. I ain't no dime show dwarf, and where I was going to stow myself was too much for me.

"Humph!" says Van. "It does look standing room only. Here, skipper; you kneel on the back seat. I'll row."

I didn't exactly kneel, but I straddled across the stern somehow, with the butt end of the hen roost in my lap and my feet over each rail just clear of the wet.

Nate's boy shoved us into deep water. He had to take off his shoes and stockings to do it, and he was laughing so that he made mighty poor headway.

"You pesky young one!" says I, losing patience. "If you don't tend to your job I'll get out and duck you. What are you giggling at?"

"I ain't giggling," says he. "I'm pushing. Ugh! Haw! haw! Ugh! There you be!"

He gave us a final shove and then went back and rolled around in the bushes. Somebody was having a good time if we wa'n't.

We moved off stately and slow, like an ocean liner leaving her dock. We didn't have any band, but the pig and hens furnished music. The skiff's rail was almost a-wash and my heels dipped on every little wave.

Van rowed like a good one till he got about two-thirds of the way across. Then the tide got a grip on us and he commenced to go slower, and groan. He'd miss a stroke and we'd swing half way around. We was going broadside on most of the time.

By and by Hartley spoke up.

"What makes this pig kick so?" says he, like 'twas some kind of a conundrum. The critter seemed to be doing his best to answer it, but his language wa'n't understandable.

"You look out he don't kick that string off his legs," I hollers. I *had* to holler to make myself heard above the choir.

He bent forward and looked down. "Why!" says he. "I'll be shot if he hasn't done it already."

"Hang on to him then!" I yells. "For the land sakes don't let him loose."

Van Brunt gives a final groan and stops the oars.

"No use, skipper," he says. "My cucumber recreation has put me out of the race. I wouldn't row another stroke for the control of the Standard Oil. You'll have to be shofer the rest of the way."

I didn't know what a "shofer" was and I don't know now; but I could see trouble coming.

"Set where you be!" I shouted. "Don't move. Thunderation! *There you go!*"

The pesky idiot had stood up to stretch, leaving the oars in the rowlocks. Course the skiff swung broadside on and a wave knocked the starboard oar overboard. Hartley see it going and made a jump and a grab. He missed it, you might know, but he let go of the pig.

I ripped out a lively kind of speech and dove

for the port oar. The hen coop was in my way and it and me went headfirst into Van Brunt's shirt front. When I got out of the mix-up, both oars was ten yards astern, the pig was doing three laps a minute over us and under the thwarts, and the hens was all out of jail and proud of it. Likewise we was drifting out to sea.

"*Well!*" says I. "This is nice, ain't it? Get out, you varmint!" This last part was to a pullet that was flapping on my shoulders.

Would you believe it, all them Heavenly loons done was to laugh. They just roared.

"Ho! ho!" whoops Hartley. "Oh, *dear* me! This is worth the price of admission."

"Ha! ha!" cackles Van, puffing for breath, and shoving the pig out of his lap. "This is the best ever! The floating garden of Eden! Or the Ark! Say, Martin; I begin to sympathize with Noah."

"Noah sent out a dove, if I remember right," says Hartley. "Wonder if it would work with a chicken? Where's our Ararat, skipper?"

I was mad clean through. Here was twice that I'd been made a fool of on salt water. I wa'n't used to it and it hurt.

"The Ark was afloat for forty odd days; you

want to remember *that,*" says I. "And this skiff won't float forty minutes, loaded the way she is, if she drifts outside that point."

"Then she musn't drift there," says Van, cheerful. "I don't want to get wet—not now, with James gone. This is the only presentable suit I've got left. If this is wrecked you'll have to press it, Sol."

My, but I was hopping! Talking about pressing clothes, and us next door to going to the bottom!

"I'll press nothing," says I. "And I'll say right now, Mr. Van Brunt, that I won't 'tend to them gardens. You hear——"

Van waved his hand. "Your salary from now on," he says, "will be——"

"No, it won't. My salary's big enough. It's me that's short—short about twenty-six hours out of the twenty-four. If I was two men I might do what's needful, but as 'tis I can't. I like you both first-rate—when you ain't *too* crazy—but either you'll have to get me a helper, or I'll have to quit. That is, if we get out of this mess alive, which ain't likely."

All the time I was preaching this way I was tugging at the 'midships thwart. Finally I got it loose and shoved it over the stern. I was going to try to scull with it.

The Heavenlies was completely upset. Not by the fear of drowning—drat 'em. I don't cal'late they was *afraid* of anything—but my talk of quitting seemed to knock 'em silly.

"By Jove! you know," says Van. "This is serious, skipper. You can't mean it."

"You bet I can!" I says, sculling like all possessed with one arm, and fighting pullets with the other.

"You're not going," says Van, decided. "You're—simply—*not*. Is he, Martin?"

"I should say not," says t'other Twin. "Sol, if you want more money—or assistants—or anything, why, all right. But *we* want *you*. And we're going to keep you."

"That's settled then," says Van, quick. "What kind of help do you want—and how many?"

"Well," I says, cooling down a mite—of course I was pleased to find they liked me so well. "Well," I says, "if you could get somebody to cook and help 'round the house, maybe I——"

"A cook?" says Van. "Good! We get a

cook—two cooks—ten of 'em, if you say so. And we get 'em quick."

"Let's get ashore first," says I. "I've got to make the point there or we'll get——"

"Our finish, hey?" he says, ending the sentence for me. "All right; *make* the point." Then he got out a cigar and went to smoking.

But I wa'n't by no means sure we would make the point. 'Twas the east'ard end of Ozone Island I was aiming for. The tide set in strong there and I could see that the skiff would pretty nigh hit the beach, if I had luck.

We zig-zagged along. Pretty soon we got to where the waves was running higher. They commenced to slop into the boat.

"She'll go under, sure's you're born," says I. "If I can only keep her up till we get into shoal water."

"I seem to have acquired the castaway habit," says Van. "Once in that other boat of yours, Sol, and now in this one. I must swear off. This is getting monotonous."

The swells run bigger as we neared the point. The skiff was half full and the slopping and the motion stirred up the menagerie. Such squealing and squawking and flapping you never heard nor saw. Them hens was all over us and the pig underneath.

We riz on a wave and begun to capsize.

"Here we go!" I yelled. "Stand by!"

Over we went. The hens had the best of us in a way—they could fly after a fashion. I wished I could. Lucky the water wa'n't more than waist deep.

I ploughed through the sand and undertow and got to the beach. Hartley come next, toting the pig by one leg. The "dear" wriggled loose and headed for the pines, hurrahing like a saw-mill. The most of the hens had gone on ahead.

"Humph!" says somebody. "You're pretty wet, ain't you?"

I rubbed the wet sand out of my eyes. There on a sand hummock in front of us was a girl. A queer looking female she was, too. Reminded me some of Hannah Jane Purvis, being built on the same spare lines and having the same general look of being all corners. She had on a striped calico dress, stripes running up and down, and her belt went across the middle of the stripes as straight as if 'twas laid out with a spirit level. I couldn't see her face good, for she had on a sunbonnet and 'twas like peeking at her through a nail keg, but she had snapping black eyes and moved quick, which wa'n't Hannah Jane's way by a good sight. I stood and stared at her.

"I say you're pretty wet, ain't you?" she says again, louder. "Why don't you say something? Are you hard of hearing?"

Before I could get my bearings enough to answer, Van Brunt comes dripping alongside. He was still holding the cigar stump in his mouth and he had one of the Plymouth Rocks—the rooster, as it happened—squeezed tight under one arm.

"Well, skipper," he says, "the Ark has stranded and the animals may now—Hello! What? Who?"

He looked at the girl and she at him. Then he says brisk—

"Can you cook?"

CHAPTER XI

EUREKA

WHATEVER that girl might have expected from us, I guess she didn't expect *that.* It set her back so that she couldn't speak for a full minute; which was something of a miracle, as I found out later.

"Can I *what?*" she says, finally.

"Can you cook?" asks Van Brunt again.

"Can I—" Then she turns to me. "He ought to be attended to right off," she says, referring to Van. "Some of that wet has soaked in and he's got water on the brain. Take that poor rooster away from him afore he squeezes it to death."

Van laughed and dropped the rooster. I cal'late he'd forgot that he had it. "Let me explain," he begun. "You see, we——"

Hartley spoke then. "Wait a minute," says he, laughing. "I suggest that we adjourn to the house and get into some dry clothes. Then we can talk business, if the young lady is willing."

The girl looked at him. " Business is what I'm here for," says she. " Which of you three is the quahaug one? "

" The which? " says I; and the Heavenlies both said the same.

" Which of you is the quahaug one? I've got some business to talk with *him.*"

" Martin," says Van, grave, and turning to his chum. " Are you a ' quahaug one '? "

" I guess he is," says I. I was beginning to see a light. Hartley's clamming cruise was turning out as I'd expected.

" Humph! " says the girl. " Well, you made a clean job, Lys says. About three buckets and a half, wa'n't they? "

You never see a man so puzzled as Hartley, unless 'twas Van Brunt. They looked at each other, at the girl, and then at me. I explained.

" I judge 'twas this young woman's quahaug bed that you and James cleaned out t'other day," I says. " You remember I told you we'd hear from them quahaugs later."

" Oh! " says Martin. " Awfully sorry, I'm sure. I hope you'll permit me to pay for——"

She bobbed the sunbonnet up and down. " That's what I come for," says she. " They was my brother Lycurgus's quahaugs. He'd just bedded 'em. Quahaugs is worth a dollar a bucket this time of year. That's three dollars and a half. I won't charge you for the sticks, though what on earth you done with *them* is more'n I can make out, and Lys says the same."

Van was grinning from ear to ear. T'other Twin reached into his pocket and fished out a sopping-wet pocketbook.

"Will the three fifty be sufficient?" he asks, troubled. "I'm really very sorry. It was a mistake, and——"

"Oh, it's all right," says the girl. "You didn't know no better. Pa says fools and children ain't accountable. You'd better spread that money out to dry 'fore you pay me with it. And you'd better get dry yourself or you'll catch cold. I can wait a spell, I guess. Why don't you go after your boat, Mister?" she says to me. "You'll lose it first thing you know."

I looked where she pointed, and there was the skiff stranded bottom up on the tip end of the point flat. I ran after it, waded in and hauled it ashore. The Heavenlies hurried up to the house. When I come back the girl was waiting for me.

"I'll walk along up with you," she says. "Say,

you're Solomon Pratt, ain't you? I heard about you. Nate Scudder told pa. He said he'd let this place to Sol Pratt and a couple of crazy men from New York. I thought sure you'd swear when the boat upset, but you didn't. You must belong to the church. What are you—Methodist?"

I grinned. "So you think a ducking like that would be apt to make a man swear, do you?" says I.

"Yup, if he hadn't got religion. Pa'd have cussed a blue streak. You'd ought to hear him when he has his nervous dyspepsy spells. Did you say you was a Methodist?"

"No-o, I guess I didn't. Let's see. Did you say your name was Dusenberry?"

She stopped and kind of fizzed, like a teakettle biling over. "Sakes alive!" she snaps. "I hope not! Do I look as if I was carting a name like that around? My name's Sparrow—Eureka Florina Sparrow. What's the matter—anything?"

"No, not 'special. You kind of fetched me up into the wind, striking me head on so, unexpected. Just say that again and say it slow. Eureka Peruna—what was it?"

She switched around and stared at me hard.

" Eureka—Florina—Sparrow," says she, slow and distinct. " Want me to spell it for you? "

" No, thanks. You might mix me up some if you did. I had to leave school early. Any more in your family? "

" Yup. Seven of us, counting me—and pa makes eight."

" What's *their* names? "

" Well, there's Lycurgus and Editha and Ulysses and Napoleon and Marguerite and Dewey —he's the baby. Great names, ain't they? Pa's doings, naming 'em that way was. Pa says there's nothing like hitching a grand name to a young one; gives 'em something to live up to, he says. His own name's Washington, but he ain't broke his back living up to it, far's as I can see; and ma used to say the same afore she died."

" O-o-h! " says I. " I see." I knew who she was now. I hadn't lived around Wellmouth so very long, but I'd heard of Washington Sparrow. He lived in a little slab shanty off in the woods about a mile from Scudder's, and had the name of being the laziest man in town.

We'd reached the house by this time and I left Eureka Florina in the kitchen and went to my room to change my duds. When I come down the

Twins was in the kitchen, too, and I could hear the Sparrow girl's tongue going like a house afire. Martin had just paid her for the quahaugs and she was telling how scarce they'd got to be in the bay, and how her brother had worked to get a few bedded and how he'd sold a couple of quarts to the Baptist minister's wife and what she said about 'em, and so on. The Heavenlies seemed to be enjoying every minute of it, judging by the way they laughed.

"Introduce us to the lady, skipper," says Van, when I come in.

I done the honors. "She's one of Washy Sparrow's tribe—I mean family," says I. "They live over in the woods hereabouts."

"I guess tribe'll do," says Eureka, cutting in quick. "There's pretty near enough of us to make a town, seems sometimes. You'd think so if you had to get meals for 'em, same's I do."

"You!" says I. "Do you cook for all that gang? How old are you?"

"Seventeen last March. Cook for 'em? Guess I do! And scratch to get things to cook, too; else we'd have to live on salt air pudding with wind sass. I take in washing, and Lycurgus he goes fishing and clamming and choring around, and

Editha helps me iron, and we all take watch and watch looking out for the young ones."

Hartley spoke then. "We're looking for a cook," he says. "Will you come and cook for us, and help about the house here? Mr. Pratt finds the job too big for one man."

She bobbed her head. "Yup," says she, dry as a chip. "I should think he might, judging by what I've seen. No, I can't come. I've got to stay home and look out for the folks."

"Why can't your father do that?" asks Hartley.

"Who—pa? I guess you ain't heard about pa. He's sick. Got his never-get-over, he says. Pa's had most every kind of symptom there is; phthisic and influency and lumbago and pleurisy. Now he's settled down to consumption and nervous dyspepsy. Afore ma died she used to try to cure him, but the doctor and pa had a row. The doctor said pa didn't have consumption nor nothing else; what he needed was hard exercise, such as work. Pa said the doc didn't know his business, and the doc said maybe not, but he knew pa. So pa told him never to darken our door again, and he ain't—except to come around once in a while and collect something from me on the bill."

"Well," says I, "maybe you know somebody else that would do for us. Who's a good cook and general housekeeper that would be likely to hire out?"

She thought for a moment or so. "I don't know," she says. "Most folks in this neighborhood is too high-toned to go out working. They'd rather stay to home and take boarders. Mrs. Hannah Jane Purvis is about the only one, and you've had her."

Martin made a face. "We have," he says.

"Yup," says Eureka. "She told Mr. Scudder that you was crazy as all get out, and sunk in worldly sin besides. She said you'd get your pay hereafter for treating her the way you did."

"We hope to," says Van, cheerful. "Now, Miss—er—Sparrow, we want you to come and help us out. We're Crusoes on a desert island and we need a Man—I should say Woman—Friday. We'll pay you so much," he says, naming a price that made even *my* eyes stick out, and I was used to high prices by this time.

"A *month?*" she says, staring at him.

"A week," says he.

She had a queer way of doing everything by jerks, like as if she was hung on wires and worked with a string. Now she straightened up out of her chair so sudden you almost expected to hear her snap.

" A week ? " she sings out. " Oh ! " Then she looked at me.

" Oh, it's so, if he says so," says I, resigned like.

" Land sakes ! A *week!* I never—but it ain't no use. What would become of pa and the children ? "

" Couldn't you come over for the days, at least ? " asks Martin. " You might go home nights, you know."

And that's the way it ended, finally. The Twins had made up their minds, and when that happened, heaven and earth wouldn't change 'em. At last Eureka said she'd talk it over with her folks, and Van Brunt said we would come over to her house next day and get the decision.

" There ! " says he, when the Sparrow girl had gone. " Skipper, the cook question is settled."

" Maybe 'tis," says I. " Looks to me as if you'd settled it the way the feller settled the coffee, by upsetting it. For chaps that pined for rest and quiet you two do queer things. Do you realize what getting mixed up with that Sparrow gang is likely to mean ? "

" If the whole flock is like the specimen bird

we've seen," he says, "it'll mean joy. If there was one thing needed to make Ozone Island a delight, a gem of purest ray serene, that original would be the thing. She's a circus in herself. I shall dream to-night of pa and the doctor. Ho, ho! By the way, what's her Christian name?"

I told the name—the whole of it. How them Heavenlies did laugh.

"Eureka!" says Hartley. "Splendid!"

"Eureka!" says Van. "We have found it! Sol, let's have lunch."

I got 'em something to eat and then the three of us put in the afternoon chasing the wild animals. The chickens was fairly easy to get hold of; I laid a trail of corn up to the door of the hen-yard and trapped the most of 'em that way. But the pig was a holy terror. He'd had his experience with Ozone Islanders that morning and he didn't want any more. Up and down that blessed sand bar we chased him, getting upset and tiring ourselves out. The pig race over to Eastwich wa'n't in it. I did most of the chasing; the Heavenlies superintended, as usual, and give orders and laughed. They pretty nigh laughed themselves sick. Finally the critter bolted into the woodshed and I locked the door on him. It was six o'clock when I dumped him into the sty. Of all the Natural Life days I'd had yet this one was the liveliest and most wearing. A week like it and *my* natural place would have been the burying ground. I cal'late I lost three pound that afternoon. I was getting so thin that when I fell down my legs made grooves in the sand.

The next forenoon me and Hartley went over to close the cook trade. Van wouldn't go. He said the gardening and the shipwreck and the steeple-chase—meaning the pig hunt—had given him sensations enough for a week or so; he had some of 'em with him yet. So Martin said he'd go, for my sake. I borrowed a couple of spare oars from Scudder, when he arrived with the morning's dose of skim-milk and cream and butter, and, as I took care to row the skiff this time, we made the passage all right. Then we walked up to the Sparrows' nest.

'Twas a pretty shabby looking shack, now I tell you. Shingles dropping off, and fence falling down, and a general shortage of man's work everywhere. But there was a bed of bachelor's buttons and old maid's pinks under the front window, and the windows themselves was clean and bright. Eureka had done her best to make the place homey; you could see that.

She let us in when we knocked at the kitchen door. Her sleeves was rolled up and there was a big basket of clothes by the steaming washtub. Editha, the twelve-year-old, was grinding at the wringer and Dewey, the baby, was setting on the floor playing with a rag doll. The rest of the tribe—except Lycurgus, who had gone peddling clams—was off playing.

Eureka, she apologized for things being so upset, but there wa'n't any need for apologies. The house was plain and poor—you could see that it took a mighty lot of stretching to make both ends come in sight of each other, let alone meet; but 'twas clean as a whistle. Even the baby was clean, all except his face and hands, and no healthy young one ought to have *them* clean.

"Good morning," says Hartley. "Have you decided to cook for us?"

She bobbed her head over the washtub. "I've decided it, if pa has," says she. "He ain't made up his mind yet. He wanted to sleep on it, he said. I guess he's done that. Anyhow he's just got up. Step right into the dining-room and talk to him. You'll have to excuse me; I've got to get this washing done afore noon, somehow."

So she pitched into the scrubbing, bending in the middle exactly like a jointed pocket-rule, and the Twin and me went into the dining-room.

Washington Sparrow was there. There wa'n't but one comfortable rocking-chair in sight and he was in that, with his stocking feet resting on the ruins of a haircloth sofa. He was pretty husky looking, seemed to me, for a man complicated with consumption and nervous dyspepsy, but his face was as doleful as a crape bonnet, and 'twas plain that he couldn't see no hope, and was satisfied with his eyesight. He had a clay pipe in his mouth and was smoking like a peat fire.

"How are you, Mr. Sparrow?" says Martin, bright and chipper. "How's the health this morning?"

The invalid rolled his eyes around, but he didn't get out of the rocker. Neither did he take them blue yarn socks off the sofa.

"Oh!" says he, groaning something awful. "I'm miserable, thank you. Set down and make yourselves to home."

There was only three settable pieces of furniture in the room. He was using two of 'em, and t'other was a child's high chair. So we decided to stand up.

"Don't you find yourself improving this beautiful weather?" asks Hartley, sympathetic.

Washy fetched another groan, so deep that I judged it started way down in the blue socks.

"No," says he. "I'm past improving. Just lingering 'round now and suffering, waiting for the end. I s'pose Reky told you what I had, didn't she?"

Hartley looked troubled. "Why," he says, "she did say that you feared tuberculosis, but——"

"Tuber—nothing! That's just like her! making fun of her poor sick father. What I've got is old-fashioned consumption." Here he fetched a cough that was hollerer than the groaning. "Old-fashioned consumption and nervous dyspepsy. Can't eat a meal's vittles in comfort. But there! I'll be through pretty soon. The sooner the quicker *I* say. Everybody 'll be glad when I'm gone. 'Don't,' I says to 'em, 'don't rag out in no mourning for me. Don't put no hot-house wreaths on *my* grave. I know how you feel and—' Get off my feet, you everlasting young one! Think I'm a ladder?"

This last part was to Dewey, who had come in from the kitchen, and was trying to climb onto the sofa.

Martin looked like he didn't know what to say. By and by he cleared his throat and threw out a hint concerning Eureka's coming to Ozone. The sick man shook his head.

"No," he says. "I'm self-sacrificing, and all that, but somehow I can't make up my mind to let her go. I can't bear to have her out of my sight a minute. You can't begin to think, Mr. What's-your-name, what a comfort 'tis to me, agonizing here and suffering, to have Reky setting down alongside of me day after day, the way she does. You can't begin to think it, Mister."

I couldn't begin to think it—not without what the doctor calls "stimulants." The amount of setting down that poor hard-working Eureka got time for wouldn't comfort anybody much, it seemed to me.

"She's my favorite child," went on Washy, swabbing his eyes. "She always was, too. Even when she was a baby I thought more of her than I done of all the others."

Eureka must have been listening, for she called from the kitchen.

"Why, pa!" she says. "When I was a baby there *wa'n't* any others. I'm the oldest."

The invalid bounced up straight in the rocker.

"That's it!" he hollers. "Make fun of your helpless, poor old father! Go ahead! pick at me and contradict me! I s'pose when I'm dead and in my grave you'll contradict me every time I speak."

He blew off steam for much as five minutes. Didn't even remember to stop and get his cough going. Hartley turned to the door. I could see he was disappointed.

"Very well," he says. "I'm sorry. I'm sure she is just the girl we need. Good day, Mr. Sparrow."

I cal'late Washy wa'n't expecting that. He hitched around in his chair. It had a busted cane seat, the chair did, and he had to roost on the edge of it to keep from falling through.

"Er—er—just a minute, Mister," he says. "I want you to understand how I feel about this thing. If I was able to do for myself 'twould be different, but——"

Eureka came to the door then, wiping her arms on her apron.

"Why, pa," she says, "I told you I could fix that."

She went on to tell how she'd get up early every morning and cook the meals afore she left, and how Editha would be there, and Lycurgus would split the wood and do the chores, and how she'd be home nights, and so on. She had planned everything. I liked that girl. At last her dad give another one of his groans.

"All right," says he. "*I* give in. *I* ain't going to stand in the way. Hadn't ought to expect nothing different, I s'pose. Work and fret and slave yourself into the boneyard bringing up children, and—and educating 'em and all, and then off they go and leave you. Well, *I'm* resigned. Mr.—Mr.—What's-your-name, she can go, Eureka can—for two dollars more a week."

I actually gasped out loud. The cheek of him! Why, the price Van had offered was enough to hire three girls. And now this shark wanted more.

Even Martin Hartley seemed to be set back some. But he was game. For a "mercenary" chap he was the most liberal piece of goods on the shelf.

"Certainly, Mr. Sparrow," says he. "That will be satisfactory. Good morning. Good morning, Eureka. I presume we shall see you tomorrow?"

We got out of the house finally. Washy come far as the kitchen to see us off. He was smiling and sweet as syrup now. When I'd got to the walk Eureka called me back.

"Mr. Pratt," she whispered, "you tell Mr. Hartley that of course I sha'n't take the extra two dollars. I'll be paid too much as 'tis. But we won't let pa know."

Afore I could answer there was a yell from the dining-room. I looked in and there was Washy doubled up in that rocker with his knees under his chin. He'd forgot about the busted cane seat and had set down heavy and gone through. Editha was trying to haul him out, the baby was crying, and the invalid himself was turning loose the healthiest collection of language I'd heard for a good while. Eureka dove to the rescue, and I come away.

Hartley and I walked on a spell without saying much. Then he asks—

"Skipper, do you suppose that fellow really has consumption?"

"Humph!" says I, disgusted; "consumption of grub."

He thought a minute longer.

"Poor girl," says he. "She has a hard time of it. We must see if we can't help her in some way."

CHAPTER XII

MISS SPARROW'S DIAGNOSIS

EUREKA was on hand bright and early the next day and it didn't take me long to see that she was worth her salt. She took hold like a good one and had breakfast—and a mighty good breakfast—ready right on time. I don't know when I've enjoyed a meal like I done that one, sure all the while that I hadn't got to turn to and wash the dishes afterwards. I went out to my gardening feeling like a sick man who had turned the corner and was on the road to getting well again.

And from then on the Natural Life was easy for all of us, for quite a spell. The new girl was a wonder, so far as doing work was concerned. She'd go through Marcellus's old home like a hurricane, sweeping and dusting and singing. She was 'most always singing—that is, when she wa'n't talking. She had a queer programme of mus. too, running from hymn tunes to songs she'd heard the boarders use over at the hotel. One minute 'twould be, "Land ahead! Its fruits are waving," and the next meeting somebody "in the shade of the old apple tree."

One day I come in and she was piping up about how everybody to her house worked but her dad, or words to that effect.

"Hello!" says I. "Did you make that up out of your head?"

"No," she says. "It's a new one that Lycurgus heard over to the Old Home House. It sounded so as if 'twas made for our family that it kind of stuck in Lys's craw and he come home and told it to me.

"'Everybody works but father,
And he sets 'round all day.'

"I tried it on pa last night," she went on. "Thought it might jar him some, but it didn't. He said 'twas funny. Maybe I'd think so, too, if I was him."

How Hartley laughed when he heard her singing that. She tickled the Twins 'most to death, anyway. She was as sharp as a whip and as honest as a Quaker parson. When her first pay day come she set her squared-toed boot down and simply would *not* take the extry two dollars wages. She said even a hog knew when it had enough, and she wa'n't a hog. Martin told me he was going to make it up to her some other way. The Heavenlies was mighty interested in her; but not more so than she was in them.

She and I had some great confabs when we was alone together. She asked I don't know how many questions about Hartley and Van Brunt; why they was living this way, and how they used to live and all. I told her some of what Lord James had told me, but not the whole. I left out about the engaged business, because I figgered it wa'n't any of her affairs, rightly speaking. Course 'twa'n't none of mine neither, but somehow I'd got to feel that I was a sort of father to them two cracked New Yorkers.

"Do you think they're crazy?" she asks. "Nate Scudder says they act as if they was."

"You've got me," says I. "I ain't made up my mind yet."

"What makes 'em go in swimming every morning?" she wanted to know.

"Why, to take a bath, I guess," says I. "Van Brunt told me he always took his 'plunge' when he was home."

She nodded, quick as usual. "Um-hum," says she. "I've read about it. They do it in the marble swimming pool in the gardens of the ducal mansion. And there's palm trees around and fountains, and nightingales singing, and music floating on the balmy perfumed air. And when they've got all scrubbed up there's velvet-footed menials to fan 'em and give 'em hasheesh to smoke."

"Want to know!" I says. "What's hasheesh? Plug cut or cigars?"

"'Tain't neither," said she. "It's some kind of stuff that makes you dream about beautiful women and things."

"Well, they don't have that here," says I. "They smoke cigars and cigarettes. And I've smoked both of 'em and *my* dreams was mainly about how much work I had to do. Nightingales are birds, ain't they? We're pretty shy on nightingales over here to Horsefoot, but maybe the gulls make that up. Gulls don't sing, no more than hens, but they screech enough for six. Where did you get all this stuff from, anyway?"

She got it out of library books and the *Home Comforter*. Seems old Miss Paine, over in the village, lent her the *Comforter* every week as fast as she got through with it herself. Eureka had never been to the city, nor anywheres further than

Eastwich, and her ideas about such things was the queerest mixed-up mess of novel trash and smart boarder's lies that ever was. That, and what she'd read in the newspapers. She said she was going to the city some day, when her " affinity " showed up.

" What's your idea of a first-class affinity ? " I asks, looking for information. I didn't know whether 'twas an animal or a cart.

" Well," says she, " he's got to be good-looking and have chests and chests of gold and jewelry. Further than that I ain't made up my mind yet."

She said when she did go she would sew up her money in the waist of her dress, and if a confidence man, or a trust or a policeman tried to get it away from her, she bet he'd have trouble on his hands.

" Policeman ? " says I. " What would he be doing trying to steal your money ? Policemen ain't thieves."

" They ain't, hey ? " she says. " *City* policemen ain't ? I guess you ain't read much about 'em."

She read the police committee trials in a stack of three or four-year-old newspapers and they'd fixed her, far's policemen was concerned.

She didn't take any stock in Hartley's being

down our way for his health. She said she had made up her mind what was the matter with him. "What ails *him*," says she, "is Girl."

"*Girl?*" says I.

"Yup. He's in love."

I set back and looked at her. Mind you I hadn't said one word about Agnes Page or the busted engagement.

"Get out!" I says, finally. "What did he come here for then? There ain't a female native in this neighborhood that wouldn't stop a clock—present company excepted, of course."

"It don't make no difference. He's in love, and he's come here to forget his troubles. You never read 'False but Fair, or the Bride Bereft,' did you? I thought not. Why, East Wellmouth is Glory alongside of some places that young men in love goes to. You wait. I'll find out that girl's name some of these days."

She said that Van Brunt wa'n't in love; which struck me funny, knowing what I did.

'Twa'n't so very long after this that the Heavenlies and me drove to South Eastwich to visit the Fresh Air School. I don't think Hartley would have gone if it hadn't been that his name was 'specially mentioned in the note from Agnes.

Even then Van had to say that he wouldn't go unless his chum did.

We left Eureka to keep house. It seemed to suit her first rate.

" You wait till that Scudder man comes," she says to me. " I want to talk to him about the milk he's been leaving."

" What's the matter with it? " I asks. " Ain't he giving full measure? "

" Not of milk he ain't," she says. " It's too white to wash with and too blue to drink. I'm going to tell him we've got a pump ourselves."

The Eastwich school was a big old farm house with considerable land around it. The youngsters had lots of room to run and carry on. All hands was at the door to meet us, Agnes and Miss Talford and Redny, and all the inmates. The Heavenlies had stopped in the village and got a big freezer full of ice cream—they ordered it ahead—and, well, I thought we'd got a warm welcome, but when the children saw that freezer——

The ladies shook hands with us and asked us in. Lord James was there in all his glory. You could see that his new job suited him down to his shoes. No hard work, no sailing or such like, good easy bosses, and plenty of picking on the side, I judged.

I turned the horse and carriage over to him, under protest, and we went into the house.

"First of all, Ed," said the Page girl, turning to Van Brunt, "I want to thank you, on behalf of the children, for your kindness in sending them the fruit. It is delicious. You should see the dears every day when the expressman comes with the basket."

Van looked puzzled. "Fruit?" he says. "I don't understand. Do you know anything about fruit, skipper?"

I pleaded not guilty. Hartley didn't seem to hear. He was busy talking with Miss Talford.

"Why!" says Agnes. "Doesn't it come from you? We have been receiving the loveliest basket of fruit from Boston every morning. I thought of course you had ordered it for us. Didn't you, really?"

Van shook his head. "It takes a man with the ordinary amount of brains and thoughtfulness to do things like that," he says. "I'm miles below the average in such things. In all but carelessness and general idiocy I'm a bear on the market. Here, Martin! Miss Talford, please excuse him for a moment, will you? Martin, are you responsible for this fruit?"

Hartley was so sunburned that you couldn't have told if he did blush. But he acted nervous and uneasy.

"It was nothing," he said. "I knew the youngsters liked such things, and the stuff you get here isn't eatable. Then James is a success, Miss Talford, you say?"

But he didn't get off quite as easy as that. Agnes looked up surprised and, I thought, pleased.

"Thank you, Mr. Hartley," she said. "It was kind of you, and very thoughtful."

Of course the Talford girl thanked him, too. He acted a good deal like he wished he hadn't come.

But I guess that feeling wore off after a while. It seemed to me that Miss Page was considerable pleasanter to him than I'd seen her yet. She talked to him more and there wa'n't so much of that chilly "hands-off" kind of manner in her voice. Two or three times they seemed almost friendly, as you might say, and toward the end of the day Hartley's blueness, that was always with him when she was in sight, had pretty nigh disappeared. He seemed quite happy, for him—not his usual careless, don't-care kind of jollity, either.

One thing that I think Agnes noticed was the way the boy, Redny, stuck to him. You could see that the little chap's idea of a first-class brick was Martin Hartley. And another sure thing was that Redny was the Page girl's favorite. She was always running after him to see what he was doing, that he didn't get hurt, or such like. One time when she'd gone on this kind of an errand, and the Twins and Miss Talford and me was left together, I spoke up and says—

"That small fire top is considerable on Miss Agnes's mind, ain't he?"

Margaret Talford laughed. "He's the apple of her eye," says she. "She fairly worships him. I'm sure I don't know why, for he's the worst mischief-maker in the school. But Agnes's sympathy seems to run to the black sheep. Were you a black sheep, Mr. Van Brunt?"

Van shook his head, very solemn. "I was," says he, "but the cleansing influence of the Natural Life has removed the upper coating. You can see that she doesn't find it necessary to run after *me*. I flatter myself that I'm rapidly becoming—what is it that our new cook sings, skipper? Oh, yes! 'Whiter than snow.' Do you notice my alabaster purity, Miss Talford?"

"I hadn't as yet," she says. "I'll call Agnes's attention to it."

"Pray don't," says he. "I'm not altogether certain of its lasting qualities. Suppose *you* keep an eye on me instead, until I'm sure that it is enamel and not whitewash."

That was a sample of the talk of them two. Just nonsense, but they seemed to enjoy it first rate.

At dinner Van entertained the crowd, as usual, with stories about the Island and our doings on it. He told how the Ark upset, and 'twas wild enough anyhow, but when he'd finished embroidering it 'twas a regular crazy quilt. Then he begun with Eureka. He didn't know much about Washy, except from the girl's talk, for Hartley nor me hadn't told much of our experience. So all he said was that the old man was sick. Agnes Page seemed a good deal interested.

After they'd finished eating she asked me considerable many questions.

"Is he all alone there, the poor sick man?" she asked.

"No, no!" says I. "There's children enough to help out a whole hospital. He's all right."

"But those children ought not to have to stay at

home," says she. "They need the air and exercise and schooling."

"They don't look as if they was wasting away," I told her. "Eureka's as good as a ma to 'em—and better than a pa—*her* pa, anyway."

She seemed to be thinking. "The poor fellow," she says, referring to Washy, I judged. "I must drive over and see him."

I told her Hartley had promised to help Eureka. She seemed real pleased. Her face kind of lit up. She walked away then and didn't say no more.

Lord James and me had our dinner together. I pumped him about the girls and how he liked 'em.

"They're all right," he says. "As perfect ladies and as generous and open 'anded as I could wish."

"Which do you like best?" I asked.

"I 'aven't no choice," he says. "Miss Page is a good 'ousekeeper. Almost too good if I may say it. A lady 'adn't ought to meddle with 'ousehold affairs, not when she has a competent man to attend to 'em for 'er. Miss Talford now, she's different. I'd like to work for 'er always."

"Pity she ain't going to be Mrs. Van Brunt instead of t'other," says I. "Then you'd have an easy berth. Don't it seem to you that Miss Page and your boss ain't any too thick for engaged folks?"

"No, indeed!" says he, scornful. "Lord love you, you'd ought to see some married folks as I've worked for. W'y Lord 'Enry and 'er Ladyship, they——"

He was on his English tack now and you never could get him off it when he was started good. I didn't get much satisfaction out of him.

I got more a while later, though. Just afore we started for home Hartley and the Page girl come walking down the porch together. They wa'n't saying much when I first saw 'em, but all at once she says—

"Mr. Hartley, there is one thing I must ask you. You paid Dennis the five dollar prize he won at the race that day. Did you collect it from the judges?"

"Oh, that's all right," he answers, fidgety. "I think probably I did. I don't remember."

"I thought not," says she. "Now you must permit me to pay it to you. The boy is under my charge and I shall insist upon it."

He was pretty short and sharp, I thought. "No, really," he said, "I've forgotten the affair entirely.

No doubt I've been paid already. It was nothing, of course, and the boy was plucky and I took a fancy to him."

She insisted, but he wouldn't give in. At last she says, looking hard at him—

"I think," she says, "that your simple life is doing a great deal for you. You have improved in many ways. I have heard things—good things—about you that surprised me. I'm very glad."

He didn't answer. Just then the valet brought the carriage up to the door and 'twas time to say good by.

I was pretty tickled with the day's work, take it altogether. Eureka got after me soon as we was back to the Island, and she asked a couple of ton of questions. She wanted to know all about the school and especially about the Page girl and her chum.

"You ain't told me all you know," says she, finally. "Tell the rest of it. What relation is this Agnes Page to Mr. Hartley?"

I said she wa'n't no relation. At last, sort of in self-defence, I told the whole yarn about the engagement—Van's engagement, I mean.

She bobbed her head. "I thought so," says she. "I don't care if Mr. Van Brunt *is* engaged to the Page one. He ain't in love with her. And Mr. Hartley is."

"What are you talking about?" says I, soon's I could get my breath.

"Just what I said. He's in love with Miss Page. And I'm going to help him get her."

"Humph!" says I. "You be, hey? Well, how about poor Van? What do you want to shove him out into the cold for? He ain't done anything to you, has he?"

She shook her sunbonnet and looked wise. "That's all right," she says. "I've got my ideas about him, too. Anyway I'm going to help Mr. Hartley."

I thought and thought. And then, without exactly meaning to, I spoke my thought out loud.

"I believe I'll help you help him," says I.

She wa'n't a bit surprised. "Humph!" she says. "That's no news. *You've* been trying to help him for ever so long."

What do you think of that? There wa'n't anything slow or dull about that Sparrow girl—not enough to fret yourself over, there wa'n't.

CHAPTER XIII

THE LAWN FÊTE

IT was August now. The nice weather held out right along and one day on Ozone Island was a good deal like the next.

And yet it seemed to me that there was little changes. For instance, take the matter of reading. When we first arrived 'twas nothing but that Natural Life book; the Heavenly Twins was at it continuous, and such a thing as a newspaper or magazine was what Van Brunt called an " abomination." I couldn't get a paper even to kindle fire with; had to use poverty grass for that. But now the Natural Life sermon laid on the dining-room mantel piece most of the time, with a layer of dust on it, and Scudder fetched the Boston and New York newspapers every day. And magazines and books begun to come in the mail.

I remember one day Hartley set reading the New York *Evening Post,* that part of it he called the " financial page." All at once he spoke.

"By Jove! Van," he says. "Consolidated Tea Lead is up three points from last week's quotations. There must be something doing."

Van looked at him, kind of sad and disappointed.

"Martin," says he, "are you falling from grace? Get thee behind me, Satan. Give me that financial sheet."

Hartley laughed and tossed it over.

"There!" says his chum, crumpling it up and shoving it into his pocket. "That disturbing influence is out of the way. Let us discuss the simple and satisfying subject of agriculture. There is an article on 'The Home Garden' in this month's number of *The Rural Gentleman*, which should be instructive to our friend Mr. Pratt, plower of sea and soil. Skipper, lend me your ears. I'll return them shortly."

Then he commenced to read that magazine piece out loud to me, very solemn, and stopping every once in a while to chuck in some ridiculous advice on his own account. This had got to be a regular thing. Every bit of farm news I had to hear. The garden was Van's pet joke.

"What," says he, when the reading was done, "is the latest crop bulletin, Sol?"

"I have the honor to report," says I, "that from the present outlook we'll have two cornstalks, one tomatter vine, and three cucumber plants really in sight by to-morrow morning. That is, if the sand don't blow in and cover 'em up in the night."

"Good!" he says. "I move that the report be accepted. Martin, don't let me see you wasting your time on the frivolity of the Street, when there are such serious matters to claim our attention."

Which was all right, only that very afternoon I saw him, himself, out behind the barn, reading that *Post* financial page and looking mighty interested.

They was more anxious to be doing things than when they first come. Hartley's health was improving all the time, and that probably accounted for his liveliness. I took 'em sailing 'most every day and they wanted to fish and shoot and the like of that.

Once we went on a cruise after shore birds. I bagged a few, but the Twins couldn't hit a flock of balloons with a cannon, so they didn't have no luck. But a little later Van went out alone with Nate Scudder and I'll be blessed if he didn't come back with a dozen peep and ring-necks. Then the way he crowed over me and Martin was scandalous, till, a week later, Hartley himself went gunning with Nate and fetched home fifteen, bigger and better than his chum's. And after this, of course, 'twas nothing but what a great hunter Scudder was, and rubbing it into me.

The hotel boarders and the town folks was mighty interested in the Ozone Islanders by this time. The picnic boats from the Old Home House generally sailed close by our point, to give the passengers a chance to look our outfit over. Sometimes the boats stopped, and then the Twins would take an observation from an upstairs window, and, if they liked the looks of the crowd, would come down and keep what they called "open house." "Open house" always meant more work for Eureka and me. Lucky for us, 'twas pretty seldom that the Heavenlies liked their callers' looks well enough to open up.

The Baptist minister and his wife came over to call. There was going to be a "lawn fête and sale" at the church pretty soon, and the idea was to get the Twins to "donate" something. Van Brunt was full of his high jinks that day, and he took that poor parson and his wife in tow.

First he carted 'em out to the henyard. He

paraded up and down in front of the coops, pointing out the scraggly Plymouth Rocks as if they was some kind of freaks, like ostriches. He said they ate a bag of corn a day and laid one egg a week, so he figgered that every egg was worth five dollars or so. What did the parson think of a donation of half a dozen of them eggs?

"Not to eat, you understand," says Van; "but as rarities, as curiosities."

The minister was a young feller, not long out of college, and pretty straight-laced. But he had some fun in him.

"If I might suggest," he says, "I think one of the hens themselves would be more acceptable and profitable. Among our summer people there is a great demand for 'antiques.' Now one of those hens——"

That tickled Van. He told Hartley afterwards that the minister was a trump. He donated liberal—not with eggs nor poultry neither—and promised that he and Hartley would attend the sale.

And they did. And so did Eureka and me. The lawn fête was held in the meeting-house front yard, and 'twas all rigged up fine with flags and tissue paper and bunting. There was a grab bag and a cake table and a fancy goods table, and I don't know what all. All the summer folks was there, and most of the town women and girls, and the prices charged for things would have been highway robbery if it hadn't been a church that was charging 'em.

The Heavenlies bought and bought and bought. They bought everything—the foolishest things. Van bought three pair of embroidered suspenders and a crocheted tidy and a pin cushion, and Martin got a worsted Afghan and a hand-painted sofa pillow, so fresh that the paint come off on your hands when you touched it. And 'twa'n't any quiet colored paint neither. And when you rubbed off one layer there was another underneath. Luretta Daniels' daughter had painted it; she was taking lessons and her ma said that she'd painted that pillow over much as a dozen times, because the colors wa'n't "blending right" or the subject didn't suit her. 'Twas so stiff with paint on top that 'twould have been like ramming your head into a fence to lay on it.

We stayed till most everything was sold but a log cabin bed quilt that the Christian paupers at the poorhouse had made. Nobody seemed to want that, although they was gay rags enough in it to build a rainbow. The minister's wife said she was *so* sorry. The poor things at the almshouse had worked *so* hard.

"You wait a minute," says Van. "*I'll* get rid of it."

He took out his vest pocket memorandum book and tore about ten pages into little squares. Then he made numbers on these squares with a pencil. Half of these he put into his hat, and, the next I knew, he was standing on a chair, waving the bedquilt with one hand and the hat with t'other.

"Ladies and gentlemen," he shouts. "Here is positively the last chance to secure this magnificent —er—er—lambrykin, made by the deserving poor to cover the restless rich. Competition has been so strong that no one person has been able to buy it. The only solution would be a syndicate, and the almshouse is opposed to trusts. Therefore I am authorized to"—then he bent down and whispered, "Mr. Morton, kindly give me whatever small change you have left."

The minister looked puzzled, but he handed up a half dollar. Van Brunt reaches into the hat and takes out one of the folded slips of paper.

"Here you are, sir," says he. "Treasure that as you would your life. Now, then, ladies and gentlemen, this is a raffle. The minister starts it. Tickets are anything you please, provided it's enough. Come early and avoid the rush."

There was a kind of gasp from all the church people. The members of the sewing circle looked at each other with the most horrified kind of faces. The parson, Mr. Morton, run forward.

"Just a minute, Mr. Van Brunt, if you *please,*" he sings out.

But Van waved him away. The summer folks come after them tickets like a whirlwind, laughing and shouting and passing up dollar bills. 'Twa'n't hardly any time afore the hat was empty and the Twin's jacket pocket was full of money. Then he fills up the hat with more pieces of paper.

"These are duplicates of the numbers sold," says he. "The drawing will now take place. Here, Bill!"

He grabs a little shaver by the coat collar and lifts him up to the chair. Old lady Patterson, the deacon's wife, set up a scream.

"Stop!" she yells. "My child shall not——"

"It takes but a moment, madam," says Van, waving to her, calm and easy. "Now, Julius Cæsar, please take one of those numbers from the hat."

The boy reddened up and grinned and looked foolish, but he stuck a freckled paw in and took out a piece of paper.

"Number fourteen," shouts Van Brunt. "Number fourteen secures the—the tapestry. Who's the lucky one?"

Everybody unfolded their papers, but there didn't seem to be any fourteen. Hartley had three, but he wa'n't in it.

"Number fourteen," Van calls. "Who is fourteen? Mr. Morton, you began this. Where is your ticket?"

The minister looked dreadfully troubled. "Really," he stammered, "I—I—it was a mistake. I——"

"Here's yours, Mr. Morton," says a little girl. "You dropped it on the ground."

The parson looked pretty sick. He reached for it, but Van got it first.

"Number fourteen it is," he says. "Our esteemed friend, the Reverend Mr. Morton, secures the prize. That's as it should be. Three cheers for Mr. Morton!"

The summer folks give the cheers, but the church folks looked pretty average wild, I thought.

I forget how much was in Van Brunt's pocket.

That bedquilt fetched in enough money to pretty nigh buy the poorhouse itself.

The Twins felt good. They figgered that they'd made a hit at that " lawn fête."

" Great success, my raffle idea, wasn't it, skipper," says Van Brunt, on the way home.

I didn't answer right off. Eureka spoke up.

" Well," she says, " it sold the bedquilt, but I wouldn't wonder if it made the new minister lose his job. You see, 'twas gambling, and that church is dreadful down on gambling. Mrs. Patterson told me that she should have her husband call a parish meeting right off. I guess you won't be invited to no more sales *this* year."

And we wa'n't. Poor Morton had an awful time explaining, and the only way he could get out of it was to lay it heavy on the Twins. He had to preach a sermon giving gambling fits, and all around town 'twas nothing but how dissipated and wicked the Heavenlies was. We wa'n't fit for decent folks to associate with.

But I ain't been able to learn, even yet, that the bedquilt money was returned to the ticket buyers.

Van got a long letter from Agnes Page a little later, saying that she had heard of him as a " disturbing influence " and that she was shocked and grieved. He thought 'twas a great joke and didn't seem to care much. Nate Scudder was glad of the whole business. He didn't want nobody else to be milking his own pet cows.

Me and Eureka was glad, too, in a way. We judged that Van's being in disgrace with his girl would help Hartley's side along. And in a few days another idea begun to develop that, when I found it out, seemed to me likely to help him more.

Eureka told me that she'd seen a dress pattern at the church sale that she wanted awful. I asked her why she didn't buy it and she said 'twas two dollars and a half and she couldn't afford it. Hartley heard her say it and he loafed out into the kitchen and begun to ask questions, pumping her, sort of quiet, to find out what she done with her money. After she'd gone home he says to me—

"Skipper, that girl is robbing herself to support that old loafer, her father."

"That's right," says I. "It's my opinion that she ain't never told him that she ain't getting that extry two dollars a week. I guess she pays every cent into the house."

"It's a shame!" says he. "Can't we make the old vagabond earn his own living?"

"When you do," I says, "I'll believe that black's the blonde shade of white. Making Washy Sparrow work would be as big a miracle as the loaves and fishes."

He thought a spell. "Well, I mean to look into the matter," he says. "Sol, I want you to find out who owns that apology for a house they live in. Don't ask Eureka. We must keep it a secret from her or she'll interfere. And we may as well not tell Van, either. He's so careless that he might give it away."

"All right," says I. "I'll ask Scudder. He knows 'most all of everybody's business and Huldy Ann knows the rest."

So when Nate come, after breakfast next morning, I asked him.

"What do you want to know for?" says he, suspicious as usual.

"Oh, nothing. Just curious, that's all."

"They ain't going to move out, are they?" He seemed mighty interested.

"No, no!" says I. "Where'd they move to? Think they're going to Washington to visit the President or the Diplomatic Corpse?"

"Well," he says, "you needn't get mad. I didn't know but they might be coming over here.

I don't mind telling you. Huldy Ann, my wife, owns the place, if you want to know."

I *was* surprised. He was a regular sand-flea for bobbing up where you didn't expect him.

"She does?" says I. "Say, Nate, for the land sakes how much more of this country belongs to you and Huldy? And how much did you pay for it?"

He went on with a long rigmarole about a mortgage and a second mortgage and "foreclosing to protect himself," and so on. All I see in it was more proof that lambs fooling with Nate Scudder was likely to lose, not only wool, but hoofs, hide and tallow.

When I told Hartley he seemed real pleased.

"That makes it easy," he says. "Scudder will accommodate me by doing a little favor, won't he?"

"Sure thing!" says I, sarcastic. "Ain't he been accommodating you ever since you struck town?"

"Yes," he says, "he has. Scudder is a generous chap."

And he meant it, too! Why the good Lord lets such simple innocents as him and his chum run around loose for is—but there! No doubt He has his reasons. And what would become of the summer hotels without that kind?

Him and Nate was pretty thick for the next few days. Something was up, though as yet I wa'n't in the secret. Hartley made one or two trips to the village and he took neither me nor Van with him. He asked me where the doctor lived and a lot more questions.

Van Brunt, too, was getting pretty confidential with Nate. I caught the two of 'em off alone by the barn or somewheres quite a good many times. They was always whispering earnest, and when I hove in sight they'd break away and act guilty. There was something up there, too, and again I wa'n't in with the elect. I begun to feel slighted.

But in a little while Hartley's secret come out. One day Van took a notion to go down to Half Moon Neck gunning after peeps. He wanted Hartley to go with him, but Martin said no. He said he didn't feel like it, somehow. Why didn't Van put it off? But Van wa'n't the put-off kind. He was going and going right then. He wanted Scudder to sail him down, but Nate was too busy, so he hired Eureka's brother, Lycurgus. The two sailed away in the *Dora Bassett* to be gone all night. I wa'n't invited. The Twins had no use for me as a gunning pilot.

That afternoon late Hartley comes over from the main, rowed by Scudder. The pair of 'em seemed mighty tickled about something.

"Well, Mr. Hartley," says Nate, "we'll see you to-morrow morning. It'll work all right; you see."

"Will *he* work?" laughs Hartley. "That's the question."

"I cal'late he'll make the bluff," snickers Scudder. "I don't know where he'll sleep nights if he don't. Land of love! Did you see his face when you sprung it on him? Haw! haw!"

When we got to the house Hartley calls in Eureka.

"You're going to stay here to-night," he says to her. "Mr. Pratt and I have an errand ashore early in the morning and Mr. Van Brunt will be back soon after, and hungry, I imagine. So you must be ready with his breakfast. It's all right. Your father understands."

Eureka was some surprised, but she said she'd stay.

All through supper Hartley was laughing to himself. Just afore bedtime he calls me out on the porch.

"Sol," he says, "what would surprise you most in this world?"

"To see Mr. Van Brunt shoot at a bird and hit it," says I. Leaving me out of all these gunning trips jarred my pride considerable.

"Humph!" he says. "He shot a dozen the other day."

"Yes, but I didn't *see* him shoot 'em."

He laughed. "You countrymen are jealous creatures," he says. "Well, this is more surprising than that. What would you say if Mr. Washington Sparrow consented to go to work?"

I looked at him. "I wouldn't *say* nothing," I says. "I'd send for a straight-jacket. What are you talking about?"

He turned around in his chair.

"You remember I told you I was going to try to make him?" he says. "Well, I think I've succeeded. Come with me to-morrow morning and see. I'm doing it for the sake of that plucky daughter of his, and it has required some engineering and diplomacy. But I think I win. Don't mention a word to Eureka, though."

I promised to keep mum. I tried to get him to tell me more, but he wouldn't. "Wait and see" was all I could get out of him.

I turned in a kind of trance, as you might say. Washy Sparrow work! Well, I'd have to see him doing it with my own eyes. I wouldn't believe even a tintype of the performance if 'twas took by Saint Peter.

CHAPTER XIV

"THE BEST LAID PLANS"

WE left the Island early next day. I rowed to the main and anchored the skiff. Then me and Hartley walked up to the Neck road. I didn't ask no questions. He could speak first or be still. I'd had *my* dose. Nobody can call me nosey.

He did speak first. "Well, skipper?" he says, finally.

"Well, Mr. Hartley," says I.

"Why don't you ask me what my scheme is? Aren't you curious?"

"Scheme?" says I. "Scheme? I ain't much of a schemer, myself. Nice weather we're having, ain't it."

He laughed. "Sol," says he. "I like you. You're the right sort—you and Scudder."

Drat him! Why did he want to spoil it all by that last?

" Virtue must be its own reward, then, far's I'm concerned," I says, pretty average dry. " I don't seem to be getting no other kind. Pity me and Nate couldn't divide the substantials more equal."

His face clouded right up. " Money! " he says, disgusted, kicking a stick out of his way. " Don't you for one minute believe that money means happiness."

" All right," I says. " I ain't contradicting you. You've had more experience with it than I have. Sometimes it seems as if I could manage to bear up under a couple of thousand or so without shedding more'n a bucket of tears; but I'm open to conviction—like the feller that said he stole the horse, but they'd got to show proof enough to satisfy him."

'Twas some minutes afore he come out of his blue fit. Then he says—

" The scheme is this: I determined to see what could be done to make things easier for the Sparrow girl. The only solution seemed to be the getting rid of papa."

" If you'd waited long enough," I says; " maybe his consumptive dyspepsy would have saved you the trouble."

" I wish I had your faith," says he.

" You have. The same kind. Washy's is different. His doctrine is faith without work. Go on."

" So I tried to think of some way to bring it about. When you told me that Scudder owned the Sparrow place I saw my chance. Scudder and I consulted. He was willing to lose his tenants provided he didn't lose the rent. The rent was nothing; I promised to make that good until our season here was over and Eureka could return home. But I made it clear that when she did return home her father mustn't return with her. He must be provided for somewhere else. Then we saw the doctor and Morton, the minister. Morton was somewhat prejudiced, owing to Van's raffle, but he's a pretty decent fellow and seemed to think what he called a good action on my part might offset even a bedquilt gamble. So between us we fixed it up.

" Old Sparrow is offered a job as general shoveller and brick carrier over there at the hotel. They're building a new addition, you know. Brown, the manager, said he'd take him on, as a favor to me. He has been offered the place. If he doesn't accept, why, out he goes. Scudder has told him he can't stay in his house any longer. You should have seen him when we broke the news last night."

"S'pose he don't accept," I asks. "What about the children?"

"They'll be looked out for. Lycurgus will board at Scudder's. Eureka will stay with us. Editha and the baby will be roomed and fed by the minister. The others are to have good boarding places and go to school. Every one is willing to help the family, but they won't keep the old rascal. It has worked out beautifully."

"Hold on a minute," says I. "It's all right, as a plan. But Eureka won't let her dad suffer, even though she knows there ain't nothing really the matter with him. And who's going to pay all the young ones' board? She can't."

"I'll attend to that," says he, impatient. "It isn't enough to signify. And it will be all settled before Eureka knows it. The old man will take the job."

"I'll bet a cooky he don't," I says. "But it'll make him scratch gravel one way or 'nother. Bully for you, Mr. Hartley! I'm glad I'm along to see the fun."

"The fun was last night," says he. "Cæsar!

how he did cough and groan. And then swear! But here's the rest of the crowd."

They was waiting for us on the corner. Dr. Penrose was there, and Mr. Morton, and Cap'n Benijah Poundberry, chairmen of selectmen, and Scudder, and Peter T. Brown, manager of the Old Home House. They was all laughing, and thinking the whole thing a big joke.

"Mr. Hartley," says the doctor, "I wish you were to be a permanent resident. There are a few more cases of this kind I'd like to have you tackle."

We walked on together the rest of the way, laughing and talking. Nobody took the business serious at all. They all thought Washy would go to work when he found 'twas either that or get out and hustle for a place to put his head in.

We marched into the Sparrow yard like a Fourth of July parade. Hartley knocked at the kitchen door. Editha opened it.

"Is your father in?" asked the Twin.

"Yes, sir," says Editha. "He's in. I s'pose you'd like to see him, wouldn't you? Pa, here's Mr. Hartley."

There was a groan from the dining-room. Then some coughs, like a string of small earthquakes. Finally a dreadful weak voice orders us to step right in. The rest of the crowd went on ahead. I stopped for a jiffy to speak to Editha.

"Where's the rest of the children?" I asks.

"I sent 'em over to the grocery store on an errand," she says. "I thought you'd be along pretty soon. They took the baby with 'em."

"How's your dad been since he heard the news?" says I.

"Oh, he was going on terrible last night. Had nerve spells and fired the chairs around and carried on so we was all scared. But he went out about nine o'clock with a letter he'd wrote, and this morning he seems better. Say, Mr. Pratt," she whispers, eager, "is it true that me and Dewey are going to live with the minister's folks?"

"Maybe so," says I. "Why?"

"Oh! I *hope* so," she says. "Then I could go to school, and pa wouldn't be 'round to jaw us, and Reky 'd have a little rest. She does need it so."

Think of a twelve-year-old young one talking like that. But the children was all grown-ups in that family.

I went into the dining-room. The delegation was gathered on one side of the table, and Washy was crumpled up in his rocker on the other. He looked some scared.

"Well, Mr. Sparrow," Hartley was beginning when I come in, "have you made up your mind about the position which this gentleman has been kind enough to offer you?" He pointed to Brown as he said it.

"Hey?" asks the invalid, feeble.

Martin said it all over again; he had to stop in the middle so 's to give the candidate for the job a chance to cough and turn loose a few groans.

And all that Washy said when the Twin had finished was another "Hey?"

Hartley begun to lose patience. "You heard what I said," he snaps, sharp. "Have you made up your mind?"

"Don't get mad, Mr. Hartley," pleads the sufferer, sad and earnest. "*Please* don't. My nerves is dreadful weak this morning and I ain't able to stand it. I've had coughing spells ever since I got out of bed. Well, I won't have to linger here much longer. Pretty soon I'll be laid away, and——"

"Have you made up your mind?" interrupts Martin. "Answer quick. The time of these gentlemen is valuable."

"Don't, Mr. Hartley. *Please* don't. How can you cruelize a poor feller this way? Don't you know that any kind of stir and rumpus is the worst thing for me? Any doctor 'll tell you that——"

"Bosh!" 'Twas Doctor Penrose that said it, and he stepped forward. "Bosh!" says he again.

"What's that? Why, if it ain't my old friend the doctor! I never noticed you was there. I'm awful glad to see you, Doc. Seems just like old times. You'll excuse my not getting up, won't you? I've wasted away so since you was here that——"

"Bosh!" says the doctor again. "You're fatter than ever. There's nothing in the world the matter with you but pure downright dog laziness. Don't cough on my account. I don't care to hear it."

Washy looked at him as reproachful and goody-goody as a saint.

"I forgive you for them words, doctor," says he. "I realize I ain't been able to pay my bill to you, and so I can make allowances."

"Allowances! Why, you confounded impudent loafer! I've a good mind to——"

He was purple in the face. Peter Brown caught his arm.

"Ain't this a little off the subject?" he says. "Look here, Sparrow. We need a good husky man about your size at the hotel. We'll pay him ten dollars a week. I've offered you the job. Are you going to take it?"

"There ain't nothing in the world I should like better, Mr. Brown. I like to work, and——"

"All right, then. Get on your hat and come along."

"Come along! Why, how you talk! If I was to stir out of this house 'twould——"

'Twas Scudder's turn. "You'll have to stir mighty quick," says he. "I won't have no do-nothing tramps in a house of mine. Either take this chance or out you go next Saturday, bag and baggage."

"Why, Mr. Scudder! Why, *Nate!* How can you talk so! Just for a little matter of rent. You don't need it. Ain't you been telling me that you had a couple of soft rich folks over to Horsefoot Bar that was paying you a good living and more, too, all by themselves. Don't you remember you said——"

"Shut up!" 'Twas Scudder who got purple now. It looked to me like the invalid was having all the fun. He seemed to be expecting something and playing for time. I guess Hartley thought so too, for he says:

"That's enough of this. It's plain that he doesn't intend to accept. Mr. Scudder, you have given him formal notice. Come on."

Then Washy broke down. He sniffed and half cried and wanted to know things. The work would kill him in a day or so, of course, but he didn't mind that. When he thought of his poor fatherless children——

"The children will be provided for," says Martin. "I told you that. Mr. Morton will care for Editha and the baby."

"Mr. Morton? Morton? Seems to me I've heard that name afore. Ain't he the gambler? The one that come near being run out of town for stealing a bedquilt from the poorhouse, or something like that? Is *he* the man to trust with innocent little children?"

There it was again. The minister was red as a beet and stammering about "impertinence" and "blackguardism." I thought he'd lick that consumptive right then and there. It took another five minutes to calm *him* down. And so far we hadn't gained an inch.

And just then a horse and buggy come rattling into the yard. The horse was all over lather, like he'd been drove hard, and the buggy was white with dust. Everybody looked out of the window. Sparrow looked and his face brightened up. I cal'late 'twas exactly what he had been hoping and waiting for. Martin Hartley looked and his eyes and mouth opened. So did mine.

'Twas Lord James that was driving the buggy, and there was a young woman with him. The young woman was Agnes Page.

Agnes jumped from the step and run to the kitchen door. In spite of the dust and her clothes being rumpled and her hat shook over to one side she was as pretty as a picture. The next minute she was in the room, staring solemn at all us men. And her eyes seemed to look right through a feller.

"Why, Agnes—Miss Page!" exclaimed Hartley. Why are you here? What's the matter?"

She didn't answer him. Just turned to Washy. And says she—

"Am I in time, Mr. Sparrow? I didn't get your letter until nearly nine, because James was delayed at the office. But I hurried right over. I was so afraid I would be too late. Am I?"

The invalid looked at her. And, if he'd been the picture of misery afore, he was a whole panorama of it now. He coughed afore he answered. She shivered, kind of, at that cough, and I don't wonder. If ever there was a graveyard quick-step, Washy Sparrow's cough was it.

"No, ma'am," says he. "I guess not, but I don't know. The shock of it, and—and all, has pretty nigh finished me up, I'm afraid. I don't cal'late I'll pull through, but I may. Let's hope for the best, anyhow. But, ma'am, if you'd heard the things that's been said to me!"

She whirled around on us and her eyes flashed chain lightning.

"Aren't you *ashamed?*" she says. "Great strong men, every one of you, and all banded together to torture a poor helpless invalid."

A feller's conscience is the biggest fool part of his insides. Now I knew that what we'd been doing was exactly the right thing *to* do, but I felt as mean and small as if I'd been caught stealing eggs. I kind of shrivelled up, as you might say, and tried to scrouge back into the corner. Maybe I'd have got there, only the rest of the crowd was trying to do the same thing.

All but Hartley. He was a lot set back, but he spoke up prompt.

"Miss Page," said he, "I'm sure you don't understand. We——"

She was back at him afore he'd begun.

"I think that is exactly what I do—understand," she says. "At any rate, I mean to understand thoroughly. Mr. Sparrow, what have they said to you?"

Washy cleared his throat. When he answered 'twas in a sort of beg-pardon voice. You could see how he hated to speak ill of anybody. *He* wouldn't hurt nobody's feelings for the world. Bless him! he was a cute shyster, if ever there was one.

"It's like I wrote you, ma'am," says he. "They've offered me a place to go to work, and I've been awful tempted to take it. I *want* to take it. My land! *how* I want to! But I don't feel able to dig cellars. I wouldn't last at it more'n a few days and then what would become of my fatherless children with nobody to look after 'em? And because I think of these things and can't bring myself to—to—passing away from 'em so soon, I'm going to be put out of my house and home. My little home, that I've thought so much of——"

He had to stop and wipe his eyes. Agnes' eyes were wet, too, and her feet patted the floor. "But why?" says she. "Why?"

"I don't know—that is, for sure, ma'am. You see I ain't been able to earn nothing for some time.

Eureka, poor girl, she's had to look out for us all. And I b'lieve the doctor there, his bill ain't been all paid; and we owe Mr. Scudder some rent; and I s'pose likely Eureka would be able to give more of her time to the Island work, and maybe for less pay, if——"

"I see," says Miss Page, scornful. "I see. And so, for a few dollars you are to be turned out of your home. You, a poor sick man! Oh! I can hardly believe there are such people in the world. And yet, I have had some experience."

She flashed a look at Martin as she said it. He turned white under his sunburn.

"Miss Page," he said, "you do *not* understand. I must insist that you hear our reasons for this proceeding."

"It is not necessary," she says, cold as ice. "I have heard enough."

The minister plucked up spunk to speak. But she snapped him up short as pie crust. Then *I* tried it—and got my medicine.

"Mr. Sparrow," says she, "let them do their worst. The children shall come to my school. As for you, I mean to—" Then she turns to me.

"Does Mr. Van Brunt know of this?" she

asks. Course I couldn't say nothing but I believed he didn't.

"Thank goodness!" she says. And just then who should walk in but Van himself.

"Hello!" says he, surprised. "Eureka told me you were at the village, Martin, so Lycurgus rowed me across. One of the children said you were here. What is this, a surprise party? And Agnes, too! Am I too late for the refreshments?"

He smiled, but nobody else did.

"Edward," says the Page girl, "will you do a great favor for me?"

"Yours to command, of course," he answers, puzzled.

"Will you find a boarding place for Mr. Sparrow?"

"Who? Eureka's father? Why, certainly. What's the trouble? Is it time for the Sparrows to nest again? He can come over to the Island with us. There's plenty of room. Hey, Martin?"

"Never mind your friend, please," says Miss Page. "If he comes will you protect him and treat him kindly? Thank you. Then that is settled. Gentlemen, I believe there is no necessity for your further inconveniencing yourselves. Your several *bills* will be paid."

I looked at the doctor and he looked at Poundberry. The minister and Brown and Scudder looked at each other. Maybe it seems queer that we didn't speak up and *make* her hear our side—the right side. It does seem strange now, I'm free to say, but, as for me, I couldn't have faced her then no more than the boy with the jam 'round his mouth could face his ma.

Hartley was the only plucky one. He says, swallowing once, as if he was gulping down his pride, "Miss Page," says he, "you are treating me most unfair. To judge without a hearing is not——"

She held up her hand. There was a kid glove on it, and even then I noticed how well that glove fitted.

"Mr. Pratt," she says to me, "I want to ask you one question. Who is responsible for this? Whose idea was it?"

I hemmed and hawed. The other fellers might not have meant to do it, but somehow their eyes all swung round to Hartley.

"I see," she says. "I thought as much. There is a proverb, I believe, concerning what is bred in the bone. Thank heaven, to me there are some things in this world which outweigh my personal convenience and—money. You needn't answer, Mr. Pratt. He pays your salary, I believe."

My, but she said it bitter and scornful. Hartley was white afore, but now he was like chalk. He bowed to her, stuck his chin into the air and marched out of that house as proud and chilly as a walking icicle. The rest of us, all but Van and Agnes, trailed along astern, like a parcel of kicked dogs.

Washy sung out to us as we went. "Good day, gentlemen," he says; "I hope you'll come and see me sometimes while I'm over to Horsefoot. I forgive you free and clear. I haven't no doubt you meant for the best."

The doctor and the rest was brave enough when we was out of Agnes Page's sight and hearing. They was talking big about what they'd do to Sparrow when they had a chance. But I noticed none of 'em said much to Hartley. He marched ahead, stiff and white and glum. Peter Brown's last word to me was this:

"Pratt," says he, "if you see a hole in the sand anywheres 'tween here and the beach, mark my name around it, will you? The way I feel now I'd like to crawl into it and pull it after me. One about the size of a ten-cent piece would do, and even then I guess there'd be room and to spare for the rest of this gang."

When I got down to the skiff Van comes running to catch up. He caught me by the arm and hauled me to one side.

"Skipper," says he, "what the devil's the matter?"

I told him in as few words as I could. He roared. "That's all right," he says. "I'll fix that."

He went over to his chum and slapped him on the back.

"Brace up, old man," he says, "it's a mistake, and a mighty good joke on you, isn't it? Of course I'll square you with Agnes."

Hartley turned on him so quick that he jumped.

"If you please," says Martin, cutting and clear as a razor, "you will perhaps be good enough to mind your own business. If you mention one word concerning me to that lady you and I part company. Is that thoroughly plain?"

'Twas the first time I'd ever heard them two have a hard word. The trip to Ozone Island was as joyful as a funeral.

CHAPTER XV

THE WHITE PLAGUE

THE fat was all in the fire. Hartley's great scheme that he thought was going to help Eureka, and that I cal'lated would be one more big boost for him in the Page girl's eyes, had gone to pot to see the kettle bile. Instead of getting rid of Papa Sparrow, it had fetched that old hypocrite right over to eat and sleep and groan under our very noses. And, instead of helping Martin's love business, it had knocked the keel right out of it and left him stranded with a bigger reputation than ever for cold-blooded, mercenary money grabbing. Sweet mess, wa'n't it?

I snum, I did hate to tell Eureka! And yet of course she was bound to find it out for herself. When she went home that night, thinks I, "I'll catch it to-morrow morning." And, sure enough, next morning she was laying for me.

She come out to the garden, where I was trying to fool myself into hoping that six inches of green string, with a leaf or two hung along it, might bear a cucumber some day, and down she sets in the heap of dry seaweed by the pig-pen.

"Now, then," says she, sharp, "I want to know all about it."

"Oh!" says I, looking innocent at the cucumber string; "I ain't give up hope, by no manner of means. If the loam don't blow off, and I'm able to lug water enough, we'll have as much as one jar of two-inch pickles off this plantation by the time the Heavenlies are ready to quit."

"Humph!" she sniffs. "You ought to pickle that understanding of yours. It's too fresh and green to keep long, out in this sun. Now you look me in the eye and tell me all about it."

"About what?" I asks, not looking at her, however.

"About the doings at our house yesterday. Why is Pa coming over here to live? And what makes Mr. Hartley so blue and cross? And how come that Agnes Page to be mixed up in our affairs? Out with it. It's my family business, and I want to know."

So I had to tell her. She was pretty mad, and mighty sarcastic.

"I thought so," she snaps. "Didn't you know no better than that? Didn't you know that a girl who's as far gone with charity as Miss Page is would be sure to go and see Pa and want to do for him? I've found out that she's been giving him money for medicine and things for over a week. Why, a sentimental city woman is Pa's best holt; he can tie 'em in bow knots round his finger. I s'pose you thought you could fetch Hartley and his girl together all by yourself. Well, you've done a good job. Now I've got to begin it all over again."

"It ain't no use now," I says. "She's down on him for good."

"Rubbish! Don't talk so foolish. It'll be my turn next, and *my* plans won't go backside frontwards, like a crab. And I've got to fix Pa, too. I've been working out a notion about him for two or three days. I guess it's time to be starting it a-going."

She wouldn't tell me what the notion was. 'Twas her turn to have secrets. She seemed pleased to have Editha and the children go over to the Fresh Air School, because there they could be studying their lessons with somebody to look after 'em. She liked the idea of Lycurgus' hiring out to Nate Scudder, too, though she did say that she guessed he wouldn't wear out his pants' pockets carting his wages around.

Next day she stayed at home and shut up the house, and that night she and Washy come to the Island to stay all the time. They had rooms in the back part of the house, three flights up, and Scudder sold the Twins bedding and truck enough to more than make up for losing the rent of the Sparrow house. Van put the wax wreath and Marcellus's picture and the rest of Nate's "presents" up in the invalid's room. He said he thought they was kind of appropriate. Washy didn't mind. He said they was lovely and made him think of his "future state." 'Cording to my notion the cook-stove would have been better for that.

Martin and his chum was pretty cool to each other for a while, but they soon got over it. Hartley was different, though, from what he'd been afore. He was more reckless and his "don't care" manner was back again; only, now that his health was so good, it showed in other ways.

The two of 'em took to raising the very Old Boy. They must be up to something all the time. The Island wa'n't big enough to hold 'em and they was crowded over into the village, so to speak. They got mixed up with some of the men boarders at the hotel and 'twas "Whoop!" and "Hooray!" all the time.

They and the boarders got horses out of the livery stable and had races right through the main street; going it licketty-cut and scandalizing the neighbors and scaring old women into conniption fits. Deacon Patterson had a new horse and the Deacon happened to be setting in his buggy in front of the Boston Dry Goods and Variety Store when the racers went by. The racket scared the critter and he bolted, and there was the Deacon going down the road in the middle of the race, hollering "Whoa!" to beat the cars, with his hat off and his hair a-flying. Lots of the sewing circle women saw him and 'twas town talk for weeks. The Deacon was going to have the Twins took up and sent to jail, but he didn't. He prayed for 'em in meeting instead.

Van Brunt got another letter from Agnes pretty quick after the race. She'd heard about it and she give him fits. Why was it necessary for *him*—she didn't mention Martin—to shock the community and public opinion? She wanted to know that and other things similar. He read a little of the letter to Hartley and that's how I heard it. I'd have heard more, probably, only Hartley got up and walked off. And he was blue as a whetstone for the rest of the day.

I guess the Talford girl wa'n't quite so shocked. Anyhow me and Van met her up in the village one afternoon and she wanted to know all about the race.

"I *should* like to have seen that old Mr. Patterson," says she. "He is always so very solemn and pompous. It must have been killingly funny."

Van told her the yarn, trimming it up fine as usual, and they laughed and had lots of fun over it. He went around with her shopping all the afternoon and I was forgot altogether. I didn't mind. I don't hanker for famousness, and the way the small boys followed Van Brunt around and pointed at him and snickered was too popular altogether. I cal'late he'd been preached up to them young ones as a horrible example till they envied him 'most as much as if he was a pirate.

Ozone Island was chock full of secrets and whisperings by this time. Van kept up his little side talks and backyard confabs with Scudder; and Hartley seemed to have caught the disease. I see him and Nate looking mysterious at each other and meeting together in out of the way places time and time again. And the mail was getting heavier and there was half burned telegram envelopes in the stove ashes more'n once. But nobody ever mentioned getting a telegram.

There was so much reading matter 'round the place now that Eureka was in her glory. She read when she got breakfast, with a book propped up on the kitchen table. She read when she dusted, holding the dust cloth in one hand and a magazine in t'other. She read when she ate. She went upstairs at night reading; and I wouldn't wonder if she read in her sleep.

Washy had been pretty decent, for him, for the first week after he landed in his new quarters. But his decency didn't last long. He begun to fuss and find fault and groan and growl. Miss Page sent him nice things to eat—and he always ate 'em every speck himself—and medicine, which he took about a spoonful of and then said 'twa'n't helping him none and give it up. He yelled for Eureka every few minutes and she'd have to drop her work and run and wait on him. He was a pesky outrage and everybody hated him, including Van, who said that he was a common nuisance and if 'twa'n't for his promise to Agnes he'd abate him with a shot-gun.

One day Eureka comes out on the porch where the Heavenlies was setting, and says she:

"Mr. Van Brunt, would you and Mr. Hartley be willing for me to cure Pa?"

"Cure him?" asks Van, surprised. "Cure him? Yes, indeed. Or kill him either," he adds, under his breath.

Hartley didn't say nothing. He never spoke to old man Sparrow now nor *of* him, far's that went.

"All right," Eureka says. "Thank you."

"What's the cook got up her sleeve concerning the afflicted parent?" asks Van of me.

"I don't know," says I. And I didn't.

That afternoon Eureka got me to help her lug the haircloth lounge from the front parlor out to the spare shed, the one we didn't use. 'Twas a little ten by six building that Marcellus had for a tool house, and the shingles was falling off and the roof and sides full of cracks and knotholes. We set the lounge down in there.

"What on earth?" says I.

"I'm going to tell you," says she. "Mr. Hartley said I could have the lounge."

Then she told me what her plan was. 'Twas a

mighty good one, and I promised to help along. I laughed over it till supper time.

That evening we was all in the dining-room. The weather had changed lately and the nights was chilly and windy. 'Twa'n't pleasant enough for the Twins to be on the porch, and Washy had come down from his room and was all hunched up in front of the stove in the kitchen. Eureka was just finishing the dishes. All of a sudden I heard her say:

" Pa, I don't s'pose you feel well enough to go to work? "

I could hear her dad's feet come down off the stove hearth with a thump. He started to speak, and then, remembering himself, he coughed, as hollow as an empty biler.

" I asked," Eureka goes on, " because I saw Mr. Brown yesterday and he said you could have that job at the hotel any time you wanted it."

" Hotel job! " hollers Washy. " How long do you cal'late I'd last lugging bricks and digging? Ain't you satisfied to see me slipping into the grave day by day, without wanting to shove me under all at once? "

" No, I knew you wa'n't fit to work. But Pa, I've been hoping to find a way to cure you some day, and now I've learned the way. And I'm going to try it."

Washy coughed again. I was listening with all my ears, and I see the Twins doing the same.

"Cure? Humph!" sniffs the old man. "I'm past curing, darter. Don't you worry about me. Let me die, that's all; let me die. Only I hope 'twon't be too slow. Cure! The doctors give *me* up long spell ago."

"Doctors give you up! What doctors? Nobody but Penrose, and you've said more'n a thousand times that *he* wa'n't no doctor. I've been reading up lately and I know how *real* doctors cure folks."

"It ain't no use—" begins her dad. She cut him short.

"Your case is kind of mixed-up, Pa," says she, "I'm free to say, owing to your consumption being complicated with nervous dyspepsy. But I've made up my mind to start in on your lungs and kind of work 'round to your stomach. You listen to this."

She come in the dining-room and took a magazine out of the chest of drawers. Then she opened to a place where the leaf was turned down, and went back to the kitchen.

"Consumption, Pa," she says, "ain't cured by medicine no more. Not by the real doctors, it ain't. You say yourself that all Miss Page's medicine ain't done you no good. Fresh air night and day is what's needed, and you don't get it here by the stove or shut up in your room. You ought to live out door. Yes, and sleep there, too."

"*Sleep out door?* What kind of talk is that? Be you crazy or——"

"Don't screech so, Pa," says Eureka, cold as an ice chest. "Folks over on the main will think this place is on fire. Listen to this. Here's a piece about consumption in this magazine. They call it the 'White Plague.' I'll read you some of it."

The Heavenlies was in a broad grin by this time. Washy kept yelling that he didn't want to hear no such foolishness, but his daughter spelt out different parts of the magazine piece. It told about how dangerous shut-up rooms and "confined atmospheres" was, and about what it called "open air sanitariums" and outdoor bedrooms.

"See, Pa," says she; "look at this picture. Here's a tent where two consumptive folks lived and slept for over a year. 'Twas thirty below zero there sometimes, but it cured 'em. And see this one. 'Twas forty-five below where that shanty was, but——"

The invalid jumped out of his chair and come bolting into the dining-room.

"Take it away!" he yells, frantic. "If you expect me to believe such lies as them you're——"

"They ain't lies," says Eureka, following him up, and speaking calm and easy. "They're true; ain't they, Mr. Van Brunt?"

Van smothered his grins and nodded.

"True as gospel," he says.

"Yes, course they be. And Pa, I'm going to cure you or die a-trying. The old tool-house out back of the barn is just the place for you. It's full of holes and cracks, so there'll be plenty of fresh air. And I took the sofy out there this very day. You can sleep there nights and set in the sun day times. You mustn't come in the house at all. I mean to keep you outdoor all winter, and then——"

The Heavenlies just howled and so did I. Washy Sparrow howled, too, but not from laughing.

"All *winter!*" he screams. "The gal's gone loony! She wants to kill me and get me out of the way. I sha'n't stir one step. You hear me? Not one step!"

"This piece says that many patients act that way first along. 'In such cases it is often necessary to use force.' Mr. Pratt, will you take Pa out to the tool shed? I'll carry the lamp."

Would I? I was aching for the chance to get my hands on the little rat. I stood up and squared my shoulders.

"Mr. Van Brunt," yells Washy, dodging into the corner, "be you going to set by and see me murdered? Didn't you swear your Bible oath to treat me kind?"

"There couldn't be nothing kinder than curing you, Pa," says Eureka. "It's all right, ain't it, Mr. Van Brunt."

Van didn't answer for a second. Then he says, like he'd decided, "Yes, it's dead right. Go ahead and cure him, for heaven's sake, if you can! I'll back you up and take my chances."

"My nerves—" begins Washy.

"Nerves," says Eureka, "come from the stomach. I'll 'tend to them later. We'll cure your lungs first. Mr. Pratt, fetch him along."

I got my fingers on the back of that consumptive's neck. He fought and hung back. Then I grabbed him by the waist-band with t'other hand. He moved then, " walking Spanish," like the boy in the school-yard.

Eureka opened the door. " Nobody can say," says she, emphatic, " that I let my Pa die of consumption without trying to cure him. Come along, Mr. Pratt."

" Remember, Mr. Sparrow," says Van, busting with laugh, " it's all for your good."

We went out and across the yard and round back of the barn. The Twins come to the door to see us off. I could hear 'em laughing even after we was out of sight. Eureka shaded the lamp with her apron. When we got to the shed there was a bran-new padlock on the door of it.

" I put it on this afternoon," says she. " I'm pretty handy at fixing things up."

We went into the shed and she put the lamp on the floor in the corner.

" I guess maybe Mr. Pratt 'll stay till you get undressed, Pa," she says. " You tell him the rest, Mr. Pratt. Good night."

She went out and shut the door. The patient set down on the lounge and looked at the cracks in the walls. The wind off the bay was singing through 'em and there was a steady hailstorm of sand coming with it. If fresh air was physic, Sparrow was certain to be a well man.

"Get undressed," says I. "Hurry up."

"I'll freeze to death," says he, shivering.

"No you won't. Not in August. Maybe, later on, in December, 'twill be different. But, anyhow, freezing's a quick death, so they say, and I've heard you hankering to die quick ever since I knew you. Get into bed."

He took off his coat and vest and camped out on the lounge. There was plenty of bed clothes. I took up the lamp. Then I looked up at him.

"There's one or two things more," says I. "To-morrow morning you'll be for coming into the house. Well, you can't come. You'll stay outside, same as Eureka says you will. And the skiff and sloop are locked and chained, so you can't run away in *them*. And Scudder won't take you, nor any letters from you, 'cause he's in the game, too. And when Miss Page comes, if she does come, don't you dare tell her one word. If you do—well, you won't die of *consumption*, anyhow."

I pounded my knee with my fist when I said it. It's a pretty average fist, far's size is concerned, and I see him looking at it.

I said "Good night" and went out and locked

the door and took away the key. The fresh air cure had begun.

Next day was raw and chilly and the invalid put in the hours chasing what few patches of sunshine happened to come along. Eureka brought his meals out to him. He begged and pleaded to be let into the house, but 'twas no go. He spent that night in the tool-house, same as he had the first.

For a week he stayed outdoor. Then he said he felt so much better that he guessed he could risk a day inside. Eureka was ready for him.

"I'm glad your lungs feel better, Pa," she says. "I thought they would. But, of course, you mustn't come in for months and months yet. I guess it's time to start in on the dyspepsy line."

She took a piece of paper out of her dress waist and unfolded it. "I sent a dollar to a doctor that advertised in the *People's Magazine*," she says, "and I got this. It's for dyspepsy, Pa, and particular nervous dyspepsy. 'A careful diet and plenty of exercise,'" she read. "We'll begin on the dieting. 'In severe cases patient should take nothing but hot milk.' We've got plenty of milk—such as 'tis. That's a comfort."

Her dad had been setting on the wash-bench back of the kitchen. Now he jumped up off it like 'twas red hot. " Do you have the face to tell me," he screams, " that I can't have nothing to eat but *milk?* Why, that's——"

" Doctor's orders, Pa," says Eureka. " I'm going by doctor's orders, and see what they've done for your lungs already."

" I can't live on *milk!* I ain't a baby. I hate the stuff! I don't believe no doctor 'd ever——"

" Well, we'll call Dr. Penrose and see what he says. I'll bet he'll back me up."

Washy didn't take the bet. He knew what Dr. Penrose thought of him and his ailments.

" Aw, Reky, please—" he begs.

" For your own good, Pa," says his daughter. " I'll fetch you the hot milk."

She did—a quart of it. He drank it 'cause there wa'n't nothing else. For another week he lived on hot skim-milk and cold fresh air. He pleaded with the Heavenlies and me, but we hadn't any pity for him. He tackled Scudder, but Nate never pitied anybody unless there was money in it. He tried smuggling letters to Agnes, getting Lycurgus to carry 'em; but Lys was in with his sister and the letters never got any further than Eureka's pocket.

'Twas fun for the rest of us, but a kind of nuisance in some ways. You see the sight of us eating three square meals a day was horrible tantalizing to a dyspeptic with an appetite like Washy's. He'd peek in through the dining-room windows while we was at the table, and groan steady and loud till dessert time. Van said it reminded him of what he called a "tarble dote" at a Hungarian restaurant in New York. He said there was music at both places, but that, on the whole, Washy's music was the best of the two.

The Sunday of the week following was a mean day. A cold rain and considerable wind; more like October than August. The invalid set in the tool-shed with the door opened and an umbrella keeping off the rain that leaked through the cracks in the roof. He looked as happy and snug as a locked-out cat in a thunder storm.

"Aw, Eureka," says he, when me and his daughter went out to the shed with the noon bucket of steaming milk. "Aw, Eureka," he says, "won't you let me have something hearty? Only a hunk of bread, say? I've drownded my insides with that thin milk till I feel like a churn. I *can't* keep on drinking the stuff. The mere sight of a cow would make me seasick."

But Eureka wouldn't give in. "It's all for

your good, Pa," she said. That was what Van told him every chance he got. I cal'late them words had come to be almost as sickening to him as the milk.

Next morning I got up early and come downstairs. 'Twas blowing hard and still raining. Eureka hadn't turned out yet. I opened the door of the kitchen and there I see a sight.

In the rocking chair by the kitchen stove was Washy Sparrow, sprawled out fast asleep. His feet was on the hearth of the stove, a piece of piecrust was on the floor by his hand, his head was tipped back and his mouth wide open. And his face—oh, say! It was perfect peace and comfort.

The critter, so it turned out afterwards, had hunted around in the night till he found a cellar window unlocked. Then he'd crawled in and tiptoed up to the kitchen.

I went upstairs again and routed out the Heavenlies. I wanted 'em to see the show. We stood in the door and looked at it. Just then Eureka come along.

"My soul and body!" she sings out.

Her dad heard her and woke up. First he just opened his eyes and stretched. Then he set up straight and turned round. He turned pale.

"*Well,* Pa!" says Eureka, sharp, "what sort of doings is this? What do you mean?"

Sparrow stared at her; then at us. He started to speak. Then he happened to notice my fist; and he never said a word.

"The idea!" says Eureka. "After all I've done to cure you. Roasting in this hot kitchen and eating—is that apple pie crust by your hand?"

She stepped across and opened the pantry door.

"My sakes alive!" she says. "I swan to man if he ain't ate everything in the buttery!"

"I—I—" stammers Washy, wild like. "I—I—I didn't mean to, but I was starved and—and half drownded, and——"

"Pie!" says Eureka. "Well, I never! Now we're in a nice mess; and all to do over again."

"I'm all right now, anyway," says Washy. "I ain't coughing none and the grub don't distress me a mite. Not half so much as that cussed blue milk."

"All to do over," says Eureka. "And I don't know as we'll ever cure you now. Get out door this minute. And you mustn't eat a thing, not even milk, for three or four days. Open that outside door, please, Mr. Pratt."

I opened the door. The rain come beating in,

with the wind back of it. It hit Washy like a cold wave.

"I'm all *right*, I tell you!" he yelled. "I feel fine. Better'n ever I was, don't knows I ain't."

"Are you sure, Pa?"

"Sure? Course I'm sure. Don't I know? I'm all cured."

"Well, that's a mercy," Eureka says. "I knew 'twas the right receipts, but I didn't think they'd work so quick. Mr. Van Brunt, Pa's cured. He'll take that job at the hotel this very day; just as soon as it clears up a little."

The Heavenlies shouted and so did I. The cured man looked tolerable uneasy. He choked up and begun to sputter.

"Course you mustn't go if you ain't real well and cured for good, Pa," says his daughter. "Maybe you'd better try the tool-house and the milk a spell longer."

The door was still open. And the wind and rain was driving in. Washy swallowed, and answered slow:

"I'll—I'll go," he says. "But I'll have to work sort of easy first along, so's——"

"Oh, no! you must work real hard, so's to get the exercise, or you'll have a relapse. Mr. Pratt, you'll tell Mr. Brown to see that Pa works the way he'd ought to, won't you?"

I nodded. "He'll work," says I, decided.

At ten o'clock 'twas clear and I rowed the ex-consumptive dyspeptic over to the main and led him up to the hotel. I give him some advice as I went along.

That afternoon the Twins did nothing but tell Eureka that she was a wonder.

"Yes," says she, "I cal'late he's cured, at least for a spell. Anyhow, that 'Everybody works but father' song don't fit our family no more."

CHAPTER XVI

THE NATURAL LIFE

WASHY SPARROW'S going to work was the biggest surprise Wellmouth had had since old man Ginn, owner of the Palace Billiard Pool and Sipio Parlors, got converted and joined the Good Templars. Nobody would believe it, of course, without seeing him do it with their own eyes, and there was so many folks round the hotel that Peter Brown said he was thinking of charging admission. Agnes Page heard the news and come posting over to find out what sort of cruelizing her pet invalid had had to bear. Van Brunt done the explaining; it was right in his line.

"It was the invigorating atmosphere of Ozone Island that did it, Agnes," he said. "When we have finished ruralizing here I'm considering turning the place into a sanitarium. One week of Pratt's chowder and Eureka's corn muffins, coupled with the bay breezes and the odor of clam flats and seaweed, would make an Egyptian mummy turn flip-flaps. I have to lay violent hands on myself every day, or I, too, would be seized with the laboring fever."

She looked at him, kind of odd. "That is most alarming news," says she, "if true. I confess I hadn't noticed the symptoms. Your temperature appears to be normal at present."

"It is," he says. "I flatter myself that I am making a magnificent fight against the disease. My most rabid attacks are in the early morning, before I get out of bed. Then I feel the insane desire for work, hard work, creeping over me. But I am firm. I reason thus: 'The governor is sixty odd and his heart is weak. Think of the shock that the news would be to him? Think'— and so forth. So I resolve to keep up the fight. By the time I am dressed and have had breakfast all yearning for work has left me. Don't you think I deserve credit?"

She said he did. Only he must be careful and not get up and work in his sleep. I listened with my mouth open as usual. Such crazy drivel from grown up men and women was too many for me. It wa'n't intended to be funny, of course, because they never smiled. It beat me altogether, and

Eureka said the same. 'Twas her notion that all the lunatics that was crowded out of the asylums, or was too rich to be put into 'em was sent to New York. It sounded reasonable enough to believe, sometimes.

Agnes saw Sparrow, of course, but Brown was by when she see him and Washy didn't dare say but he'd gone to work of his own accord. I cal'late that he figgered that the gang of us would have killed him if he had. So the Page girl went back to Eastwich satisfied. And Eureka went home again nights and kept house for Lycurgus and her dad. But Hartley looked out that the most of the old man's ten dollars a week was turned over to her.

The Heavenlies quiet Naturalness had pretty nigh disappeared altogether now. They was restless all the time. Mail was heavy and the telegram envelopes in the coal hod and around was thicker than ever. And Scudder come to Ozone three times a day.

By September I thought sure they'd be ready to quit and go home. They acted to me as though they was tired of the whole thing. I thought I'd sound 'em, so I says:

"I s'pose likely you'll be for shutting up this

shop and getting back to the city 'most any day pretty soon now, won't you?"

Van Brunt looked at his chum and Hartley looked at him. Then they caught themselves doing it, and looked away quick.

"Why, skipper!" says Van, "what makes you say that?"

"Oh, nothing 'special," says I. "Only it seemed to me that you was kind of nervous and fidgety lately. Didn't know but you was anxious to be 'dealing' them stocks of yours, or something. You've been away from 'em a good while."

It was Hartley that answered. "Van is done with the stock market," he says, quick. "He has sworn never to touch it again."

"That's so," says I. "I remember hearing him swear that every ten minutes when we first come. But he's kind of knocked off swearing lately, so I forgot. But I did think you fellers weren't quite so keen on the Natural Life business as you was. You ain't read the gospel for a considerable spell."

They both looked sheepish and guilty.

"That's so," says Van. "We haven't. But we've been so confoundedly busy, gunning, and White Plagueing, and so on, that we haven't had time. And we've mislaid the book. If I knew where it was I should be——"

"Here 'tis, right on the mantelpiece," says I, reaching for it and knocking off the dust. "Why don't you take a set at it now? It's too foggy to do much outside."

So they done it, Hartley reading, and Van listening. But 'twas a short session. When I come in, about fifteen minutes later, the book was bottom up on the floor and the Twins was dealing what they called "cold hands" with cards, for a quarter a hand.

That week was when we reaped our harvest from the garden. Two middling lean cucumbers and a tomatter that was suffering from yellow jaundice. They was pretty sick vegetables, but the Heavenlies seemed to think they was something wonderful. They made more fuss over 'em than if they was solid gold. And they digested as if they was, too.

News come that Dewey, the Sparrow baby, was sick with a cold over to the Fresh Air School and Eureka was worried. Finally she decided to go over there for a day or so and see to him. Lycurgus would look out for Pa. So she went and me and the Twins was left alone.

The day she went was beautiful and clear. Hot as July, and not a breath of wind. It acted to me like a weather breeder, and I said so; but all I got for the prophesying was Van's calling me a Jeremiah again. He had planned a gunning cruise for the next day.

That night I woke up about twelve o'clock and Marcellus's old slab castle was shaking like as if it had the palsy. The wind was roaring and screeching and the rain was just swashing against the windows. I turned out and put in a lively half hour shutting blinds and making things fast. Usually September is a pleasant month down our way, but sometimes we get a regular gale, and, when we do, we get all the back numbers without subscribing for 'em. I was soaking wet when I got to bed again.

Next morning 'twas worst than ever. The bay looked like a tortoise shell cat in a fit, just a whirligig of black and white and yellow water. Scudder managed to get across, but his milk cans had upset in the dory and he said he wouldn't risk another trip till she faired off some.

Along about noon the tool-shed—the late lamented Washy's boarding house—blew down with a bang. Then the *Dora Bassett* broke loose from her moorings and drove into the cove head first. She was bound to bang herself to flinders unless somebody got to her quick, so out I went into the storm. I did think maybe the Heavenlies would offer to turn to and help, but they was pitching half dollars at a crack in the floor and was too busy to think of anything else.

I had a sweet time ploughing through the sand against that wind and rain, and when I got to the cove my job was cut out for me. The sloop was hard and fast aground on the flat and the tide was coming in. She couldn't stay where she was, so I worked for two hours up to my waist in ice water, and more a-pouring on to me from the clouds, getting her off and made fast. The Twins *did* help me long towards the last part of it. That is to say, they set in an upstairs back window and pounded on the glass and made signs—superintending, as usual. I wish they could have heard some of the language I hove back at 'em. Then they'd have realized how grateful I was.

I got supper without changing my wet clothes, and when I woke up next morning I decided without no argument that something else had happened. I was took with the galloping rheumatiz—my old trouble—and couldn't move, scarcely, without howling same as a dog with his tail shut in a door. The fire was out — the old chimbley had unloaded half of its top rigging in to the wind—the storm was bad as ever, and there I was laid up on the corn-husks. The Heavenlies was worried. Breakfast was somewheres 'round the next corner.

"Too bad, old man," says Hartley. "What can we do?"

"Do?" I answers, between yells. "I don't care what you do. Only don't bother me. Ow! O-o-o-o! my shoulder!"

"But what'll we do for eatables?" asks Van Brunt.

I liked them fellers first rate and they knew it. But now they made me mad.

"Do?" says I. "*Do?* Why, scratch for your living, same's I've had to all my days! Work, consarn you! *work!*"

I said considerable many other things. 'Twas a sort of jerky talk—I had to stop every minute to attend to my shoulder—but there was meat in it. They heard some plain truth that nothing but rheumatiz could have fetched out of me. I didn't skip nothing—leastways I tried not to. I hope it done 'em good; it seemed to help *me* a heap.

They went to work, but they was way down in

the primer class so far as that branch of learning was concerned. I could hear things falling around in the kitchen and a million matches, more or less, a-scratching, and I judged that Hartley was trying to build a fire. And under my window there was the dickens of a thumping and a most astonishing number of cuss words, so I gathered that Van was chopping wood.

I managed to hobble downstairs about half past ten, but I was in plenty of time for breakfast. I was feeling too mean to have any appetite—which was a mercy, and I'm thankful for it. We had smoked mush, Wall Street style, and fried eggs with cinders, and one cup of coffee for three. But that cup was strong enough—owing to Hartley's letting it bile for two hours—so nobody wanted any more.

The Twins was pretty well wore out by this time, so neither of them would wash dishes. They chucked 'em into the kitchen sink and left them there. Then they put in three or four hours looking out of the window and swearing at the weather. I stayed in the armchair by the fireplace and did little or nothing but groan and rub alcohol on my lame shoulder. 'Twa'n't a joyful kind of experience, but 'twas the first real daytime rest I'd had since I got Naturalized. And, I own up, I got a good deal of comfort watching the Heavenlies try to do for themselves.

Mind you, if the thing had happened when they first lit on Horsefoot Bar, when they was full of simplicity and the love of it, I cal'late they'd have stood it better. But now they was about sick of the Island anyway, only one was afraid to say so and t'other dassent. So the more the work piled up the uglier they got.

Dinner was served at four o'clock; scorched eggs again, and coffee. No dishwashing. 'Twas storming hard as ever and the draft kept both the stove and fireplace roaring, so more wood had to be chopped.

"Martin," says Van Brunt, "go out and cut that wood, will you? The axe is by the woodpile—that is to say, it's there if this blessed cyclone hasn't blown it out to sea."

Hartley was poking at the stove, with his face and clothes all covered with ashes.

"Cut it yourself," says he, brisk. "You're doing nothing."

"I cut it before," snaps his chum. "Think I'm a steam engine?"

He grabbed up the day-afore-yesterday's newspaper and went to reading. Hartley poked at the stove a spell and then went to the closet and got a cigar. Van looked up and saw him.

"Hand me one of those," says he, motioning towards the cigar.

" There isn't any more. This was the last one in the box."

" The devil it is! And you take it? Well, by George!"

" Now, see here. I saw you take four this forenoon, and this is only my second. Don't be a prize pig."

The stove ashes got into his mouth and nose just then, so he had a fit of sneezing. When 'twas over he slammed the poker into the corner and went to the window.

" Where's that idiot Scudder? " he asks.

" You mean Nature's Nobleman? " says I, smooth and calm. " Oh, he won't show up for a day or so. Sea's too high to risk his dory. Dories cost money."

Van sat up straight. " You're bluffing, aren't you, skipper? " he asks, troubled. " It isn't possible that that rascal will stay at home and not come near us."

" Rascal? " says I. " Rascal? Oh! yes, yes.

No, the 'rough diamond' won't trust himself afloat this weather. He's too expensive a jewel for that. We'll have to do without milk."

"Milk be hanged! It's my mail I want. Why, I'm expecting——"

He bit the sentence in two and looked quick at his partner. But Hartley was scowling and staring out of the window. I guess he hadn't heard.

"That fireplace needs filling," says I, after a while. "It'll be mighty damp and chilly here if the fire goes out."

"Why don't you chop that wood, Van?" asks Hartley, kind of fretful.

"Chop it yourself. My hands are blistered enough already."

"No more than mine. That confounded stove has fixed me. Where I'm not burned I'm scraped raw."

Then there was another spell of saying nothing.

"Fire's most gone," I suggests, by and by.

"Let it go," says Van. Hartley didn't speak.

"Now see here," I says, decided. "I've got the rheumatiz and I don't want to get any more cold. You fellers have pretended to think something of me. If you don't want my remains on your hands, and a funeral to pay for, you'll chop that wood."

Martin got down from the window seat, moving stiff and lame.

"You're right, Sol," says he. "We *are* ungrateful beasts. I'll chop that wood."

"Hold on, old man," breaks in his chum. "You sha'n't be the only game sport. I'll match you for the job."

So they matched cents and Van Brunt got stuck. He yanked on his hat and coat and went out, banging the door. Hartley tackled the cookstove again. 'Twas time to be thinking of supper, if we was going to have any.

Van was gone a long time and he come in soaked with sweat and rain and broke up generally. The wood looked like it had been chewed. I cal'late they don't do much chopping in the Street.

He slatted himself into a chair, wet clothes and all. Then he commenced to cuss the Island and everything that grew or moved on it.

"What we ever came to this lonesome fag end of creation for, anyway," says he, "is——"

"*What?*" I hollers. "I don't understand you. You can't mean—what place are you talking about?"

"This place. This sand-scoured, blown out heap of desolation. Ozone Horsefoot Bar Island, or whatever you call it."

"*Well!*" says I. "Are you crazy? Mr. Van Brunt, I've heard you yourself say that this island was all that's lovely."

"Oh, shut up!" he snaps.

"Jolliest old ark you ever saw," I went on, quoting from memory. "'Air to breathe, veranda to set on, ozone by the keg. Man alive, it's Paradise!'"

He ripped out an order for me to go somewheres as far away from Paradise as a feller could think of.

Supper was ready by seven. All we had to eat was a hunk of dry cornbread and two eggs. Oh, yes! and the tea. Hartley biled some tea that was a kind of herb mush. Strong and thick enough for a stick to stand up straight in. And there wa'n't clean dishes to go around, so some of 'em *had* to be washed.

I was having a fairly good time. Wood must be chopped again and they matched cents. Blessed if Van didn't get the short end, as usual. His talk was pretty nigh pitiful. It would have brought tears to a mule's eyes; I know it did to mine. The sight of Martin's upsetting the tea-kettle and getting next door to scalded was the only thing that comforted him.

He got a letter out of his pocket and went to reading it. The envelope dropped on the floor. It had printing on one corner and Hartley happened to glance at it. Then he tiptoed up behind his chum and peeked over his shoulder.

"Ed Van Brunt!" he sings out. "What's that you've got there?"

T'other Twin jumped and looked scared. He stuffed the letter back into his pocket.

"It's nothing," says he, stuttering. "Nothing but an old letter."

"It's a broker's letter," says Hartley. "You villain, you've been *speculating!*"

First off, Van Brunt was for denying everything. But 'twas no use. His chum had read the letter.

"You've been trading in stocks," he says, solemn. "You, that have sworn over and over again never to touch the market! *You!*"

"I'm mighty sorry, Martin," begs Van. "It was a miserable cheap thing to do. I don't know what you must think of me, old man. But, you see, it got so deadly dull here, and when I saw the *Post* that day, it said that Tea Lead was a good purchase. I wrote Smythe and he——"

"Tea Lead?" breaks in Hartley. "Have *you* been buying Tea Lead?"

"Yes, I have. I'm carrying a pretty good load of it, too, worse luck. Scudder has been bringing my letters and telegrams, and now that he doesn't come, why——"

"Wait a minute! Has Scudder been looking out for your wires and orders?"

"Yes, he has. Oh, I've played you mean and low enough, Martin. Might as well make a clean breast of it, though it will probably smash our friendship. I've paid Scudder three dollars a day to attend to things, and say nothing to you. It's——"

Hartley didn't seem to hear nothing but the last sentence. Now he interrupted.

"Three dollars!" he says, low. "*Three* dollars! Why, the confounded grafter's been charging me *five!*"

And there it was! The cat out of the bag and both Heavenly Twins tarred with the same brush. That's what Nate's secrets and the talks behind the barn, and all, had meant. Van Brunt had been bucking the Tea Lead deal ever since he read the *Post* that day, and Martin had begun after his row with Agnes. And both of 'em bribing Nate Scudder to keep his mouth shut.

First they was provoked and mad at themselves and each other. Then they got to laughing.

"Whew!" says Van, wiping his forehead; "you and I came here to rest and break off from business worry. And I've worried more in the last month than I have before since my big deal. It's hard to teach old dogs new tricks, isn't it, Martin?"

"You're dead right, old chap," says Hartley.

They was going to turn in soon after this, but when they went upstairs they found the rain had leaked in through the ell roof and their feather beds was sopping wet. Down they come again, mad clean through and calling Marcellus's heirloom everything but a nice place.

"You'd better set down and rest yourselves a spell," says I. "It'll do you good. I'm sorry I ain't been able to help you more to-day, but there's one thing I *can* do; I can help you do what you call 'improve your minds.' I'll read you some out of that Natural Life book. Hand it to me, will you?"

Van jumped for the book. But he didn't hand

it to me. Not much! He drew back his arm and banged that book into the fireplace so hard that I thought 'twould knock the bricks out at the back.

"Well!" says I, my mouth opening like a clam shell. *"Well! The Natural Life!"*

"The Natural Life be d—d!" says Edward Van Brunt.

And Martin Hartley says "Amen."

CHAPTER XVII

ACROSS THE BAY

MARTIN," says Van Brunt, "I guess it's the only safe way. I'll go out on the next train."

We was at the dinner table when he said it. 'Twas one o'clock of the day after the Natural Life sermon went up in smoke. The weather was still pretty mean, the sky being all clouded over and the sea running high. But it had stopped raining and the gale seemed to be petering out. I was a whole lot better and was able to turn out and work.

I had my hands full that morning, too. All three of us was close to starvation, after twenty-four hours of short rations, and it took some time to get us filled up. Then I had the pig and hens to see to. The poor critters' lives had been more Natural even than ours—*they* hadn't had *nothing* to eat. The pig was in particular trouble. The rain had turned his pen into a sort of lake and he was playing Robinson Crusoe on a seaweed island in the middle of it. The way he grunted for joy when I looked over the fence was human—yes, sir, human.

Scudder hove in sight about ten and the Heavenlies fairly fell on his neck when he stepped out of the dory. But they warn't so happy when he'd spun his yarn. It seemed that the gale had blown down the telegraph poles and tangled up the wires and no messages could get through either way, and wa'n't likely to for two or three days.

'Twas that that upset the Twins. The Tea Lead market might be tied up in a knot, for what they knew, and their "friends" in the Street might be robbing 'em right and left. I picked up from their talk that now was the most ticklish time, something about "passing a dividend," or the like of that. So that's what they argued about at the dinner table; and it was decided that Van should go to New York right off, and pick up what might be left after their chums and the rest of the forty thieves had got through shaking the contribution box.

"I'll leave at once," Van says; "and be in town to-morrow morning. If all goes well I'll be back here next day. Meanwhile, you, Martin, can be arranging matters with Scudder."

He meant arranging for our quitting Ozone Island for good. They was as anxious now to get out of "Paradise" as they had been to move into it. If I mentioned a word of Natural Life they all but threw things at me.

I expected for sure that they'd lick Nate Scudder for charging his dry-season rates for secret keeping. But they never mentioned it to him. When I spoke of it to Van Brunt, he laughed.

"Oh, Scudder's all right," he says. "He had a corner in secrets and squeezed the shorts, that's all. That's legitimate. Scudder has a talent of his own."

"Yes, and he's making it ten talents in a hurry, like the feller in Scripture," says I.

"Well, he doesn't hide it in a napkin, anyway," laughs Van.

"No," says I. "I believe he uses one of Huldy Ann's stockings."

About three o'clock we got into the skiff, the three of us, and rowed to the main. 'Twas a hard wet row. I judged the gale wa'n't all over yet. We walked up as far as Nate's and there he was waiting in his buggy to drive Van Brunt to the Wellmouth depot. Martin and Van said good-by and had a final pow-wow over the Tea Lead.

"Good-by," says I. "Ain't got any real gilt-edged expensive secrets you want kept while you're gone, have you? I'd like to squeeze a short or two, myself."

You ought to have seen Nate Scudder bristle up and glare at me. But his passenger only laughed, as usual.

"No," he says, "not a one. My conscience is clear. But I may unearth a few while I'm away."

Well, he did. But not the kind he expected.

I had to step into Nate's house to get a few eggs. Our own hens was too weighted down under the Natural to be working overtime. Huldy Ann had the remnants of a nicked blue set of dishes that was handed down from her great aunt on her grandmother's side, and she thought maybe Hartley 'd be interested at a dollar a nick. It took so long to make her believe he wa'n't, that we wasted an hour or more there. When we got to the hill by the beach 'twas 'most five o'clock.

"The wind's hauled clear around," says I. "We ain't had all the dirty weather yet. This 'll be a bad night in the bay."

Just then from behind us come the rattling of a wagon and the thumping of a horse's hoofs. Somebody was driving our way like all get out.

"Who in time—?" I says. "Runaway, ain't it?"

But 'twas no runaway. In another minute, a horse all lather, hauling a buggy all mud, comes bouncing over the hummocky road and down the hill. A girl was driving it.

"Whoa!" she screams, shrill. The horse stopped like he was glad of the chance.

"Eureka Sparrow!" I sings out. "What in the name of goodness——?"

'Twas Eureka, and the team was the one that the Fresh Airers had hired for the season. The girl looked as if she'd been through the war. She had a shawl pinned 'round her but it had slipped down 'most to her elbows, and her hat was over on the back of her neck.

"What's the matter?" I asks. "Is Dewey ——"

"Dewey's all right," she says, leaning from the buggy. "It's little Dennis—Redny. He's awful sick—and—where's Mr. Van Brunt?"

"Gone to New York," says Hartley, stepping up to the wheel. "What is it? Tell me about it."

She was almost crying. "The poor little feller," she says; "he was took this morning.

Pains, and such suffering. We sent for Dr. Bailey and he was sick in bed himself. Then James drove over for Dr. Penrose, and he'd gone up to the city to a medical society meeting. There wa'n't nobody left but that new doctor at West Eastwich, Doctor Duncan, and nobody likes him. *I* wouldn't have him to a sick cat. He says it's appendi—appendi—something or other."

"Appendicitis?" asks Hartley.

"Yup. That's what he says. And he wants an operation to-morrow. And Miss Agnes don't trust him, and she's all upset. She thinks more of that boy—! And she sent me for Mr. Van Brunt, and——"

"Sol," asks Martin, quick. "Is this new doctor a good one?"

"No, no!" says I. "If he said I had diphthery I'd be sure 'twas gout. And there ain't another doctor nowheres around."

"There's one," says Eureka, "if we could only get him. Miss Talford read in the paper day before yesterday that Doctor Jordan, the big sturgeon——"

"Surgeon," says I.

"All right, surgeon then. He's at the Wapatomac House for a week. But he probably wouldn't come and the telegraph wires are down and nobody thought to write in time. And that Doctor Duncan thing, he says he'll operate to-morrow morning. If he does he'll kill the boy sure, just as he done to Emeline Macomber's child. What *shall* we do? Poor Miss Agnes! Can't *nobody* help her?"

"How can I get to Wapatomac?" asks Martin, sharp and quick.

"You can't," says I. "Not in time to get the doctor. He must reach Eastwich on that morning train or 'twill be too late. The last train has gone to-night. There ain't another till eight o'clock to-morrow. If you took that 'twouldn't reach Wapatomac till ten, and that's no good."

We was silent for a second. Then Eureka jumped up in the buggy and clapped her hands.

"You *can* get him!" she cries, her black eyes snapping sparks. "Oh, you *can!*"

"How?" Martin and me said together.

She pointed towards Ozone Island.

"The sailboat!" she said. "The *Dora Bassett!* Sail over in her. Then he'll come on the morning train."

I swung around and looked at the waves and the clouds. Wapatomac was clear across the bay, miles and miles away. And a night like this was likely to be!

"Lord!" says I. "It's crazy! We'd never live——"

But Martin Hartley was already half way to the skiff. Of course he didn't know the risk, and I did, but—well, there.

"I'll go," says I to Eureka. "You head for the school fast as your horse can travel. Tell the Page girl not to let Duncan touch the boy till the Jordan man comes or the train comes without him. You understand?"

"You bet you!" says she. "It's splendid! We'll save the boy and Mr. Hartley will be all right with *her*. Oh, I'm *so* glad Mr. Van Brunt wa'n't here!"

She whirled the horse around and off she went. I give one more look at the weather and then ran after Hartley. Save the boy! A considerable bigger chance of not saving ourselves. Well, my school teacher always used to say I'd be drowned some day—if I wa'n't hung first.

I had one reef in when the *Dora Bassett* swung clear of the outside point of Ozone Island cove. I hated to take another, for I wanted to make time.

But I had to take it afore we tacked at the end of the first leg. 'Twas pretty nigh a dead beat and the sloop was laying over till I thought sure she'd fill. The waves was as big, almost, as ever I see in the bay, and when one would fetch us on the starboard bow the biggest half of it would shoot clean from stem to stern. We was soaked afore we'd hardly started. It couldn't have been much worse unless 'twas the middle of February.

I had the tiller and Hartley was for'ard in the cockpit. I was using the mainsail altogether, although later on I did use some of the jib to help her point up to wind'ard. There was plenty of water and would be for hours, so I could give her the centerboard full. That didn't bother us—not then.

I was too busy to speak and Martin didn't seem to care to. He set there, looking out ahead, and when he turned, so's I could see his face, it was set and quiet. And in his eyes was the look that I'd seen there once afore—the day of the pig race. I wouldn't have known him for the reckless, lazy chap he'd been for the last month or so.

The only thing he said to me at this time was, as I remember it, something like this:

"I know that Doctor Jordan," he says. "I

met him at Cambridge at a football game. I was there at college and father came over for the game. The doctor was one of father's friends."

"That's lucky," says I. "Maybe that 'll give you some pull."

"Perhaps so," says he.

"If he won't come," I asks, "what 'll you do?"

"He'll *have* to come," was all the answer he made.

Even this little mite of talk meant hollering your lungs loose. The wind was rising all the time, the sea kept getting more rugged as we got where the bay was wider, and the splashing and banging was worse than a waterwheel working double watches. After awhile I made Hartley set side of me, so that, when I wanted anything, I could grab his arm.

This was after it got dark. And it got dark early. Likewise it begun to rain. The storm that we'd had for the last few days seemed to be blowing back over us. Seems as if it ought to have rained and blown itself out by this time, but we had proof that it hadn't.

We wa'n't making scarcely anything on our tacks. The *Dora Bassett's* a good wind'ard boat, too, but she'd fall off and fall off. By and by the dark and rain got so thick that I couldn't see the shore lights, and I had to run by compass and guess. There wa'n't likely to be any other blame fools afloat to run into us, still I gave Hartley a horn to blow in case there should be.

'Twas lucky I did. Along about twelve, when we was somewheres in the middle of the bay—off Sandy Bend, I should think—it seemed to me that I heard a toot in answer to one of Hartley's. He heard it, too, I guess, for he commenced to blow hard and fast. 'Twan't much use, for anything that was to wind'ard of us wouldn't have heard a sound. And we only heard that one, I judge, as the noise was blown past us down the gale. We listened and listened, but no more come.

All at once we both yelled. Out of the muddle of rain and black comes poking a big jibboom and a bowsprit. Next minute a two-master, with only a jib and reefed fo'sail set, went booming by just under our stern. I could see a wink of her for'ard lights, and a glimpse of a feller holding a lantern by her rail and staring down at us. His face was big-eyed and scared. I've wondered since how ours looked to him. All the rest was black hull and waves and roaring. A mackerel boat trying to run into Naubeckit Harbor, I guess she was. I cal'late the afternoon lull had fooled 'em into trying.

We didn't say nothing. Only Hartley looked up at me and grinned. I could see him in the lantern light. I shook my head and grinned back.

All the time I kept thinking to myself, " Sol Pratt, you old gray-headed fool, this is your final bust of craziness. You can't make it; you knew afore you started you couldn't. You'll be in among the shoals pretty soon and then you and the *Dora Bassett* 'll go to smithereens and cart that poor innocent city man with you. *He* don't know that, but you do. And all on account of a red-headed little toughy from the back alleys of New York, and a girl that ain't none of your relations. You deserve what's coming to you."

And yet, even while I was thinking it, I was glad I was making the try. Glad for Redny's sake; particular glad on account of what it might mean to Martin and Agnes; and glad, too, just out of general cussedness. You see, 'twas like a fight; and there's a heap of satisfaction once in a while in a real old-fashioned, knock down and drag out, rough and tumble fight—that is, when you're fighting for anything worth the row.

The storm kept on; seemed as if 'twould never let up. And we kept on, too, three reefs in by this time, and the jib down. And with every tack I cal'lated we was making better headway towards the bottom than anywheres else. I couldn't see nothing to get my bearings from, and hadn't no idea where we was, except the general one that, up to now, and by God's mercy, we was afloat.

Then, at last, the gale begun to go down. A landsman wouldn't have noticed the change, but I did. It stopped raining, and the wind was easing up. By and by the haze broke and I caught a glimpse of Middle Ground light, almost abreast of us. I unbuttoned my ileskin jacket and looked at my watch. Half-past two, and only three-quarters of the way to Wapatomac. We'd been eight hours and a half coming a distance that I've made over and over again, in that very sloop, in less than three. Hartley caught my sleeve.

"Will we get there?" he shouts. His face was all shining with the wet and his hair was too heavy with water even to blow in the wind.

"Don't know," I hollers back. "We'll try."

He nodded. The clearing of that haze had

helped me considerable. I could sight my marks, the lights, now, and we made faster time.

At last, after what seemed a fortnight more, come the first streak of gray daylight. The clouds was breaking up and it would be a nice day later on, I judged. But there was a living gale still blowing and the waves was running savage over the shoals ahead. The channel was narrowing up and I had to watch out every second. I sent Hartley amidships to tend centerboard.

We beat in through Long Point Reach. The life-saving station is on the Point, just abaft the lighthouse. I see the feller in the station tower open the window and lean out to watch us. I cal-'late he wondered what asylum had turned that pair of lunatics loose.

Past the Point, and now we come about for the run afore the wind up the narrows. Wapatomac village was in plain sight.

"With any sort of luck," says I, "we'll be alongside the dock by quarter-past five. The down train leaves at twenty-five minutes to eight. You can thank your stars, Mr. Hartley."

'Twas a pretty cock-sure thing to say, and I ought to have known better than to crow afore we was out of the woods. But we'd come through so far enough sight better than a reasonable man could expect.

The narrows is a wicked place. The channel is fairly straight, but scant width, and on each side of it is a stretch of bars and rips that are bad enough in decent weather. Now they was as good an imitation of as salt-water Tophet as I want to see. Strip after strip of breakers, with lines of biling, twisting slicks and whirlpools between. And the tide tearing through.

I sent Hartley for'ard to look out for shoals. He had one knee on the edge of the cabin roof and was climbing up, when I happened to glance astern. There was an old " he " wave coming—a regular deep water grayback.

" Look out! " I yells. " Stand by! "

That wave hit us like a house tumbling down. I'd braced myself and was, in a way, ready for it, but Hartley wa'n't. He was knocked for'ard on his face. Then, as the bow jumped up, he was chucked straight backwards, landing on his shoulder and left arm against the centerboard well. He turned a full somerset and his feet knocked mine from under me. Down I went and the tiller was yanked out of my hands.

Waves like that hunt in droves, generally speaking. The next one was right on schedule time. Up we went, and sideways like a railroad train. Then down, " Bump! " on the bottom.

Up again, and down. " Thump! Crunch! "

That time we struck with all our heft. The *Dora Bassett* shook all over. She riz, still shaking, and the next wave threw her clean over the bar. We was in deep water for a minute, but just a little ways off was another line of breakers. And astern was the rudder, broke clean off, and floating away.

'Twas no time for fooling. Hartley got to his knees, white, and holding his left arm with his right hand. I jumped and cast off the sheet. She floated then on a more even keel. Then I yanked loose the oar from its cleats alongside the rail and got it over the stern to steer with.

This got her under control, and down the lane, between them two lines of breakers, we went, me with the sheet in one hand, the oar braced under t'other arm, and the three-reefed mainsail well out. The cockpit was half full of water.

The lane of deep water narrowed up ahead of us and there was a kind of gate, as you might say, at the end. Hartley looked at me and I at him.

"Can you?" he asks. He was white as paper, but not from being scared I was sure. His left arm hung down straight and he kept rubbing it.

"Lord knows," I says. "Are you hurt?"

He didn't answer; just shook his head. On went the *Dora Bassett*. Bless the old girl's heart! She was doing her best to pull us through.

The gate was just in front of our nose. I set my teeth and headed her for the middle of it. A jiffy more, and the crazy breakers jumped at us from both sides. Their froth flew over us in chunks. Then we was through, and I fetched my first decent breath.

We was in a kind of pond now, where we had elbow room.

Martin looked astern. "Here comes a boat," says he.

'Twas the lifeboat from the station. They'd seen our trouble and was coming full tilt. I hadn't ever been took off my own boat by no life-savers, and I wa'n't going to begin.

"Heave to!" hails the crew cap'n from the boat. "We're coming to take you off."

I didn't answer.

"Heave to!" he yells again. "Heave to!"

I turned my head a little ways.

"Go home and get your breakfast," I sings out. "We're busy."

They kept on for a ways, and then they give it up. I ran two or three more of them lanes and then, when I had the chance, I dropped my mainsail and histed the jib. And with that jib and the oar I picked my way for another spell, in and out and betwixt and between. At last we slid past the Wapatomac breakwater and up to the wharf. A nice piece of work for anybody's boat, if I do say it.

Hartley seemed to think so, too, for says he, "Skipper, that was beautiful. You're a wonder."

"Twenty minutes of six," says I. "We're on time."

There was an early-bird lobsterman on the wharf, come down to see how many of his pots had gone adrift in the night. He stood and stared at us.

"God sakes!" says he. "Where'd you come from?"

"Wellmouth," says I, making fast to a ring bolt.

"In *her?*" he says, pointing to the sloop. "In this gale? Never in the world!"

"All right. Then we didn't." I hadn't no time to waste arguing.

"Good land of love!" he says, kind of to himself. "Say! she must be something of a boat."

I looked at the poor old *Dora Bassett*. Rudder gone centerboard smashed, rail carried away, and hull nigh filled with water.

"She *was*," says I. "Considerable of a boat."

CHAPTER XVIII

POOR REDNY

HARTLEY had climbed on the wharf and now he was heading for the village. I got the sloop fast, after a fashion, and then run over and caught up with him. He was walking with long steps and looking straight ahead. His left fist was in the side pocket of his jacket and his face was set and pale under the tan. I happened to bump into him as I come alongside, and he jumped and gave a little groan.

"What's the matter with that arm of yours?" I asked, anxious. He'd stopped for a second and was biting his lips together.

"Nothing," he says, short. "Bruised a little, I guess. Where's the hotel?"

"Up the main road a piece. That's it, on top of the hill."

"Come on then," says he, walking faster than ever.

We went through Wapatomac village like we

was walking for money. Some of the town folks was just getting up, and you could see smoke coming from kitchen chimneys and window shades being hoisted. Once in a while, where the families was particularly early risers, I smelt fried potatoes cooking for breakfast; them and smoked herring. In the center, by the post-office, the feller that keeps the market was just taking down his store shutters. He looked at us kind of odd.

" Good morning," he says. " Going to fair off at last, ain't it? "

" Guess likely," says I, keeping on.

"You been on the water, ain't you? " he asks. " Get caught down to the Point? "

Long Point's a great place for Wapatomac folks to go on clamming and fishing trips. I suppose he thought we'd been out the day afore, when it cleared that time, and had had to put in at the station over night. We must have looked like we'd been through the mill. Both of us was sopping wet, and I had on rubber boots and a sou'wester. I'd thrown off my ileskin coat at the wharf.

I didn't stop to explain. I had to save my breath to keep up with Martin. The nigher he got to the hotel the faster he walked.

The Wapatomac House is about the toniest summer place on our part of the coast. A great big building, with piazzas and a band stand, and windows and wind-mills and bowling alleys till you can't rest. We turned in between the stone posts at the end of the driveway and went pounding across the lawns and flower beds.

There was a sleepy-looking clerk behind the desk in the big hall. Nobody else was in sight, and the whole outfit of empty chairs and scattered newspapers had that lonesome look of having been up all night. Oh, yes! and there was a colored man mopping the floor.

Hartley went up to the desk, leaving muddy foot marks right where the darkey had been scrubbing.

"Good morning," he says to the clerk. "Doctor Jordan, of Providence, is one of your guests, isn't he?"

The clerk put down the book he was reading and looked us over. He done it deliberate and chilly, same as hotel clerks always do. If there's any one mortal that can make the average man feel like apologizing for living without a license, it's a slick, high collared, fancy shirt-bosomed hotel clerk.

"What?" says the clerk, frosty and slow.

"Doctor Jordan, of Providence. Is he here?"

His Majesty looked at his book again afore he answered. Then he put his thumb between the pages to mark the place, and condescends to drawl out:

"What do you want with him?"

For once he'd made a mistake. There are times when it ain't wise to judge a feller by his general get-up. Martin stiffened, and he spoke clear and sharp.

"Answer my question, if you please," says he. "Is the doctor here?"

"No, he ain't."

"Where is he?"

"Gone."

I felt sick. Maybe Hartley did too, but he didn't show it.

"*Where* has he gone?" he asks.

"I don't know that I've got to——"

"*I* know. And for your own good, my friend, I advise that you tell me. Where is Doctor Jordan?"

The Emperor come down off his throne a little. I cal'late he figgered that 'twas good policy.

"He's gone to Brantboro," he says. "He went yesterday morning and he's to leave there for Boston this forenoon. Then he's going to Bar Harbor for the rest of his vacation. Anything else you'd like to know?"

This last part was loaded to the gunwale with sarcasm.

"Yes," says Hartley emphatic. "Where is the Doctor staying in Brantboro?"

"Cold Spring House. Want to know what he pays for his room?"

Martin didn't answer. He walked to the door. I stopped for a jiffy.

"See here, my smart aleck," says I to the clerk, "you'll have some more fun from this later on, when your boss hears of it. Do you know who 'tis you've been sassing? That young man is John D. Vanderbilt of New York."

There is some satisfaction in a first-class lie. It done me good to see that clerk shrivel up.

Martin was calling to me. "Sol," he asks, like a flash, "how can I get to Brantboro?"

"You can't—in time to catch that morning train. Brantboro's ten mile off, and the train that gets here at twenty-five minutes of eight, leaves there at seven-fifteen. That was the one we was to have the doctor on. And it's past six now."

He spun around on his heel. "Is the telegraph

line to Brantboro working?" he asked the clerk.

"No, sir! no, sir." My! but he was polite. "I'm sorry to say not, sir."

"Can I get a horse here?"

"The livery-stable is right around the corner; but I don't think——"

We was at that livery-stable in less than two shakes. The feller that took care of the horses and slept in the stable loft was up and sweeping out.

"Have you got a horse that will take me to Brantboro in half an hour?" asks the Twin.

The feller stared at him. "Be you crazy?" says he.

Martin didn't answer. "Whose machine is that?" he asks.

He was pointing to a big automobile in the stable. A great big red thing, with a shiny painted hull and nickel-plated running rigging.

"Mr. Shearer's. He's away for a week and we're keeping it for him."

"Can I hire it?"

The feller's mouth fell open like 'twas on hinges. "*Hire* it? Hire Mr. Shearer's automobile?" says he. "Well, I'll be darned!"

"Where's your employer?" asks Hartley, quick.

"Hey?"

"Your *boss!*" I sings out, dancing up and down. "For the land sakes wake up! Where is he?"

"In the house, I guess. Where do you——"

We met the livery-stable owner just coming out of his kitchen with a pan of leavings for the pig. He'd just turned out. I knew him; his name was Ben Baker. Martin went at him hot-foot, speaking in short sentences.

"I want to hire that auto in your stable," he says. "I must get to Brantboro before seven o'clock. I'll pay any price. But I must have it."

Then there was more arguing. Baker said no. Was we crazy? He couldn't let another man's auto to the Almighty himself. And Mr. Shearer's auto, of all things! Why, Shearer would kill him. And so forth and so on.

But Hartley kept cool. He must have the machine. He'd be responsible for damages. He explained about the doctor.

"I'll pay you—so and so," says he. Never mind the price he offered. It was so big that I wouldn't be believed if I told it. Baker didn't believe it either till Martin pulled out a roll of bills and showed him.

"I'll *buy* the thing if necessary," says he. "But I'll have it. Come, skipper."

"The shofer's up at Shearer's house," says Baker. "He——"

"Never mind the shofer. I can run it. Send your man with us, and I'll leave the machine in his care at Brantboro. Then the shofer can come after it. I'll write to Mr. Shearer and explain. Come on."

"It's all right, Ben," I says. "He'll do all he tells you, and more. You'll never make a chunk of money any easier."

Baker followed us to the barn, saying "No," all the time. He kept on saying it while the Twin was getting up steam, or some such trick, in the auto. He said it even after he'd got the money in his hand. The hired man climbed in behind. Hartley and me was in front. We chuff-chuffed out of the stable door.

"For heaven's sake!" hollers Baker, "take care of the thing. I don't know what 'll come to me for this job when Shearer hears of it."

We got down to the street. I looked at my watch. It was twenty-five minutes past six.

"Now, Sol," says Hartley, "you must help me if I need you. I can use only one hand, so you pull whatever lever I tell you to. Hold your hair on *We're* going to *go*."

We went—oh yes, we went! I'd never rode in a buzz cart afore and inside of five minutes I was figgering that I'd never live to ride in one again. Suffering! how we did fly!

Lucky 'twas early. We didn't meet a soul on the road. If we had they'd had lively times getting out of our way. Away ahead somewheres there'd be a house with a dog scooting out of the gate, his mouth open ready to bark. Next minute we'd go past that house like a sky-rocket, and the pup would be digging a breathing hole through the dust behind us. I didn't have to pull a lever, for we had a clear field. Good thing I didn't, because I was too scared to know my hands from my feet. The stable man was actually blue. Next time I see Baker he told me that the feller had nightmare for a fortnight afterwards, and they could hear him yelling "Whoa!" in his sleep as plain as could be. And they in the house with the windows shut.

Afore I had time to think straight, scarcely, or remember to say more than a line or two of "Now

I lay me," we was sizzling through Brantboro. We whirled into the big yard of the Cold Spring House and hauled up by the steps. Hartley piled out and I followed him. We'd used up just eighteen minutes.

"Here!" says he to the clerk, a twin brother of the one at Wapatomac; "take this to Dr Jordan's room."

He scribbled something on a slip of paper and chucked it across the desk. The clerk yelled for a boy and the boy took the paper and lit out. Pretty quick he comes back.

"He wants you to come right up, Mister," says he.

"Good!" says Martin, tossing him half a dollar. "Lead the way."

The youngster started for the stairs, grinning like a punkin lantern. I flopped into a chair and felt myself all over to make sure I hadn't shook no part of me loose on the trip. Likewise I watched the clock.

In ten minutes more the Twin comes downstairs, and Doctor Jordan was with him. The doctor was a big gray-haired man with a pleasant face. He looked as though he'd dressed in a hurry, and he had a traveling satchel in his hand.

"I'll send you a check for my bill later," he says to the clerk. "All ready, Mr. Hartley."

We went out to the automobile. Martin started her up and we whizzed for the depot.

"Great Scott!" says the doctor, "I feel as if I had been pulled out of bed by the hair. Nobody but your father's son could do this to me, Hartley. Have you fellers fed yet?"

The Twin was too busy with the steering wheel to answer. I done it for him.

"No, sir," says I; "not since yesterday noon. Nor slept since night afore last."

Martin run the automobile into one of the horse sheds by the depot. Then he passed the stable man the bill that happened to be on the outside of his roll. 'Twas a tenner, for I caught a glimpse of it.

"Here," he says; "take this and wait here till the shofer comes for the machine. Well, skipper, we're on time, after all."

So we was, and ahead of it. We waited on the depot platform. I noticed that Hartley wa'n't saying much. Now that the excitement was over, he seemed to me to be mighty quiet. Once, when he walked, I thought he staggered. And he was awful white.

"Sol," he says to me, just as the train hove in sight; "you needn't come with us, unless you want to. Maybe you'd like to stay and attend to your boat."

I looked at him. "No," says I. "I'm going to see it through. The boat can wait."

I had to give him a boost up the car steps. As he got to a seat, he staggered again.

"Skipper," he says, quiet and with little stops between words, "I'm—afraid—you'll—have—to—look—out for the doctor. I'm believe I'm going—to—to—make a fool of myself."

And then he flops over on the cushions in a dead faint.

Doctor Jordan was at him in a second.

"It's his arm, I guess," says I. "He bruised it aboard the sloop."

The doctor pulled up Hartley's coat sleeve and felt of the arm.

"Bruised it!" he says. "I should say he did. The arm is broken."

Now you can bet that Martin Hartley wa'n't the only sick man aboard that train just then. There was another one and he'd been christened Solomon. When I heard that doctor say that the Twin's arm was broken I give you my word I went cold all over. Think of the grit of the feller —the clean up and down grit of him! Rampaging around, running automobiles and chasing doctors, and all that with a broken arm. And never even mentioning it. I took off my hat to that New Yorker. Crazy or not he could have my vote for any job from pound-keeper to President.

I wa'n't much good, but Doctor Jordan was a whole team and the dog under the wagon. He sent me for the conductor and between us we got Hartley into the baggage car and away from the crowd of passengers.

Then we rigged up a kind of bed for him on a pile of trunks and the doctor went to work.

He got Martin's coat off and his shirt-sleeve up and had a good look at the arm. Hartley opened his eyes while the examination was going on.

"Broken, doctor, isn't it?" he asks, weak.

"Yes," says Jordan. "Only a simple fracture of the forearm though. We'll get off at the next station and find a comfortable place for you."

But he wouldn't hear of it. Not much he wouldn't. He was going to see that that doctor went straight on to Eastwich. Said he'd had too much trouble getting him on that train to let him off it now, even if 'twas his neck instead of his arm that was cracked. There was considerable pow-wow, but finally Jordan give in.

"All right," he says. "Needs must if the old gentleman drives. The arm is in better shape than you deserve, considering how you've treated it. I'll make a temporary bandage, put you off at your home station, and come back and set the bone as soon as I can leave the boy. Hand me that box over there, conductor, please."

With a slat off a box in the baggage, and pieces of Hartley's shirt, he spliced that arm as pretty as a picture. Then he rigged up a sling made of a couple of handkerchiefs, and there was the patient in pretty fair shape, considering.

When we got to Wellmouth the conductor—a mighty decent feller, he was—held up the train while I made arrangements with the driver of the Old Home House depot wagon to take Martin to the hotel. I was for going with him, but he put his foot down on that plan in a hurry.

"No, sir!" says he. "I want you to see that the goods are delivered. You get Jordan to the school on time and find out if there's anything else you can do to help over there. *Then* you can come back if you want to; but don't you show your head around me till the contract is carried out. If you do—well, my right arm's in pretty good condition yet."

In spite of the pain I knew he was in he managed to pump up a grin. I grinned back, but there was a big lump just astern of my swallowing gear.

The train got to Eastwich on time, and Lord James was waiting with the team at the depot. We drove to the Fresh Air farm like we was going to a fire. Miss Talford was at the door.

"Here's the doctor," I says. "How's the boy?"

"The pain is a little easier now, we think," says she. "Come right upstairs, Doctor Jordan. It was *so* good of you to come. Agnes hasn't slept since he was taken ill."

I followed the doctor and the Talford girl up to the bedroom. A mighty pretty room 'twas, too; all flowered paper, and colored pictures and sunshine. But I didn't notice these things much.

Poor little Redny! There he laid, in the middle of the big bed, his brick top shining against the pillow and the freckles on his nose like red paint spots on a whitewashed wall. He knew me and the first thing he said was, "Hello, Andrew Jackson." That was the name I'd always called him.

Agnes Page was there, sitting by the bed, holding the little feller's hand. She looked mighty hollow-eyed and pale. She shook Doctor Jordan's hand and thanked him for coming. She shook mine too, and I noticed how her hand trembled.

The Duncan doctor was there, ready to begin his carving. Dried-up young squirt, with whiskers as scattering as corn-stalks in the Ozone garden.

"Er—Doctor Jordan," says he, "awfully sorry you've been put to all this trouble. Entirely without my sanction, I assure you. A most simple case of appendicitis. I should have operated immediately whether you arrived or not."

Jordan went across to the bed. He looked the boy over, careful as could be, thumping him, and listening, and asking questions about where he felt the worst, and all that. After a while he looked at Duncan, and says he:

"The pain doesn't seem to be localized as yet."

"No—er—not yet," answers t'other doctor, pompous. "But, of course, that's quite usual—often the regular thing. Er—yes."

Jordan nodded. Then he asked a few more questions; when the youngster was took sick, and how it begun, and the like of that. Finally he says to Redny:

"What have you been eating lately?"

"Aw, I don't know, sir. Miss Agnes give me some jelly and some mush and cream and——"

"Yes, I know. But those are what you've had inside the house. What have you eaten outside? I noticed an orchard back of the farm here. There were some very pretty late apples on the trees. How do they taste?"

Redny looked worried, seemed to me. He fidgeted with the edge of the bed-spread.

"I ain't et only a few of 'em," he says. "The ones on the ground was wormy, so——"

Miss Agnes broke in here. "He couldn't have eaten those apples, Doctor," she says. "I've expressly forbidden the children to touch them."

"Yes, of course," says Jordan. "But I've had the advantage of being a boy once myself. The apples on the ground were wormy, you say. How were those on the trees? And how many did you eat—well, say night before last?"

"Only six," says Redny, beginning to snuffle. "I knocked 'em down with a rock. They was ——"

"I see," Jordan smiled, quiet, and stood up. "Doctor," he says to Duncan, "I wouldn't operate yet awhile. He seems to be much easier now. I think it will be safe to wait."

Duncan bristles up and waved his hand, pompous. He was going to speak, I guess, but all at once the sense of what Jordan meant seemed to work down through his skull. He looked at me. I was beginning to grin. Then he looked at Agnes and Margaret; they looked queer, and Miss Talford's mouth was twitching at the corners. He turned as red as a smallpox flag.

"I—I—why didn't you tell me about those apples, boy?" he asks, sharp.

"You never asked me," snuffles Redny. "All you asked me was what I had for supper, and I told you."

"Green apples, hey?" says I, more to myself than anybody else. "Humph! Well, they never operated for *them* when *I* was a boy."

I went down to the kitchen pretty soon after that. Eureka was there and she and me had a big talk. Duncan come stomping down a little later and went out and slammed the door.

"Humph!" snaps Eureka, bobbing her head the way she always done; "he ain't going to get the chance to try his tricks on *that* boy. Pesky thing! Why don't he run a butcher shop? Then he could cut up and saw and be happy, and nobody 'd be killed except them that was dead already."

By and by Agnes came to the door and called to me.

"Mr. Pratt," she says, when her and me was in the hall together, "how can I thank you for what you've done for me and for that poor little child?"

"You can't," I says, short. "Because I ain't done nothing. It's Mr. Hartley that——"

"I know. Doctor Jordan has told me some. Please tell me the rest. How is he? Is his arm badly hurt? Is he suffering? Do you think there's any danger?"

Here was my chance. And I just spread myself, too, now I tell you. I spun the whole yarn, from the time the *Dora Bassett* pulled out of Horsefoot Bar cove to when Hartley was loaded into the Old Home depot wagon.

"He's a brick, that's what he is," says I, finally. "And he always was one. And there's one thing more I'm going to tell, now that I've got my hand in, Miss Page. That's about that business with Washy Sparrow. Mr. Hartley wa'n't no more to be blamed for that than a——"

She stopped me. "Please don't," she says. "I know; Eureka told me. And Mr. Pratt," she adds, and her face lit up like there was a glory inside it; "I'm not going to ask you to beg his pardon for me. But will you tell him that, as soon as I can leave Dennis, I'm coming to Wellmouth to ask his pardon myself, and—to thank him? Tell him that, please."

Eureka and me drove back to Wellmouth together. If that old buggy had been trimmed up to match the feelings of the two inside it 'twould have been the gayest turnout that ever come down the pike road. No circus cart would have been in it.

But poor Van!

CHAPTER XIX

SIMPLE VERSUS DUPLEX

I LEFT Eureka at Nate Scudder's. She was going to have him take his dory and row her over to the Island. She was to see to things there till I come. Dewey was all right and over his cold, she told me, so she could take up her regular job again. Scudder was glad to see us. I don't know but he'd been scared that his whole gang of lodgers had cleared out and left him in the lurch. I told him about the doctor chase. His eyes stuck out.

"Godfrey scissors!" says he. "It must have cost that Hartley man a lot for that automobile."

"Cost!" says I. "You bet it did!"

"I presume likely that'll come out of the doctor's bill, won't it?"

"No," I says, scornful. "Land of Goshen! No. Why should it?"

"Well, if 'twas me I'd take some of it out. The doc hadn't no right to be way over to Brantboro after giving folks notice through the papers that he was to Wapatomac." He thought a minute more and then he says, "Say, Sol; don't you cal'late there's a commission coming to us from Ben Baker? He'd never let that auto wagon if we hadn't provided the customer."

Didn't that beat all? Sometimes I think Nate Scudder 'll rise up in his coffin afore they bury him and want a commission from the undertaker. He'll never rest easy and see all that cash going to somebody else when he's furnishing the center of interest.

I found Martin planted easy and pretty comfortable in an upstairs front room at the Old Home. His arm was hurting him some, of course, but other ways he felt better, having had a nap and something to eat. He wa'n't sick in bed at least; and that's how I expected to find him.

I told him the good news from Redny, and it pleased him 'most to death. Then I give him the Page girl's message. He didn't say much, but 'twas plain to see how he felt. I promised to be back next morning, and then I said good-by. His good-by to me was sort of absent-minded. I left him smoking and looking dreamy out of the window.

I was in a hurry to get to Ozone but I couldn't

help stopping where they was digging the cellar for the new part of the hotel, and looking for our old friend Washy Sparrow. He was wheeling dirt in a wheelbarrow and he seemed mighty willing to let go of the handles and talk to me.

"Hello, Washy," I says. "How's the stomach and lungs these days?"

He groaned. "Pratt," says he, "I'm dying on my feet."

"Well," I says, looking down at his cowhides, "you'd ought to have plenty of room to do it in. What are you dying of—dropsy? You're five pounds heavier than when I see you last."

He shook his head. "Tell Reky I'm doing my best to forgive her," he says. "When I'm gone maybe she'll think of how she treated me. Say! how soon's she coming home? Lycurgus can't cook fit to eat."

I told him Eureka 'd be home that night. It seemed to give him a little more hopes.

"When you see Miss Page," says he, "just tell her I want to talk to her, won't you? Tell her I'm 'most through with this world and I want to speak to her about providing for the children. Ask her to come over and see me."

Just then the foreman yelled to him to stop

gassing and hustle that wheelbarrow along. He done it, surprising prompt too, I thought. I asked the foreman about it.

"Oh!" he says, "Mr. Brown's give me the receipt for him. Every time he groans or coughs I set him to lugging stones; the louder the groans the bigger the rocks. He's getting well fast."

I took Nate's dory and went across to the Island. Eureka was up to her elbows in work.

"Sakes alive!" says she. "Who's been letting this house get this way? The tea kettle bottom's burnt out and somebody's been trying to eat the axe. And the beds are so wet that the feathers are beginning to grow."

"That's the Natural Life," I told her. "The Heavenlies lived it for a whole day."

"I thought they lived it afore I come here at all," she says. "Things was bad enough then, but nothing like this."

"'Twas me that was the Natural then," says I. "This last attack hit the Twins."

"Do you know who I think ought to live the Natural Life?" she asks.

I said I didn't.

"Nobody but natural born idiots, that's who."

"I guess that's who's *been* living it," says I.

Next morning I went over to see Hartley. He was feeling like a new man. Doctor Jordan had been there ahead of me and set the arm. Redny was pretty nigh well. Jordan had the right cure for green apple appendicitis and it worked tiptop.

I drove up to the depot in the Old Home wagon and met Van Brunt. He was in fine spirits. The Tea Lead deal had been closed up—the Street pirates having decided not to pass the dividend—and the Heavenly Twins had made money by the keg, I judged.

"How'd New York look to you?" I asked him.

"Hush!" says he. "Don't speak lightly of sacred things."

When he heard about what had happened while he was away hc was the most surprised man in the county.

"Skipper," he says, grabbing my hand, "you're a star of the first magnitude. You and Eureka are the redeeming features of this Natural experiment. You pay the freight and a large rebate over. And Martin! bully old boy! I want to see him."

Him and his chum was shut up together for a

good half hour. When Van come down to the porch he beckoned to me.

"Sol," he says, "there's another question I want to ask you. Of course I know that Martin liked the boy and all that, but that reason won't quite do. What's the real one?"

'Twas a ticklish place for me. But I couldn't see but one way clear; that is, but one way which was best in the long run for all hands. So I spunked up and answered.

"Mr. Van Brunt," says I, "I hate to say it, but of course you know that your partner and Miss Agnes set considerable store by each other at one time. And you can't break off feelings like that same as you'd bust a piece of string. I——"

He nodded. "All right," he says. "I'm not altogether a blockhead. That'll do. I've been sure of it, myself, for some time."

"I understand," I went on, "that the reason she give him the mitten was on account of his being too grasping after money. If she'd seen him, like I have, just throwing it away as if 'twas shavings, I guess likely she——"

He interrupted and looked at me queer.

"How did you know that was the reason?" he asks.

I'd put my foot in it away over the shoe laces.

"Well," I stammered, "you see I—that is, 'twas told to me—and—course I can't swear——"

"Who told it? Oh, never mind. I see. Dear James! Well done, good and faithful servant. You've been faithful over a few things, and general superintendent and advertiser of all the rest. Sol, I learned something when I was in New York. Considering all you've done and know, I think you're entitled to know more.

"When I was in God's settlement yesterday," he went on, referring to his home town, I judged, though I'd never heard afore that it belonged in that neighborhood, "I met an old friend of Hartley's governor—of his father, I mean. This friend had been abroad for some time and had just returned. He spoke of Martin, and what a fine fellow he was; to all of which I set my hand and seal, of course. Then he said that the way in which young Hartley had paid his father's debts and saved the family honor and credit was one of the biggest things he knew of. I expressed surprise. Then he was surprised to learn that I didn't know, being Martin's closest friend, and told me the rest.

"It seemed that Hartley senior was heavily involved when he died. He had speculated and his affairs were in horrible shape. Martin didn't know of this until the old gentleman, on his death bed, sprung it on him. So then the plucky chap started in to save the name. He arranged with the creditors—this man who told me the story was one of them—for time, and set to work. He worked nights and days and in his sleep, I guess. He had promised his dad, for his mother's sake, not to tell a soul, and he didn't. Every creditor was pledged to secrecy. Even his own mother didn't know it to the day of her death. But he paid dollar for dollar and broke down when it was over. That's why he was willing to join with me in this hunt of ours after the Natural Life. Agnes' cutting him made him reckless, I suppose. And when he was on his feet again financially, he lost interest in the whole game."

"And now that he's well and husky," I says, "her mistake about his doings with the old man Sparrow set him going at it again. I suppose his digging in the hardest and keeping it quiet on account of his promise, was what made her call him a money grabber. I might have known 'twas something like that."

"So might I," he says, "if I wasn't such a careless, happy-go-lucky idiot. You see I always thought that the 'mercenary' business was only a cloak for the real reason of their breaking off. She only took up with me because our people wanted her to. I've been sure of that for a good while. But why Martin didn't come to me when he was in trouble, instead of going it alone like a bull-headed chump, is——"

He stopped and went to thinking. I looked at him and I guess there was a question in my face, for he answered it without my saying a word.

"Certainly I shall tell her," says he. "When is the next train to Eastwich?"

He went to the school that afternoon, and stayed at the Bay View House over there that night. Next day, afore I left the Island, Hartley comes rowing over with Scudder. He was feeling chipper as could be and, except for the arm in a sling, you wouldn't have known there was anything the matter with him.

About eleven or so that forenoon Eureka comes running out to the hen-yard where I was. Her face was on the broad grin.

"They're coming," says she. "The whole of 'em!"

"Who?"

"Why Miss Agnes and Miss Talford. Nate Scudder is rowing 'em and Mr. Van Brunt is along, too."

And so they was. I could see the dory half way across already.

"Hooray!" I sings out. "Let's tell Hartley."

"Don't you *dare* tell him," she orders. "He's in the house. You let him stay there. It's your job to meet that boat and keep the rest of 'em out of the way."

I was at the beach when the dory landed. Miss Talford and Van got out first. Then comes Agnes Page. She stepped up to me and held out her hand.

"Good morning, Mr. Pratt," she says. "I'm very glad to see you."

"Same here, ma'am, I'm sure," says I. "How's Redny?"

"Who? Dennis? Oh, he's almost well. We left James in charge of the children. Are you all well here? Is——"

"Yes, ma'am. He's doing first-rate. You'll find him in the dining-room."

She reddened up like a climbing rose-bush in June, but she left me and headed for the house.

The minute she stepped her foot on the porch, that wise critter Eureka dodged out of the kitchen door. She knew her business, that girl did, and whether it had come to her by instinct or from *Home Comforter* reading don't make an atom of difference.

About twenty minutes after that I happened to have an errand in the kitchen. I made a dickens of a racket on purpose when I went in, but 'twas good work wasted. Hartley and the Page girl was standing by the parlor window looking out, and didn't appear to hear a sound. They'd left the doors open and I could see 'em. Martin hadn't only one whole arm, but he seemed to know what to do with that.

Van Brunt come into the kitchen after a drink of water. He see the tableau in the parlor. When we was outside again he spoke.

"Well," he says, with a kind of sigh, "that settles it. And yet, by George! I'm glad. Yes, sir; it's as it should be and I'm thoroughly glad of it."

I couldn't think of nothing to comfort him, poor feller. But I squeezed his hand hard. I guess he knew what I thought of him and his self-sacrifice.

And yet, a couple of hours later, when I told Eureka, she didn't seem to think so much of it.

"Humph!" says she. "Self-sacrificing's all right, but you look here."

She took me by the arm and led me to the woodshed window. Down by the cove on the beach was Van Brunt and Margaret Talford, walking up and down together. They was both laughing and acting perfectly contented.

Eureka gave me a nudge and a wink. "I told you I had my ideas about *him*," says she.

The Fresh Air girls went back to Eastwich that afternoon. When they had gone Van turns to me.

"And now, skipper," says he, slapping his hands together brisk; "now then for packing up, and back, back to little old New York. 'Oh, Uncle John! isn't it nice on Broadway?' or words to that effect."

They was all going together; the Heavenly Twins and Lord James and the Fresh Air girls and all their tribe. Redny's sickness and the worry that it brought had made Agnes and Miss Talford anxious for the city, where doctors was plenty and green apples scarce. And the Twins was pining for what Van called " the intoxicating degeneracy of an effete " (whatever that is) " civilization."

We packed up. That is to say, me and Eureka packed up, while the Heavenlies superintended and enjoyed themselves. Scudder's face, when he heard that his private gold mines was going to leave, was a sight to see. But, after a couple of lengthy interviews with the Twins, he seemed to feel better.

" I shall miss 'em terrible," he says to me. " But this world's a valley of dry bones, anyhow, ain't it, Pratt? "

" Valley of dry bones," and " fleeing to the ark of safety " was his pet words when he testified in prayer-meeting.

" I guess so," I says. " Still I wouldn't kick if I had your knack of getting double price per pound for the bones. You've managed to fertilize with 'em pretty well, Nate."

He fetched a sigh. " They're such nice obliging fellers," he says. " And such good hands at business. Never no beating down nor jockeying for a trade. I always feel perfectly safe in dealing with 'em."

I cal'lated that statement wa'n't exaggerated.

Most likely a shark feels the same way about dealing with a school of porgies.

Nate had agreed to take back the hens and the pig, as an accommodation. He was to pay three dollars for the hog and the fowls was hove into the scales for good measure. There was a lease of the Island, too, that had to be canceled. Them simple-minded Tea Leaders had, in the first fever of Naturalness, signed a lease on Horsefoot Bar to run till November. Now that their pulse was normal again they wanted to break that lease, and the job was considerable more painful and expensive than breaking Hartley's arm had been. But Nate let 'em break, though I thought he'd break them afore he got through.

Him and Eureka and me had a good many talks about the Twins when we was alone together. The last of these talks we had on the afternoon of the day afore the grand final emigration. Lord James was over on an errand and he was in the kitchen with us. Eureka begun the talk.

" I ain't quite made up my mind whether they're really crazy or not," she says, referring to the Heavenlies. " They don't act much more loony than some of the earls and such in books. And yet they must be some out of their minds or they wouldn't do such fool things. Once they was all for living poor and Natural. Now they're all the other way. Switching 'round like that is a sure sign of weakness in the top stories."

"Most city folks act to me some crazy," says I. "And perhaps these two, being the toniest kind, is crazier than others. Maybe the higher up you go the loonier they get. I read in a paper once about how some rich big bug give a swell dinner to a pet monkey. The Twins are Solomons alongside of *him*. And, anyhow, they're mighty nice young fellers. Money may have got to their heads, but their hearts is in the right place."

"'Taint a question of hearts," says Scudder. "Way I figger it out the Almighty sends 'em down here on purpose. We poor folks alongshore don't have much chance to earn an honest living, and so the Lord takes pity on us and makes men like these two get cracked and hanker to live in the sand and spend money. You put your trust in the Higher Power. He evens matters up in the long run."

His Lordship broke in then; and my! but he was top-lofty and scornful.

"Crazy yourselves!" he sniffs. "My 'eavens, I've done some traveling in my time, with Lord 'Enry and the rest; I've been all over. And never in my life 'ave I seen such a Gawd-forsaken country as this, or such a blooming lot of ignorant 'ayseeds as is 'ere. W'y, you don't know 'ow to live at all and yet you're proud of it. You 'aven't no conveniences, and you eat with your knives, and you've no manners. Lord 'elp you, I say! You're all crazy together, and don't know 'ow to act in good society. Mr. Van Brunt and Mr. 'Artley is gentlemen, and what you call their craziness is nothing but the eccentricities *of* gentlemen. And if you think *they're* eccentric! W'y compared to some I've worked for, like Lord 'Enry——"

'Twas high time to stop him. "But they're so crazy loose with their money," says I.

He was hotter than ever. "Do you suppose," he asks sarcastic, "that a real gentleman 'as time to 'aggle over a few dirty pennies?"

Nobody said any more for a spell. Then Eureka says, like she'd been thinking:

"I cal'late," says she, "that it's all in the way you've been raised. Maybe I'd act just as queer and looney if I went to the city; that is, if I hadn't posted myself up by my reading. I'll lend you the *Comforters* with "False but Fair" in 'em, Mr. Pratt, some time."

Next day we all met at the Eastwich depot.

Agnes Page and Miss Talford and the Fresh Air tribe, including Redny, who was chipper and gay because he was going back to New York. The Heavenly Twins was there. So was me and Eureka to see 'em off.

We spent fifteen minutes or more in saying good byes. I felt real bad and so did everybody else, I guess. Hartley and Agnes couldn't say enough to me about my sailing through that gale for 'em in the *Dora Bassett*. The poor old sloop was still tied up to the Wapatomac wharf. Baker had been looking out for her and I was going over that afternoon myself.

Agnes said she and Hartley would surely come back next summer. I must write and so would they. Eureka's brothers and sisters was to have money to help along their schooling, and Washy Sparrow would keep wheeling rocks, or, if he didn't, Squire Poundberry would attend to him.

"Pa wanted a holiday on account of your leaving, Miss Page," says Eureka. "But I told him 'twould be a bigger celebration if he kept on to work."

Scudder wa'n't at the depot. He was too busy moving the duds off of Ozone Island to get away. But he'd sent a package by Eureka. 'Twas a present for Van Brunt; something to remember him by, he said.

Van opened it. Then there was a general " haw haw." 'Twas that worked worsted motto, " What is Home Without a Mother? "

" James," says Van, bubbling over with laughter, " this is your property. I couldn't deprive you of it."

His Lordship was disgusted. " I wouldn't 'ave the blooming thing in the 'ouse; with all respect to you, sir," says he.

Agnes said she'd take it. It would be a splendid souvenir.

" Scudder's a kind-hearted chap," says Van. " He means well."

That was too much for me. I took a piece of paper out of my pocket. 'Twas a little bill I'd made out the night afore.

" Here," I says; " just run your eye over this, will you? "

Van took it. It read so:

"The Natural Life, Dr., to Nathan Scudder, Nature's Nobleman, Rough Diamond, and the like of that.

15 loads of dirt, at $3.00 a load. That's....$45.00

11 hens and 1 rooster at 30 cents a lb. That's 12.60 and the hens and rooster.

1 hog—sold for $6.00 when he was little

and thin, and bought back for \$3.00 when he was big and fat. That's.... \$3.00 and the hog.

160 quarts of skim-milk (he kept the cream and made it into butter to sell us) at 9 cts. a quart. That's.............. 14.40

About 50 lbs. of butter (made out of our cream) at 25 cts. a lb. That's...... 12.50

Vegetables and truck (mostly from the store). That's somewheres nigh........... 10.00

Bedding and furniture and kitchen stuff. That's about........................ 75.00 and all the stuff back again.

Lease of Ozone Horsefoot Island for 3 months at \$50 a month (a cent more than \$4.00 a year is like robbing your grandmarm). That's........................... 150.00

For cancelling the lease which was to run till November. That's.............. 40.00

About 60 days, altogether, of secret keeping at \$8.00 a day (\$3.00 from E. V. B. and \$5.00 from M. H.). Call it, say 480.00

Total (it ain't nigh all)..................\$842.50

And twelve hens and one hog and all the furniture and land knows what else besides."

"And that don't count in half of the Ozone cost," I says; "let alone what you fellers paid for hiring his house and Huldy Ann and all."

Hartley looked over his chum's shoulder.

"Humph!" says he. "I wouldn't wonder if I could add an item to that. What did you pay for those shore-birds you got when you went gunning with Scudder, Van?"

Van blushed up some, but he answered prompt.

"Well," he says, "to tell the truth, Scudder sold 'em to me for five dollars."

"Yes?" says Martin, laughing. "I thought so. I paid him six for mine."

"There's no use talking" I put in; "there may be some good things about *living* the Natural Life, but——"

"But," interrupted Martin, "the financial profits appear to lie in Scudder's plan; that is, to have the 'good things' live it for you."

The train whistled up the road. Van leaned over and tapped me on the shirt front.

"Skipper," says he, "I won't prophecy concerning next summer. Sufficient unto the day, etcetera. And I won't answer for Martin. But for me, and for this winter, if anybody asks, you tell 'em I've gone back to New York to live the most compound, double duplex life to be found from Harlem to the Battery. That's what!" says Edward Van Brunt.

THE END